The Guilty Ones

Joanna Crispi

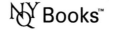

NYQ Books™

The New York Quarterly Foundation, Inc.
New York, New York

Also by Joanna Crispi

Soldier in the Grass

Roxane und Alexander

The Guilty Ones

NYQ Books™ is an imprint of The New York Quarterly Foundation, Inc.

The New York Quarterly Foundation, Inc.
P. O. Box 2015
Old Chelsea Station
New York, NY 10113

www.nyqbooks.org

First Edition

Set in Myriad Pro

Layout and Design by Seth Cosimini

Cover image used courtesy of the Hotel Hassler Roma
www.hotelhasslerroma.com

Library of Congress Control Number: 2012932119

ISBN: 978-1-935520-50-4

For my editor, Bill Packard, who said it was finished

Part One

1

They say all roads lead to Rome, and so they do. On this August night the torches in front of the Vittoriano in Piazza Venezia fed off the heavy air; street lights burned like votive candles. Tomorrow it might rain, suddenly, violently, rains of the kind near the earth's girdle. But tonight the city was as still as the palm trees that lined the villa in Tunisia where François and Juliet de Fournier had spent the past two weeks.

At Fiumicino airport, Juliet and François had just stepped off the Alitalia flight from Tunisia to Rome that landed almost two hours behind schedule.

"*Maria Gesù*, we should strike next week," an airport guard grumbled. "This is the third night this week the planes have come late."

The passengers from the flight began to form lines at the customs windows. Juliet brushed her cheek against François's shoulder, leaning on him in a lazy intimacy as if they had just awakened from a nap. He kissed her lightly on the ear before heading to the line for EU passengers.

It was a cumbersome detail of their marriage, that because he was French and she was American, they had to stand on separate lines when going through Passport Control. From across the room she took him in as a stranger might, his dark hair, his fine, manly features. His long, dark eyes, warm and sensual, seemed darker against the frame of black eyelashes and smooth tanned skin, but melancholy too, she thought as she gazed at him. After a moment, he looked over and smiled at her, reaching into his pocket for his passport and adjusting the slightly worn black leather carry-on suitcase in his other hand.

She pushed back the long strands of chestnut hair from her face as she stepped to the customs booth and slid her passport beneath the window. The officer looked up from the passport, inspecting her features as he might inspect a box for the correct postage. Apparently he determined all the postage was in order, for he stamped the passbook, closed it, and slipped it back through the window in what seemed a single automatic gesture.

Juliet saw the *carabinieri* rushing past her, but at the time she made no mental note; she was busy putting her passport safely back in her purse. She turned back casually to see whether François had passed through customs. Four *carabinieri* had surrounded someone who in the next instant she recognized to be her husband.

"François," she called, but her voice carried badly. She rushed over to where he was being held. A *carabiniere* turned and pointed his gun. There seemed to be confusion suddenly. Someone grabbed her from behind.

"*C'est ma femme,*" François said to the two *carabinieri* who held his arms.

The man in the dark suit asked for her papers. She opened the purse and handed him the passport.

"Juliet Mason," he read the name aloud, and glanced skeptically over at her.

"Mason is my maiden name," she said.

She took a French driver's license and a Bon Marché card bearing the name Juliet de Fournier from her wallet and gave them to the man in the dark suit. She glanced at her husband, asking with her eyes for an explanation.

"*Calme-toi*," he said quietly to reassure her.

A moment later the man in the dark suit, apparently satisfied that Juliet was indeed François's wife, announced that they were to follow him. Two *carabinieri* held François's arms as they walked. She had the disconcerting feeling of walking swiftly and purposefully, yet with no idea where she was going. After a few seemingly interminable minutes, the man in the suit stopped abruptly outside an office near the main airport exit. François was taken into a room off the reception area. When she attempted to follow she was prevented.

"I am a lawyer. If you intend to question him, I want to be present." She could hear her voice quivering with nerves as she tried in vain to steady it.

Without answering her, the man in the dark suit directed a *carabiniere* to escort her into the hallway.

Her hands shook as she opened her purse to find an aspirin. A terrible headache had come on suddenly. She looked for a water fountain. Finding none, she held the useless aspirin in her open palm, waiting in the hope that it might only be a matter of minutes before François was free to go, but he remained behind the closed door. She remembered the luggage, and it occurred to her that someone might steal it. But she would not leave until she knew what was happening. She gave up trying to find water and put the aspirin back in her purse.

She heard the hum of the electronic door opening and closing onto the sidewalk, and each time the door opened she felt the night air waft through the stale hallway. An hour went by. The airport became deserted except for a few employees. A janitor swept the floors with a wide broom. It was nearly midnight.

She was anxious, annoyed by the delay, concerned, even frightened, but her emotions were kept in check by the thought that whatever was going on behind those doors was the result of some bureaucratic stupidity that at worst might ruin their stay in Rome. On the way to the hotel François would give his own amusing rendition of the incident, she thought, filled with the contempt that French people have for police.

The door to the office opened. She heard voices speaking in Italian. The man in the suit came out holding François's suitcase. Then she saw François. He was handcuffed and two *carabinieri* had their hands on his arms as they escorted him out of the room.

"I would like to speak to my wife," he said in Italian to the man in the suit.

Juliet felt her heart pounding; at first she could not find her voice in her throat.

"What's happening?" she asked, shaken.

"I'm not sure."

"What do they say? Why are they arresting you?"

"They don't say."

They kept their voices low, speaking in English. The *carabinieri* stood close by, and could hear every word.

"What were they doing for the last hour?" she asked.

"Phone calls. They were not sure where to bring me, I think. I am not sure—my Italian is not good. I want you to call Alessandro Pucci, a lawyer I know. His office is on Via Veneto."

"They can't arrest you without telling you why. I don't understand."

"This is Italy; they can do whatever they want."

"Where are they taking you now?"

"A place—a jail I think called Rebibbia."

"Don't let anyone question you," she said. "Tell them you want me present."

"You're not an Italian lawyer, so it won't matter to them."

A *carabiniere* pulled at François's arm.

"I'll follow you in a taxi," she said.

"Go to the hotel," he said, his eyes shifting to the faces of the men who stood at his side. "They won't let you see me anymore tonight. We'll know what to do tomorrow."

She put her hand lightly on his face and kissed him as the *carabinieri* pulled him away and ushered him into the police car that waited on the curb. She remained standing there, the rear lights streaking across her eyes like light through tears as the car disappeared down the dark strip of road.

A sense of urgency overwhelmed her, as if she should be doing something, and yet that feeling seemed to paralyze her. She felt incapable of moving from the sidewalk. *"Call Alessandro Pucci, a lawyer I know."* She had no idea how François knew him, though, she reassured herself, as head of Compagnie Financière de Fournier, a French merchant bank, naturally, he would know lawyers throughout Europe.

Someone tapped her lightly on the shoulder, touching her bare arm, and she pulled back with a start. It was the man in the dark suit, still holding François's suitcase.

"Let me introduce myself, Signora de Fournier. I am Lieutenant Carlo Vincenzo. I have summoned a taxi for you," he said in perfect English, seemingly indifferent to the irony that before this he had refused to address her in any language other than Italian.

"I have luggage—" she began, but as she said it, she saw that he had brought it with him.

"Why have you arrested my husband?"

"I am sorry, I am not free to say. Let me say only that I too wish the young customs officer had not been so careful. You and your husband would be at your hotel, and I would be home in time for dinner."

"At least tell me where he is being taken."

"Ah, *sì*. Rebibbia," he answered somberly. "*Allora*, here is your taxi."

"We must do our jobs," he said, apologetically, as he opened the door for her.

2

At the Hotel Eden, Juliet handed the taxi driver francs instead of lire. He took one look at the handful of francs, turned around and started to swear at her. For the first time all night, she was relieved not to speak Italian.

At the front desk she gave her name, "A reservation for de Fournier."

The concierge glanced back up at her. "According to the reservation you will be two."

"My husband has been delayed."

To avoid another scene like the one in the taxi, she wanted to change francs into lire, but when she opened her wallet she found she had less than a thousand francs; François had been holding the cash.

"I need a telephone number. Alessandro Pucci, Via Veneto." She wrote it out neatly on a piece of hotel notepaper.

She forced a polite smile as the bellman seated behind the desk took her to her suite, the same one she had stayed in the last time she was in Rome with François, two years before. The memory was still fresh in her mind. She took in the room like a breath, the bed where they had made love, the sitting room with its yellow silk chairs. It was just after they were married, when the honey was sweetest, the happiest time of her life, and afterwards she had always loved Rome.

Noise from the street wafted through the windows. The curtains blew in the night breeze as she looked out onto the gardens surrounding the Villa Borghese. She remembered the night they stayed up getting drunk on champagne; "François sat in this chair," she thought, caressing the back of the chair. She pictured his dark eyes with their hint of gold smiling back at her, and she was struck by a feeling of panic.

Her mind went back to the events of the past few hours, but before her thoughts could take shape, the phone rang.

"This is the front desk. The numbers you wanted—

"*Sì, grazie*," she said, jotting the numbers on the small pad beside the phone.

She tried the first number. A woman answered.

"I am trying to reach Alessandro Pucci, the lawyer. Forgive me, I don't speak Italian."

"Is all right," the woman said. "I speaks English. He is not here," the woman answered.

Juliet thought she sounded annoyed. "I'm sorry to bother you at this hour. It's important I get in touch with him. My husband, François de Fournier, was arrested at Fiumicino airport, and he asked me to call."

The woman's voice softened. "I am so sorry. I do not know where he is. I am so sorry. I can give to him the message when he returns."

"Please, I am at the Hotel Eden, room 316. He can call me at any hour."

The woman hung up. Juliet sat clutching the receiver in her hand; she had the sense of something repeating, of having the same dream a second time, or of something that has happened before happening all over again.

Before moving to Paris she had practiced as a criminal defense lawyer in New York. It had been five years last spring since she had given up the practice of law. Five years since she had seen the inside of a court room or appeared before a supercilious face in a black robe.

Like the majority of her class at Harvard Law School, she went to New York to practice. She had done her best to be a good lawyer, and she was good. No one could take that away from her. And no one did take it away from her. She had done that all by herself, she thought.

Lawyers spoke of their reputations as if that gave them a stake in an outcome. Losing never hurt a reputation: to the outside world, when a lawyer lost it was because the client was guilty. The law was not about people. It was about pieces of paper. A case always began and ended with a piece of paper. Things stood a certain way depending on which piece of paper was used—arrest, indictment, judgment of conviction, judgment of confinement, and sometimes, with a little luck, the card turned up acquittal.

But none of this had played any part in why she had left the practice of law. And she had known at the time that something was at stake, and she had known too when she lost.

"We make this motion on behalf"—like a prayer, those words, a motion, a gesture, her hand caressing François's face as he was led away.

She got up and took an airline-size bottle of scotch and a mineral water from the wet bar. After pouring the scotch into a glass, she undid the white cotton shift she had been wearing and tossed it over the back of a chair. She lay on the bed with the night air washing over her bare arms and legs, sipping the scotch. Something more than the events themselves was upsetting her. She had come to Paris for a fresh start. François was like a savior to her. Tonight as they were separated by the *carabinieri*, she sensed the harmony of their life together coming undone. Through the dark she saw the empty space beside her in bed, and she felt François's absence as something physical pulling deep inside of her. Tomorrow we will post bail, she thought. This will only be for a night. He'll be out tomorrow and, whatever it is, we will straighten it out.

It had begun to rain, softly at first, the rain glistening across the silhouette of black trees in the Borghese Gardens. The last time she was here with François, it had rained then too, and she remembered lying in bed listening to the rain, her body against his, stealing the warmth of his sleep. How happy she had been lying awake in the dark then. How different it was tonight. The sound of the rain was like the drone of sleeplessness, and the darkness seemed interminable. *Tous songes sont mesonges*, she whispered into the darkness. All dreams are lies.

3

Alessandro Pucci returned her call at eight o'clock the next morning. She had not slept well. Sunlight filtered through the crack in the shutters in a bright dazzling line that seemed to divide the room in half. They agreed to meet in the hotel restaurant at ten.

The restaurant was on the roof with a view of all of Rome, beautiful and golden beneath an azure sky. Alessandro Pucci was seated at a table drinking a coffee and reading some papers when she arrived. He took off his glasses and held them in his left hand as he stood to greet her. From her first impression of him she thought of him as short, but he was not short, merely not as tall as most American men. He was dressed smartly in a gray pinstriped Valentino suit, and his dark hair was graying at the temples and thin in the back. Juliet guessed he was closer to fifty than to forty.

"I was using this opportunity to read what I took home with me to read last night," he said, as he put the papers away in his briefcase. "Somehow there is always too little time and too much work."

Juliet smiled. She was glad to be meeting with him. She caught herself giving in to the feeling of reassurance people seek from a lawyer, the wish that this person will make everything right. But she knew better.

The waiter brought a basket of bread. Alessandro passed the basket to her. She took a *cornetto*.

"*Un caffè?*" Alessandro asked.

"With warm milk, please."

He turned to the waiter, "*Due caffé latte.*" Then, turning back to Juliet, he said, "Forgive me for not calling last night. I was working late and I did not see the note my wife had left for me. This morning at breakfast she asked if I had called you. Poor François, where is he, my dear?"

"The officer last night told me they were taking him to Rebibbia. Can you meet with him there this morning?"

He seemed to be sorting out his schedule in his head.

"Where is Rebibbia?" she asked.

"Via Montagna, in Rome, but on the outskirts. I have to call my office and rearrange a meeting for later in the day," he said.

The waiter brought the coffee.

"François has told me you are a lawyer," he said.

"I stopped working after we got married. Will it be easier to visit if I go in my capacity as a lawyer?"

"I would imagine, though each jail has its own rules. We must obtain permission first before they will admit either one of us to see him. I can accomplish this hopefully with a phone call. I say hopefully because in these situations it is quite often the case that someone will invent a rule before your eyes that makes it impossible, regardless I might add, of whether the day before you did the very thing they are now telling you is forbidden. In any case you will need proof when we arrive."

"I have only my business card," she said, and she handed it to him. Though she was no longer practicing she still carried it with her. It was worn from having been in her wallet for so long.

He put on his glasses to read it. "Juliet," he said, studying the card. "You spell your name the English way rather than the French."

"My father taught Shakespeare."

"He wanted to give you a romantic name."

"I don't know that he knew what he wanted," she said. Immediately she was sorry; it was too personal a thing to say to a European on a first meeting; he would think she was just another American willing to tell her life story to every stranger.

A flicker of sunlight diverted her attention and her eyes wandered to the view of Rome from the window. How still it seemed, like a postcard, stilted and frozen in time, she thought. The last time she was here the light was alive, and the rooftops seemed to sparkle.

"How is it that you and François know one another?" she asked, turning her attention to Alessandro.

He put his glasses back in his jacket pocket. "I have represented Compagnie Financière on matters in Rome. I represented Compagnie Financière before François took over, when his father ran it. Did you know François's father?"

"He died before I had an opportunity to meet him."

Alessandro spread confection over his bread as he continued. "He was very old-world French, aristocratic, arrogant, but a good man." Putting the knife down, he glanced up earnestly at her.

"Do you know what is involved? Why is François being detained?" he asked.

"He said he was not told."

"This happened at the airport as you were entering Rome?" He took a small bite of the bread, afterwards patting the corners of his mouth with a napkin.

"We were on our way back from Tunisia. I wanted to stop in Rome for a few days. Once we were back in Paris François would be busy again." The wistfulness left her voice. "Will we need to post a bond this morning for his release?"

"I'm sorry, my dear. It is impossible. There is no such thing. Because he is a foreigner, the case will be referred first to the Ministero di Grazia e Giustizia, Ministry of Justice, in English."

"There is no bail," she repeated as if it could not possibly be true. She felt a shock of nerves through her body like the feeling she had last night when he was first arrested.

Alessandro reached across the table and placed his hand on hers, "Forgive me, my dear, it is an unfortunate thing to say. François is lucky to be at Rebibbia. It is a women's prison, though they also keep men there. It is so much better than if he had been brought to Regina Coeli."

"Queen of Heaven," she said. "A strange name for a prison."

"Yes, I have often thought so too. But, this is Rome and everything must have a religious name."

4

Juliet waited impatiently at the front of the hotel for over an hour, indifferent to the beautiful day and the stream of people going in and out of the hotel. When Alessandro finally arrived he explained that it had taken several phone calls to Rebibbia before he was able to arrange for their visit.

"We must go first to the Ministry of Justice before we can be admitted to the jail," he said.

"Were they aware of the arrest?" she asked.

"They wouldn't say over the phone."

When they stopped at a traffic light, gypsies ran over to the car, girls in colorful skirts, with long, straggling dark hair, who made eyes at Alessandro. Juliet looked away to prevent them from giving her the evil eye—a superstition, she knew, and yet today she felt superstitious.

Her thoughts drifted back to the time François had taken her to Saintes-Maries-de-la-Mer in the south of France where the gypsies came every year for their festival. She remembered the story he told her about Sara, the queen of the gypsies, who threw her coat onto the water for the Virgin Mary to walk to shore.

"How is it possible for Christ's mother to have come to the south of France?"

François laughed at her. "It's a miracle. Why are you so literal? Don't you believe in miracles?"

"*Resta a casa*," Alessandro shouted, throwing up his arms as he passed the woman driving the car in front of them.

Alessandro glanced over at Juliet, smiling. "They want to move like sheep in the middle of the road, and everyone is supposed to stop for them." He lifted his hands from the steering wheel and shrugged. "Here everything is slower. The streets run in circles. You cannot go in a straight line across Rome."

At the Ministry they went first to the office of a clerk named Di Pietri, whose job it was to arrange the schedules of all of the magistrates. He was small and bald and wore eyeglasses. When Alessandro introduced Juliet, Di Pietri said, simply, "*Francese.*"

"By marriage," Alessandro answered.

Di Pietri scrutinized Juliet for a moment, "*Inglese?*"

"*Americana.*"

"*Sì, Sì.*"

To Juliet it sounded like a judgment. "*Inglese, francese, americana.*"

"*Aspettate.*" Di Pietri told them to wait while he called the magistrate's office.

Nearly half an hour passed without Di Pietri picking up the phone.

Alessandro began to pace and look at his watch. "What is the delay?"

"I must finish what I am doing first," Di Pietri answered.

"What are you doing?"

Di Pietri did not answer. It seemed he was merely copying something from one leather-bound notebook to another.

Five more minutes passed before Di Pietri called the magistrate's office.

"Magistrate Melazzo is expecting you," he announced, carefully pointing out the elevator down the hall as if it would have been otherwise impossible to find.

"Idiot," Alessandro muttered under his breath. "I'm always here, and suddenly today he thinks he has to officiate."

Magistrate Melazzo stood and greeted them from behind his long desk with a warm smile. He was dressed well, in a dark suit, and his hair was full and graying. He had a square face and a prominent nose with a high, pronounced bridge. Juliet felt as if she had looked into dozens of faces in the last day, and all of this measuring of features and eyes and shades of hair had told her nothing.

Alessandro made introductions. Melazzo nodded when he took Juliet's hand. Behind his desk the shutters were swung wide open, and sunlight fell into the room in long streaks of gold, but instead of the jasmine scent of summer, a trace of autumn was in the warm afternoon air.

He summoned his secretary and told her to bring three coffees. Juliet and Alessandro sat across from Melazzo's ornate desk with its stacks of colored files wrapped in different color ribbons. He joked with Alessandro briefly, before everyone's face again became serious. During these spells when they spoke in Italian, Juliet had the impression that they had forgotten she was there.

"De Fournier, your husband is French, of course," Melazzo said, addressing her in English.

"Yes," she answered.

"And you are an American citizen?"

She nodded. "Does that make a difference?"

"Possibly. I will explain." Melazzo turned to Alessandro as he took a folder from the top of a stack and undid the ribbon.

As if pursuant to a ritual, Alessandro and Melazzo took their eyeglasses from their jacket pockets and put them on.

"The ministry received this on the morning of your husband's arrest. Unfortunate timing for you," he said, pushing the paper toward Alessandro. "It is in Italian, of course. I apologize for not having a translation," he said turning to Juliet.

"If I may summarize for you, it is a warrant from the United States, requesting the arrest of Signor de Fournier under the Extradition Treaty between the United States and the Italian government."

"The United States is trying to extradite my husband? On what charges?"

"At this stage we have only these," Melazzo said, referring to the papers Alessandro was holding. "The Americans have time before they are required to make the formal request. I was provided with an English version of the treaty, which perhaps would interest you."

Juliet skimmed the pages of the treaty in search of the relevant sections, reading silently to herself. *Article XII, Provisional Arrest. . .Provisional arrest shall be terminated if, within a period of 45 days after the apprehension of the person sought, the Executive Authority of the Requested Party has not received a formal request for extradition. . .*

"But what are the charges?" Alessandro asked. "I have now finished with the papers; they say nothing of what is involved."

"We know no more than you at this point. You realize it is all an unfortunate occurrence that your husband entered Italy when he did. The more probable occurrence was that his arrest should take place in France, if he had not been taken at the airport here."

Melazzo took the papers back from Alessandro and placed them in the folder before closing it. The news that the United States was seeking François's extradition struck a fresh blow. No longer could she hide behind the hope that any of this could be resolved quickly. The matter was serious; the United States would not seek extradition over a trivial offense. If François decided to fight extradition, he would be in jail in Rome for a long time.

"I have told you all I know," Melazzo said. "You should feel free to come to me, Alessandro, in a few days. I might know more then, though as you can see from the treaty, it is as likely that we will find out nothing for a while."

This seemed to signal an end to the meeting. Alessandro stood up, folded his glasses and put them back in his jacket pocket. Melazzo followed suit.

"Will it be possible to see François today?" Juliet asked Alessandro when they were outside.

"Visits must take place before one o'clock. We can try today to reach him by telephone."

"It's not something I want to tell him over the telephone."

Alessandro nodded understandingly. "May I bring you to your hotel?" he asked gently.

"I want to walk," she said.

"Then I will see you tomorrow," he said, kissing her lightly on both cheeks before leaving.

As she walked she thought back over the events of the past few weeks. In Tunisia, he had several business calls, nothing out of the ordinary, but she remembered observing a few days before they left that he seemed upset after getting off the phone. They went for a swim and afterwards whatever was bothering him seemed to have passed.

She wondered what the next few weeks would bring for François? For herself? Tomorrow she would see him the way she would see him in the weeks and months to follow, a prisoner inside a jail. She would tell him the bad news. They would both try to be optimistic. She imagined that he would be stoic and she would be supportive. His new life as prisoner and hers as wife of the defendant would begin. As a lawyer it had been easy to separate the defendant from the accusations. She doubted whether that was possible when the defendant was her husband. The uncertainty and the waiting were unbearable.

She stopped in a church, small, humble rather than glorious, with dark walls; a beautiful mosaic of Christ's serene face decorated the floor. Votive candles burned in an alcove at the altar. She dropped a coin into the coin box and lit a thin wooden stick on the flame of a candle burning with someone else's prayer. The flame ignited onto the end of the stick as the two prayers for an instant became one before she lit a new candle and snuffed out the flame in the sand.

Outside she felt the sun on her face, the warm Mediterranean sun. The breeze was sweet, and she gave in to the simple pleasure of a sunny afternoon until she thought of François inside a jail and the beautiful sky and the sweet breeze made it all somehow worse.

5

It was almost noon before Alessandro arrived at the Hotel Eden.

"I'm sorry, my dear. My client cannot keep from repeating himself. And I wanted to stop for chocolates and cigarettes for the secretaries in the office at the jail." He sighed and tossed the raincoat and umbrella from the front seat into the back. Juliet noticed he was driving a different car, an old tan Fiat. The door on the passenger side was stuck, and he had to get out of the car and open it from the outside so she could get in. The backseat was cluttered with magazines and papers.

"As you can see, the car is a disaster," he said. "My wife needed my car to go to the doctor. My sons use this car. But today unfortunately for them, they have to go by motorcycle."

He drove very fast, hugging the car in front of him. Juliet braced herself by holding onto the door.

She looked at her watch; they had been driving for about twenty-five minutes.

"We're almost there," he said. He pulled over suddenly into a parking lot of dirt and grass.

"We have to walk from here."

Juliet looked at the sky, which had been darkening gradually since morning. It was hot and sticky and it was going to rain for sure, she thought.

"Why don't we take the umbrella?" she said, as she reached into the back seat to get it.

They walked through an open gate and up a hill along a road that led to a group of pavilions. She noticed the wire fence beneath the ivy. From the outside the jail resembled a run-down villa; the grass was tall and parched, and yellow and brown mums grew wild like weeds.

They entered through the main door of the first pavilion. She took a seat while Alessandro talked to the man at the desk. An old man, a woman and a small boy were sitting on the bench next to her. The boy tugged at the woman's sleeve, *"Mamma, Mamma, vieni, vieni."* He seemed to want to show her something on the other side of the room. The old man took the boy's hand and the boy led him to the end of the bench where a grasshopper rested motionless as a blade of grass. Juliet watched the old man bend down and catch the grasshopper in his hands. At the boy's insistence, the old man held his cupped hand out to the boy's mother and she peeked inside.

Juliet smiled at her. "He's beautiful," she said.

"Do you have children?" the woman asked.

Juliet shook her head.

The woman nodded. "Not yet."

A memory of waiting as painful as what she felt at that moment came back to her, and she felt empty in a way only a child could fill. They had tried to have a child. François had been good to her. She was the one who stopped. And he had told her at the time, "You need to rest, to get over the disappointment, but it will happen. When you are ready we will start again." And it had been a comfort to her to know that he felt that way. But as she sat on the jail bench waiting for permission to see him she realized that the opportunity to have a child together might be taken from them along with everything else and it made the empty feeling she had worse.

Alessandro approached her. "We have to go to the *infermeria*," he said. "Apparently François is there."

"Why? Has something happened?"

"No, no, they assure me simply they did not want to put him in a cell and they did not know where else to put him."

They entered a building that looked like a garage, ducking to pass through a large metal sliding door that was open only halfway. A fluorescent bulb gave off a blue glare distorting all sense of time; it could have been day or night. They were greeted by two prison guards in military fatigues and armed with attack rifles.

Alessandro asked Juliet for her passport. The guard at the desk said something in Italian to Alessandro.

"He wants to see your business card," Alessandro said.

She took the card from her wallet and handed it to the guard, who glanced at it before carefully turning the pages of a loose-leaf binder and checking the card against the name on the passport and the name in the book. Then he put the passport to the side.

"Why won't he give me my passport back?"

"He has to keep it until we are ready to leave," Alessandro explained.

She had to get used to everything being filtered to her through other people, she thought.

The guard pointed to the umbrella and shook his head.

"You have to leave the umbrella here," Alessandro said.

Alessandro undid the wrapping of the package he was carrying and went through an explanation in Italian.

"*Sì, sì,*" the guard said, shaking his head up and down as Alessandro explained.

Then Alessandro handed him the cigarettes, after which he made a characteristically Italian expression, bringing his lips together and jutting the lower lip forward. Juliet took it to signify not exactly approval, but something like, *What can I do if you want to bribe me?*

They went outdoors again and walked past a neat row of bungalows, each one the size of a small room, with flat roofs and a small window close to the roof covered by a grate with no screen.

A white sign, "Infermeria," hung from a large square stone building at the end of the walk. They entered through a screened door that to their surprise was unlocked and un- attended. A tall African woman, dressed in a colorful floor- length skirt and wearing a scarf wound tightly around her head, sat on a hallway bench nursing an infant. Paintings done by inmates decorated the walls, giving the appearance more of an elementary school than a jail, Juliet thought.

They walked to the end of the hallway where behind a rail half a dozen women who appeared to be secretaries or clerks were seated in three rows of neatly arranged desks. They were all dressed alike in a uniform of white short-sleeve blouses and navy blue straight cotton skirts, and again it seemed to Juliet more like a school than a jail.

Alessandro spoke to the woman at the first desk. Juliet watched him gesture with his hands as he spoke, standing with his weight shifted to one side of his body. He had a re- laxed, warm manner that put people at ease.

A secretary escorted them to a small conference room off the hallway. The walls were bare and dirty white, almost gray like the rug. The window looked out on a high metal fence lined with ivy. Juliet was surprised to find Jean Dugommier, a lawyer she associated with Compagnie Financière, sitting at the table. His distinctly French face, with its contrast of features, the thin bony nose and long dark brown eyes against his pale complexion, made him appear cold, just as the refined shape of his lips suggested a judgmental quality. Seeing Alessandro standing beside him, Juliet thought, was like the feeling she got going from Paris to Rome, of going from a place where the light was violet and blue to the hazy ochre pallor of Rome.

Alessandro broke into a big smile. "Jean Dugommier, how many years has it been?"

"Alessandro." Dugommier stiffly embraced the other man. "François mentioned that he had Juliet call you. *Comment allez-vous?*"

"Ah, still working too hard and not making any money." Alessandro laughed.

"Juliet." Dugommier kissed her on both cheeks, gently taking both of her hands in his.

"Have you seen François?" she asked.

"Not yet. I had to make arrangements with the French Consulate before I could visit."

Alessandro began to recount to Dugommier what they had learned from Melazzo at the ministry, and she stepped away and took a seat at the table. It was disturbing to find Dugommier at the jail. François would not have called him unless he was already aware of the nature of the allegations, she thought.

The sky was dark and the air smelled of rain. Sparrows fluttered in and out of the shrubs that lined the path. The window was open, with no bars, only a flimsy screen. She touched it, and the dirt made a black mark on the end of her finger.

"*Prigioniero Fournier, Infermeria*," a secretary called out.

After a few minutes a guard escorted François to the conference room. To her relief, his hands were free. He wore the white t-shirt and gray cotton pants issued by the jail. He had neither shaved nor showered.

She caught him acknowledging Dugommier at once with a knowing glance, before turning to Alessandro, whom he greeted generously, and lastly, to her.

"*Chérie*, you haven't slept," he said.

"I couldn't," she said. "Are you all right?"

"I think of you," he said quietly.

She wanted to tell him that she missed him at night; the night without him in bed beside her was hardest. And whereas before the words would have slipped with ease from her tongue, Dugommier, Alessandro, the guard at the door—all of it—made it seem impossible and she held back.

The guard told him to take a seat and to put his hands on the table. It upset her to see him spoken to in that way. If it upset him, he did not let on.

She took a pack of cigarettes out of her purse and put it on the table for him. He nodded in thanks. She tried to catch his gaze, but since he came into the room he seemed to want to avoid eye contact with her.

"They said my things could be picked up at the office. I had five thousand francs in my wallet. I remembered too late, Juliet, you had no cash," he said.

"*Ce n'est pas grave*," she answered. She gazed straight at him, waiting for him to look at her, but he turned to Alessandro instead.

"It's better to speak English," he said. "I do not mean to offend you, Alessandro, but they do not understand English."

"I am all too acquainted with their limitations," Alessandro said.

"Has anyone told you yet why you have been arrested?" Dugommier asked.

"I made a request of the director, but there has been no response. I ask the guards; they say they are not told."

Juliet glanced toward the window. Black clouds now covered the sky and the air was very still and heavy. She had given bad news to people in the past, but she had never loved them.

"You must have spoken to someone who knows something by now," François said to Alessandro.

"We went to the ministry yesterday," Alessandro began. "I am afraid the United States is seeking your extradition."

"Extradition?"

"Yes, they want to bring you to the States to face charges," Alessandro said.

"What are the charges?" The muscles in his face tightened as he strained to stay calm.

"There we are in the dark," Alessandro said.

"*Comment?*"

She caught him glancing at Dugommier again as if he were waiting for him to say something. Dugommier said nothing, continuing to listen to Alessandro explain the procedure involved. It struck Juliet that Dugommier did not seem surprised by the extradition.

"The Americans have forty-five days to present written charges to the Italian court," Alessandro continued. "Before that time they need say nothing, but the obligation of the

Italian government under the extradition treaty persists because the Americans have sought your arrest."

"How long is this going to take?" François asked. He seemed shaken.

"Forty-five days—from there, who knows?"

"And until then, I stay here?"

"Unfortunately for you, yes," Alessandro said. "The warrant was received by chance on the day you entered Rome. I say by chance, I should say, an unlucky chance. Unbelievable—you should enter Rome on that day, a day earlier and no one would have looked for you here. But now, because you are here, in the custody of the Italian government, the American prosecutors will insist that you remain here and fight the extradition from here."

"Incredible. You are telling me I have to stay in this jail, and there is nothing I can do."

His voice was raised and he seemed indignant and nervous and no longer capable of containing his frustration. She tried to put her hand on his wrist to calm him, but he became more upset and pulled away.

"François, I am so sorry. *C'est dommage*," Alessandro said.

François turned to Dugommier. "*Maître*, why can't I go back to Paris—anywhere in France? You realize, don't you, it is harder for them if it is France."

"They realize too; that is why they like you in Italy," Dugommier answered.

For an awkward moment no one could find anything to say. It began to rain, a heavy summer rain that splashed through the screen. François took a cigarette from the pack she had put on the table. Dugommier offered his lighter. The first few drags seemed to restore his composure. "*Vous per-*

mettez?" he said, looking over toward Dugommier and Alessandro, who seemed to understand that he wanted them to leave.

They were alone. The sound of the rain seemed to fill the silence between them. He looked out the window as he smoked.

"You know what this is about, don't you?" she said.

She waited for his eyes with their familiar light to meet her gaze, but he continued to look away, his head slightly bowed, the cigarette poised between his fingers. The room smelled of rain and cigarette smoke.

He turned away from the window though he did not look up from the table, his eyes lowered, his head bowed.

"Yesterday I spent the day on a cot waiting for someone to arrive and tell me I could leave. When I began to lose hope I told myself steps were being taken and I would not have to wait much longer."

He stopped to smoke, looking up and glancing back at the door. Alessandro and the guard were speaking in Italian. The guard seemed to have forgotten that they were alone in the room.

"The day ends early here, before dark. I asked for something to sleep, and because I was new I was given something. I woke up thirsty, and I had forgotten where I was. I reached for you until I heard the man in the cot next to mine cough. Someone was crying in the dark; I could hear it for a long time. That was the worst."

He took a last hard drag on the cigarette before putting it out. Then he got up and stood by the window where the air was fresh. She went to him and rested her hand on his shoulder, so familiar she kissed it. This time he did not push her away.

"How long have you known?" she said. "Weeks? Months maybe? How many nights did you come home as if nothing was wrong? When you slept next to me, when you made love to me, you knew and you never let on."

At last he turned and let his gaze meet hers. "You are right. I knew and I did not tell you. I am the one who has everything at stake."

"No," she said. "Whatever you lose, I lose too. Do you think it's easy for me to see you this way? Because I pulled myself together today, don't think last night I didn't fall apart."

He caressed her cheek, looking at her as if there were something he wanted to say, but he stopped himself.

"Tell me," she said, gently.

He caressed her face with his eyes and, taking her hand in his, brought it to his lips and kissed it. He no longer seemed to care about the guard as he wrapped his arms around her and drew her against him. And feeling his arms holding her, she brought her mouth to his and kissed him. She remembered the last night in Tunisia, the last night they were together, the fan beating the torpid air into a breeze, his tanned body against hers and the taste of the sea on his skin, and the desire she felt for him overwhelmed everything, the jail seemed flimsy and insubstantial; none of it mattered for as long as he held her.

She felt him let go, though she did not, wanting it to last, her head buried in his shoulder as if she could make whatever was about to break them apart disappear by something as simple as refusing to let go.

"There are gentlemen from the United States here to see you." Alessandro called from the doorway.

When she turned around, it seemed that what was happening could not possibly be true. The breath caught in her chest and she felt confusion, shock, disbelief, and she could not speak or react.

"Mr. de Fournier, I'm Michael Chase, Assistant United States Attorney for the Southern District of New York. This is Richard Giordano, an investigator with DEA, United States Drug Enforcement Agency. We'd like to speak with you."

In the silence that followed everything seemed frozen. It struck her that François sensed something, for he stepped in front of her protectively and, shielding her from the gaze of the man who had just introduced himself as Michael Chase, he extended his hand as if this were the start of a business meeting.

"This is my wife, Juliet."

"The woman at the desk told me you were meeting with your wife," Michael Chase said, directing his remark at Juliet. A trace of a smile showed at the corners of his mouth. "It's been a long time, Juliet."

"Hello, Mike," Juliet said quietly, as if she had not yet found her voice. She swallowed hard. Suddenly she wished everyone in the room would go away.

She looked across the room at Michael Chase. He was just six feet tall, but he could make himself look taller or shorter. He was good at creating illusions. He was not handsome. In fact, from certain angles, he was almost ugly, but there was something undeniably charismatic about him, something in his voice and his large blue eyes that drew people to him.

He turned to Richard Giordano. "Tell them to bring in two more chairs. See if we can get some coffee, too."

Giordano spoke to the guard in Italian. "He wants to know if he should take her outside," he said, gesturing toward her while looking at Mike.

"Tell him Mrs. de Fournier is a lawyer; she should stay," Mike said.

She could sense François watching her as if he were aware of something taking place that had nothing to do with him. Whereas earlier he had refused to look at her, now it was she who avoided his gaze.

Chairs were brought in and everyone took their places around the table.

"François, if you agree, I will speak for you," Alessandro said in French.

François seemed satisfied to let Alessandro speak.

"You will give me your assurance neither of you is using a recorder of any kind," Alessandro said.

"We can give you that assurance," Mike said.

"There must be something you have to say or you would not have come all the way to Rome—not that Rome is not a place to come. But now, during the weeks of the Caesars—" he said, as he raised his eyebrows, "only the mosquitoes like Rome."

"You gave us a little bit of an advantage by getting arrested in Italy," Mike said to François.

Juliet felt her face go flush. She would never forgive herself for insisting that they come to Rome.

"We're here because I was hoping to wrap all of this up quickly, which would be in our interest as well as yours," Mike said.

"Perhaps first you will tell us what Mr. de Fournier is supposed to have done to warrant his sudden arrest," Alessandro said.

Juliet caught Mike looking over at her again, "It's a little unusual to ask someone to give up before you've told him what the charges are," she said.

Mike laid his briefcase on the table as if he were about to take something out, though he never opened it.

One of the women from the office brought a pot of coffee and six cups, and placed it on the table in front of Mike. He poured a cup and passed it to Juliet. She felt her hand shake as she took it and she caught him watching her as if he had been testing her. Then he poured a second cup for himself. The others helped themselves.

"Your wife is right; I should tell you the charges first," Mike began. "You have been arrested because we have evidence that five years ago when you purchased the Great American Bank in New York, you were in fact acting as a front for a group of Saudi investors. You lied on disclosure forms and in testimony before the Federal Reserve Board to make it appear that the bank was being purchased by you. You never owned the bank; you were merely a nominee, using your name to conceal the true ownership of the bank by the Saudi investors."

"Forgive me," Alessandro interrupted, "but you are insisting that Mr. de Fournier remain here in jail for this! Perhaps I am making judgment in haste, but perjury is not an offense for which extradition is possible under the treaty."

"Perjury, fraud, violations of the United States securities laws and the Bank Holding Company Act to be precise. In any case, the charges don't end there." Mike took the coffee pot and poured himself another cup. The rain was falling pretty heavily, loud enough to be distracting.

Mike looked over at François. "By the way, the ten million you were paid to do this—not a bad fee for telling the same lie three or four times," he said.

Juliet caught him looking at François as if he was waiting

for his reaction, yet François gave away nothing of what he was thinking.

"You do speak English?" Mike asked. "Maybe it was presumptuous of me. I'm not trying to be sarcastic; I just want to make sure."

François nodded.

Mike glanced at her and she quickly averted her eyes; then he continued.

"Mr. de Fournier, the United States government can prove that Great American Bank was being used to launder funds out of the Middle East. After you took control, the bank began making loans to untraceable foreign entities for millions of dollars; there was defaulting on the loans. Some of this money was used to purchase arms and explosives for terrorist organizations in Pakistan, Afghanistan and Lebanon. We have evidence that the proceeds of at least one of these loans went to the organization that claimed responsibility for the bombing outside the American Embassy in Cairo in which five people died.

François sipped from his coffee and rested the cup on the table, folding his hand around the cup.

"There's another charge," Mike said. "This is more recent, and I don't have to tell you, but I'm not trying to trick you— here our investigation is only in the early stages. Which, I might add, is why it is to your advantage to try to reach some agreement with us at this stage. We believe we can link you to the recent murder of Alain Gilbert in New York. I think you knew that he was under investigation. Two weeks ago he decided to cooperate. Your name was on the short list of people he said he could give up. Within days of his agreeing to cooperate, he was murdered. We weren't sure who he had called in Tunisia until two days ago when you were arrested."

Juliet felt her throat tightening as if the air were about to be cut off. However much she wanted to look over at François, she was afraid of what he might tell her with his eyes.

Mike turned toward Alessandro. "This is terrorism. People have been killed. I think we can agree that these are extraditable offenses."

"If the allegations are as you have recited them, then yes," Alessandro answered, "the allegations themselves fall within the treaty. But it is not enough simply to accuse: there must also be the evidence to support the allegations. Here I will tell you that I am confused. You say Mr. de Fournier is 'linked' to the death of Alain Gilbert. Mr. de Fournier was on the other side of the world when Alain Gilbert died. What evidence exists to support this accusation?"

"I'm not here to discuss evidence," Mike said, staring hard at François. "The United States government is committed to devoting its resources to prosecuting this case. Under the extradition laws we can keep you in jail here for a long time." He seemed to pause to emphasize what he had just said. "The only way you can get out any sooner is by consenting to extradition, coming to New York in the custody of the U.S. marshals, and pleading guilty to something. We think you have information that would be helpful in our investigation of certain individuals."

He paused again, looking around the room and directing his steady gaze at Juliet. But she was resolved not to give away anything of what she felt, and he turned back to François as he continued.

"In particular, Saudi banker, Etienne Dufois, who our records indicate is responsible for approximately seventy percent of the investment capital in Compagnie Financière. In exchange for your assistance in our prosecution of Dufois, we would be willing to help you at sentencing. It's simple. You save us time: we save you time."

François turned the cup in his hand. Juliet saw all eyes turn to him, though he remained inscrutable.

"If you don't believe me," Mike said, "ask your wife. I think she'll tell you the same thing—it's better to cooperate at the outset."

"I'd appreciate it if you didn't speak for me," she said coldly. Her full voice had returned. "If you want to know what I think, a few phone calls are nothing. He's not going to do anything until you tell him what your evidence is."

"You know how the game is played, Mrs. de Fournier. If he wants to hear the evidence, I'd be happy to present it at a trial in New York. That's at least six months away if he fights extradition."

"I'm not playing a game," she said.

"Bad choice of words," he said, his eyes lingering on her face.

"There is nothing to say," François said.

He took the pack of cigarettes and offered it to Giordano, who took one, and then to Mike.

"I quit," Mike said.

François nodded. Then he lit a cigarette. A cloud of blue smoke hung over the table.

"Mr. Dugommier, you've been silent," Mike said, turning to him. "Perhaps you have something to add."

"Not at this point," Dugommier said.

"I guess we're finished," Mike said. He waited a moment before he stood and took his briefcase from the table.

François stood to shake his hand. Dugommier and Alessandro did the same, and it seemed to Juliet, who remained seated, that everyone was acting as if nothing more than a mere business meeting had just drawn to a close.

"If you need to get in touch with me, here's where I'm staying," Mike said, placing a piece of hotel stationery on the table. Hotel Sardinia, Juliet read silently before handing it to Alessandro.

"Allow me to walk you out," Alessandro said.

She looked out the window at the rain. It seemed to have let up. She had not been prepared. Not for seeing Michael Chase, not for the things he had said. Alain Gilbert dead and François implicated in his murder. He must have known when they were in Tunisia, and his hiding it from her was a betrayal, a silent lie that cut a wedge between them. But Dugommier remained in the room and she wanted to be alone when she spoke to him.

"Michael Chase knows you," François said.

She turned to face him. "Yes, we knew one another in New York. I represented a client he prosecuted."

She wanted to say something more, and she felt the pressure of time, but for the second time that afternoon, the words would not come. Yet it angered her that he had put her on the defensive when it should have been the other way around.

He turned to Dugommier. "*Alors, maître,*" he began, and he folded his hands together as if he had nothing more to say, she thought, though so much remained open and unaccounted for.

"I will go to the consulate this afternoon and appeal to the French government to intercede for your extradition to France," Dugommier said. "In France we can be more confident of the outcome."

In the eye contact between the two men she sensed an understanding beyond the conversation that was taking place.

"I have friends in the Ministry of Justice. They have helped me before—"

She interrupted, no longer able to contain herself. "François, we are talking about terrorism—not a business deal. Be realistic."

"You believe the Americans. You think what he said is true. I am a terrorist? Is that what you think?"

He sounded hostile; he was not shouting, but she knew if he were anywhere else he would have been.

"I didn't say that. I'm saying it's going to be hard to find people who are willing to do you a favor under the circumstances."

"Juliet, *s'il vous plait*," Dugommier interrupted. "We don't have much time."

"No, she's right," François said quietly. "It will be hard."

"We will try to persuade the consulate to act quickly," Dugommier said.

"Until then?" François asked. He seemed calm again, inscrutable.

"Until then we wait," Dugommier answered.

"What about Compagnie Financière? I need to run things. It is not possible from here."

"We have to see what happens in the next few days," Dugommier said.

"I have to be concerned that Compagnie Financière will be forced to shut down."

"François, you have twenty-five employees," Dugommier smiled. "*Alors, nous sommes bien en France*. They will not put twenty-five people out of work."

46

"Juliet will need money in an account if she is going to stay in Rome." He turned to her. "Is that what you want?"

"I'm not going to leave you here," she said. But part of her wondered if he wanted her to leave, and what Dugommier said a moment later confirmed her feeling.

"Juliet, I need to speak to François alone. I am sorry." From her own experience as a lawyer she knew her presence inhibited their ability to speak freely. And yet she resented the conspiracy of silence she felt growing around her. She remained, her gaze steady in François's direction, hoping for something more from him, a protest, an explanation.

"We will talk tomorrow," he offered, though from the way he said it, he seemed to comprehend that even that was uncertain and outside his control.

"*A demain*," she said, forcing herself to smile.

6

They had to go to a separate building for François's things. A gray-haired little woman stood behind the desk as if she were selling religious artifacts in a tourist shop outside the Vatican. The buttons of her cotton dress pulled across her large stomach. Her hair was tied in a bun and her skin was smooth, without a wrinkle. A few minutes passed before she returned with François's black carry-on suitcase and a package wrapped in brown paper tied like pastries with a taut ribbon instead of string.

The woman asked Juliet to sign for the package.

Juliet opened the wrapped bundle. Inside was François's blazer, his watch, the keys to their Paris apartment and his wallet. When she opened the wallet the francs were missing.

She pointed to the empty billfold. "He had five thousand francs. The money is gone."

The woman shrugged and spoke rapidly in Italian.

Alessandro turned to Juliet. "She says she has nothing to do with that."

"I'm not going to sign for it like this," Juliet said.

Alessandro turned to the woman and gave his own rendition in Italian of what Juliet had just said.

The woman reached to take the package out of Juliet's hands.

"She can't give it to you unless you sign," Alessandro said.

Juliet clutched the package. "*Voleur.*" She felt her voice getting thin and high. "I too have rights. I have the right not to be robbed blind by a bunch of—" the sentence was left unfinished as she broke into tears. It came over her unexpectedly, a mixture of fatigue, confusion and anger coupled with fear for the future. Everything that she felt, the words that she had been at a loss for all morning seemed captured by having been robbed of the money in François's wallet. She did not care about the five thousand francs; it was everything else that was being taken from her in the same gesture, the bundle of her husband's clothes in a brown paper wrapper, the feeling it gave her of holding it in her arms as if he no longer existed. François had been taken from her, not just physically, but everything he was, everything she thought she knew about him had been shattered and smashed into pieces like a room ransacked by a thief. The old woman with the button pulling over her stomach insisting that she sign for it was just the last straw. She felt Alessandro's arm around her and she tried to stop herself from crying, but with each attempt, a fresh sob burst from inside her.

The old woman asked if she would like a drink of water. Alessandro nodded, and the old woman disappeared behind the desk, coming back with a tiny paper cone filled with water and a handful of tissues.

Alessandro signed for the package. The old woman was willing to accept this, and she handed it to Alessandro, who gently led Juliet outside.

It was raining hard again and they waited for the rain to stop before going out to the car.

"I suppose there are things François needs to discuss with Jean Dugommier concerning Compagnie Financière. Actually, I have no idea what François needs to discuss. I'm sorry, Alessandro. I don't know what to say."

"My dear, you do not have to say anything on my account."

They stood watching the rain, which showed no signs of relenting.

Too much had happened and she needed time before she could think clearly. She crossed her arms as if she were holding herself.

"Are you cold?" Alessandro asked with concern.

"No, no, just thinking," she said quietly.

When she first learned of the extradition, she assumed that it must have something to do with Compagnie Financière; in that sense she was prepared to hear the allegations relating to François having served as a nominee and had already begun to rationalize them to herself. But the loans to terrorist organizations and Alain's murder—Alain who was François's friend—these were different. It was no longer a question of his having broken a rule that to a foreigner might have seemed overly formalistic. If he had crossed the line in an overseas business deal, guilty or not, she would not view him any differently. But these other things frightened her. And Michael Chase—it was too much all at once.

"What did those imbeciles in the garage think we were going to do with an umbrella?" Alessandro said, annoyed.

"Listen, can't we run to the garage? I really don't care if I get wet; I just don't feel like being here anymore," she said.

"Let me go ahead, and I will come back for you with the umbrella."

"It's not necessary. I couldn't possibly feel any worse than I already do. Besides, isn't rain supposed to bring good luck?"

When they reached the garage, they were both drenched, and she noticed that Alessandro was a little out of breath.

"Then it's true; American girls are tomboys," Alessandro said. "You ran very fast, and in heels, my God!"

"Now you can be satisfied that the jail was safe while you held our umbrella," Alessandro told the guard.

The guard muttered something in Italian as he handed Alessandro the umbrella.

As they walked to the car, she slid her arm inside Alessandro's so they could both fit under the umbrella. A little puddle had formed inside the toe of her shoe, and it made a squeaking sound with each step she took. By the time they reached the car, she had a chill. She felt her hair dripping down her back. Alessandro turned on the car heater, which seemed to help.

It was almost three o'clock and Alessandro suggested stopping at a roadside bar for lunch. They took a seat at one of two tiny tables in the front. The bar was empty except for an old man smoking and drinking a coffee and the boy behind the counter. Alessandro ordered ham and cheese sandwiches and a large bottle of mineral water. To Juliet's surprise she was hungry and the sandwich tasted good. When they had finished Alessandro ordered two espressos.

He put a cube of sugar in his coffee.

Juliet smiled. "The sugar has made a little island in the middle of your cup," she said.

"Ah yes, well, coffee is better when it's sweet. Don't you take sugar?"

"No," she said.

"You are sweet enough without it, my dear."

He took two sips, finished the coffee and placed the sugar-coated cup onto the table.

"You would like to return to the hotel, I presume."

"Please."

Traffic was slow because of the rain, and the silence began to seem awkward.

"Forgive me," Alessandro said, "but I am presuming you have worked with the American prosecutor, Michael Chase, in the past."

"We had a case together several years ago; I represented someone he was prosecuting."

"You won, of course," Alessandro smiled.

"There was a plea negotiation."

"You say plea negotiation." Alessandro stumbled a little over the pronunciation of negotiation. "In other words, your client made a plea of culpable?"

"My client said he was guilty and didn't want a trial. So in exchange he spent less time in jail. That in the United States is called plea bargaining."

"And the prosecutor, Michael Chase, recommends that this is what François should do? Is there a reason why he would make such a recommendation?"

"People like Mr. Chase always start out saying the same things, whether they have the evidence or not."

She saw no reason to admit to Alessandro at this point that even if Mike were bluffing, there had to be some truth to the allegation; as much as she might wish otherwise, it could not all be a complete mistake.

"They are offering François very little to ask him to make testimony against a man like Etienne Dufois," Alessandro said. "Dufois." He smiled as if he were thinking aloud. "Short, fat, bald and married to the most beautiful woman I have ever seen." His voice resolved into a laugh. "What money can buy! He, I am sure, will not be pleased by this turn of events."

"I take it you know Dufois?" Somehow it did not surprise Juliet that Alessandro would know Dufois.

"Know him?" Alessandro hunched his shoulders. "Not in the sense that I would call on him or he would call on me. But I have met him on a few occasions. Without the money of the sheiks, Dufois would have been just another poor Arab. Luckily for him, they have made him incredibly rich. And you, I imagine, have also had the pleasure of meeting him?"

"We would receive invitations to his parties, the big ones, never anything intimate. Why would someone in Dufois's position involve himself with terrorist organizations?" she asked. "I find it hard to believe."

"My dear, I could not possibly tell you—if I could fathom myself." He shrugged. "Money? Perhaps some obligation to someone more powerful in the Middle East? What can I say? This is a most unfortunate situation. You say the word terrorism to these judges and suddenly they become excited. Dufois, François—terrorists. Forgive me, my dear, you are right, it sounds fantastic."

"Fantastic, yes. As if it couldn't possibly be true," she said. Any of it, she thought, then she felt her heart sink.

"It might be best for François to remain in Rome," Alessandro said. "Unless, of course, he can return to France. You are free to disagree, as this adversary is someone you know—in Rome it is not inconceivable that the tribunal could decline the request for extradition." After a pause he added, "This is my view for the moment."

She considered Alessandro's advice; if going to New York meant remaining in jail there, then it was true, there was no rush. It also struck her that by moving the case to New York, they would be restoring Mike's home court advantage; in Rome both parties were foreigners.

"My wife and I are having guests to dinner. She would chastise me if I did not invite you."

She wanted to be alone now, but she knew she would feel differently at night.

"I will come to the hotel for you at eight-thirty. There is no need for you to wait outside. I will call to your room when I arrive."

7

The day before Mike Chase left for Rome, he had received a call from the Deputy Attorney General, advising him that François de Fournier had been picked up at Fiumicino Airport in Rome. The Deputy Attorney General explained that de Fournier was someone of importance in the European business community. Because of the possible political ramifications abroad, Justice wanted Mike to handle the case. He was told to drop everything and leave the next day for Rome. He had been waiting for the right case to make his move into the world of fancy law firms and million-dollar fees. When he got off the phone he felt as if he had just been handed his ticket to private practice.

It was his idea to involve Richie Giordano. They had worked together during the years Mike headed the Narcotics Division of the U.S. Attorney's Office. Like most second-generation Italian Americans, Richie was half Sicilian, half Neapolitan. Unlike lawyers, who spend a good part of their lives wishing they had done something else, Richie had never wanted to be anything other than a DEA agent. Regardless of whether drugs were involved, Mike did not try a big case without his help. Here it had been easy to justify since Richie spoke Italian.

Upon arriving in Rome, Mike knew almost nothing about the case. What he did know, he had read on the flight. He was not prepared for what happened when he got to Rebibbia. He was not prepared for the woman in François de Fournier's arms to turn around and be Juliet.

"Fucking Juliet Mason. Can you believe it? I bet she was loving life until two days ago," Richie said once they were outside the jail.

Fucking Juliet Mason. Richie was right, Mike thought.

When they got back to the hotel, he wanted to sleep for a few hours. He barely had taken off his jacket when Richie knocked on his door. He seemed excited.

"Your friend Juliet Mason is staying at the Hotel Eden. I made a call over to the embassy and to Interpol. They're willing to expedite the warrant. I told them we'd meet them at the embassy at five."

"Who told you to call Interpol?" This annoyed Mike. "We're not in a position to put a wiretap on her phone."

"We discussed this on the plane."

"Yeah, so what," Mike said flatly.

Richie seemed confused. "You said we should try to expedite putting a tap on de Fournier's wife's phone. As a matter of fact, you said that his wife would probably try to surface money in the next few days, and it was important to get the wire in a hurry."

"I changed my mind."

"We looked at the file together. You pointed out that his wife was making day trips to Switzerland." Richie threw open his hands in exasperation. "Come on, the airline records are there. You were the one who said he probably set up the accounts through her."

Mike merely nodded. "When I said it, I didn't know who his wife was."

Richie lifted his eyebrows. "You're backing off because of her, aren't you?"

"You're right. I am backing off. If you want to accuse me of backing off because of her, go ahead. She's a lawyer and you don't go around putting taps on the telephones of lawyers without knowing what you're doing. I don't care what country we're in—when this case gets before a federal judge in New York, we'd better be damned sure that we met all the requirements for a wiretap. We haven't even tried to trace de Fournier's other accounts. From everything I read, not a single bank record has been subpoenaed. You can't ask for a wiretap under those circumstances."

There was a knock on the door. Mike had forgotten that he'd ordered a bottle of mineral water from room service. The waiter looked for a place in the narrow room to put down the tray. The desk was crowded with papers. The waiter handed him the bottle, put the tray with the glasses on the bed and walked out of the room.

Richie seemed anxious to return to the discussion. "A wiretap didn't bother you yesterday."

"Because yesterday as far as I knew she was just some French housewife. It would have been close, but I thought we could get away with it. But she's not a French housewife, she's a lawyer, and the odds are good that the case will wind up in front of a judge who knows and likes her. I do not want to be in the position of having to explain a wiretap under those circumstances."

Mike poured himself a glass of water, drank and then put the glass down on the desk. "Justice said to be careful, this guy de Fournier is someone in France, and I want to avoid rushing out and doing something that down the road might appear to have been stupid. If Justice wanted that, they would have let any amateur handle the case."

"You're worried about what's going to happen in front of a federal judge. Yeah, well without a wiretap we may not make it to a federal judge."

"I read the file. I don't agree," Mike said. He was feeling exhausted, and he just wanted the conversation to be over, but Richie persisted.

"I read the file too. I didn't see anything in there that says de Fournier got any money. Maybe I had a few drinks on the flight over, but I wasn't out of it when you said we were on thin ice."

Mike started organizing the papers on the desk into neat piles. "It's a mistake to jump to conclusions," he said.

"You're the one who says that the best things in a case happen as a result of mistakes," Richie said.

Mike stopped what he was doing and turned to Richie. "I'm getting tired of listening to this. I make the decisions here. I've decided it's too soon to apply for a wiretap. We lose nothing by waiting; the hotel keeps records of every outgoing call she makes for billing purposes, so all our leads are there, and all we have to do is subpoena them. I'm not going to rush out to do something I could be criticized for when there's nothing to gain. She's not stupid; the woman is a defense lawyer. She's not going to say anything over the phone."

Richie shrugged. Mike could tell that he was not convinced.

"Look," Mike said, "I have more riding on this case than you, because if I win, it's my chance to get out of the government."

Richie smiled, ironically. "Then you better win." He put his hands in his pockets, a gesture signaling to Mike that for the time, at least, he had been out-argued. Rather than leave on an angry note, he seemed to want to diffuse the tension.

"Did you speak to the warden?"

"Yeah," Mike said, "They're moving him to a cell. You know, the more unpleasant it is, the sooner he'll fold."

"You think he's gonna cooperate?"

Mike shrugged. "Maybe," he said. He looked out the window. "It stopped raining. Why don't you go to one of those cafés on Via Veneto? I need to sleep for an hour. Let's meet in the lobby at six-thirty and we'll get a drink."

8

Mike unbuttoned his shirt and took a beer from the wet bar, then got the file and lay down on the bed. Richie was right about one thing: he was not comfortable with the evidence the government had. The government's only informant against de Fournier, Saed Abdul Radwan, was a Syrian national whom the United States Attorney's Office had given immunity from prosecution for a shady loan in exchange for his testimony in this larger investigation. Saed was a bit player; Alain Gilbert had been on the inside, but the government never had the chance to talk to Gilbert.

Mike took out the forensic report. Gilbert was killed with a .22 caliber weapon. The first shot was fired through the backbone at a distance of about two feet; a second bullet fired from the same distance pierced his heart. A third bullet was fired into the back of the head; whoever killed him wanted to make sure he was dead. The murder took place in Gilbert's Manhattan apartment on Sixty-sixth Street near Lincoln Center, with no evidence of a break-in; the killer entered with a key. Nobody heard anything. To Mike it had all the markings of a professional assassination; it was unlikely they would ever catch the gunman. No doubt the gun had already been disassembled and disposed of, and without a gun it was impossible to prosecute.

The last call Gilbert made to Tunisia took place from his home forty-eight hours before his death. The telephone number of the villa in Tunisia where de Fournier was staying was found on a notepad in Gilbert's apartment. All of this led Mike to conclude that Gilbert was trying to protect de Fournier by tipping him off to his decision to cooperate. De Fournier was the only insider he called during this period. No evidence existed that anyone else knew he was going to cooperate, which was why Mike believed de Fournier had to be behind Gilbert's murder.

He read the arrest report again: "François de Fournier, 37-year-old Caucasian male, 5′11″, 160 lbs, French national, arrested at 21:07, 29 August." There was a tape of a call from Gilbert to de Fournier's apartment in Paris. Mike had listened to it on the plane; it had seemed inconsequential at the time. He took out his recorder and listened to the tape again; there was a transcript in English, but he wasn't interested in what they were saying. It was Juliet's voice on the tape. He hadn't recognized it before because she was speaking French.

He finished the beer, and was starting to feel a little drowsy. He had been asleep for a few minutes when the phone rang and woke him.

"Hello, Mike, it's Juliet. I was wondering if you'd meet me for a drink at my hotel. I'm staying at the Eden. There's a bar off the lobby. Is an hour from now good?"

Mike reached for his watch, which he kept set to New York time no matter where he was.

"Five. Fine."

"See you then."

He showered and, catching his beard in the mirror, decided he needed to shave again. From the lobby he called Richie's room; there was no answer.

The man at the desk told him it was a fifteen-minute walk to the Hotel Eden. The sun was out now, and between jet lag and not having slept, it no longer felt like the same day. He cut across Via Sardegna onto Via Veneto, walked past the Excelsior Hotel and the American Embassy and turned right at Via Ludovisi.

He was a little early, and he was surprised to find Juliet already in the bar. She was seated at a table facing out onto a small courtyard.

Mike took her in with the room; her hair was swept up and her neck looked long and graceful. She wore a sleeveless black dress. She had beautiful arms, Mike thought. Her ring sparkled on her finger from a distance and she wore a three-strand pearl bracelet. Mike remembered she never wore pearls around her neck, only on her wrist. He stayed watching her for a long minute until he saw the bartender look over at him; then he went inside.

"How've you been, Mike?"

He took a seat across from her. Her face was poised; nothing seemed to move as she spoke, but for some reason he felt like there was a dig in there.

"I'm all right, I guess."

"Good for you," she said. "Will you join me in a drink? I think it would be better if we were both playing on the same field."

"A drink sounds fine. What have you got there?"

"Finlandia, straight up."

"Sounds all right."

"*Un altro, per favore*," she said to the bartender.

"You speak Italian?"

"No."

She folded her hands on the table, like a good girl from a good family, Mike thought.

"It's the universal language of poseurs and fakes—I can say 'hello' and 'please' and 'thank you' in whatever language anyone happens to be speaking."

"I don't think you're a fake," he said.

He was expecting her to be hostile, but instead she was taking it out on herself.

The bartender put the drink on the end of the bar. Mike got up to get it.

"Want anything?" he said.

"No, I'm fine for the moment."

Mike took his drink, and sat down again.

"Drink fast," she said. "You have to catch up."

She kept her hand with the diamond wedding band on top of the other one. Mike had the feeling she was doing it on purpose.

"It's been five years," he said. "You left without saying good-bye." He felt his voice softening without his wanting it to, just as he couldn't help himself from feeling happy to see her.

"I didn't think it was necessary."

"I called your office and they said you'd moved to Paris."

She lowered her eyes and put the hand with the wedding band around her glass.

"In Paris it was as if you had died," she said. "I couldn't let it go on, waiting at night for the phone to ring. You had your wife, but what did I have?"

"Elizabeth and I divorced three years ago."

She looked up at him. "I'm sorry," she said. She seemed to him surprisingly sincere.

"It's better really. We weren't meant for one another."

"What does it mean—'meant for one another'? Does it have a meaning to you?"

"I don't know; it's what people say. We weren't getting along."

"Who has custody of the two boys?"

"They live with Elizabeth and I see them weekends, vacations. Elizabeth is good about letting them spend time with me."

Juliet took a sip from her drink. "Was it acrimonious?" she asked.

He caught her looking at him as if she were studying his face. "It wasn't pleasant." He was anxious to change the subject. "Are you still working?"

"I would have thought you already knew the answer."

"I don't really know that much."

She lowered her eyes and put her fingers around her glass, holding it without drinking. The conversation seemed to have come to an end until she looked up again and her gaze met his.

"How long have you been investigating my husband?"

Husband—Mike was struck by the power of the word; she seemed so much a woman now. When she was with him all the pieces were there, but they hadn't really fallen into place, not before now when she referred to François as her husband.

"Juliet, maybe you won't believe me, but I was as surprised as you were. I'm telling you, I had no idea. I got the call from Justice the day before I left for Rome. I'm not sure anyone realized it."

"It can't be a coincidence, Mike. There are things that just can't be accounted for that way."

He put his hands around hers. Then he remembered how cold her hands always were. She pulled away from him, and he didn't quite understand why, but it hurt him.

"No one is trying to brush this aside. I'm just telling you that I didn't know before I walked into that room and you turned around."

"You ruined things for me once, isn't that enough? Aren't we only entitled to ruin someone once? Instead you came halfway across the world for a second shot." She banged her hand against the table. " Why are you doing this to me?"

He thought she might cry, but she didn't. Her eyes were like two pieces of ice.

"Tell me, what was it you couldn't stand? Was it the money? Was it because I married someone rich? Or was it because I found someone who loved me?"

"You know I loved you." He was immediately sorry he said it. He stopped himself from saying anything more, stopped short of telling her how often he thought about her.

"I want to talk about what's going to happen to François," she said. This time her voice was sharp, aloof rather than hostile.

He looked away and, out of the corner of his eye, caught a glimpse of the man sitting at the bar. Something about the way he was sitting, close enough to eavesdrop in an otherwise empty bar, gave Mike the impression that he was watching.

"Why don't we get out of here?" he said. "Let me take care of this," he said, referring to the bill.

"Don't bother," she said. "He'll put it on my tab. If it's all right with you, I'd like to skip having to say thanks to the U.S. government."

They got a taxi in front of the hotel. She told the driver to go to the Via Santa Cecilia in Trastevere. Mike had the impression she had some place in mind.

It was dusk and the streetlights were not yet lit. Everything appeared vague and covered in shadow.

"I didn't like the guy sitting at the bar," he said.

She shrugged, looking straight ahead, "I didn't notice."

"Be careful if you're going to stay in Rome."

"It's Rome, not Naples."

"I'm not talking about pickpockets. Your husband's friends are not nice people."

She turned toward him; the dusk light obscured her face.

"You have the wrong idea of him," she said.

Somehow he thought it was better not to answer.

The driver pointed to the church on the left. "Santa Cecilia, a very famous church," he said as he pulled over.

She suggested an outdoor bar nearby. "It's still too early for dinner," she said. "The work day doesn't end here until eight or eight-thirty. "

By remarks like that, he knew she was claiming the turf for her own. He looked at his watch. It was almost seven. Richie would be waiting for him in the lobby of their hotel. He looked around for the nearest phone. A woman was using it and a few people were waiting, so he decided to let it go.

They ordered coffee. He paid for it and waited at the counter while she went over to a table.

A gypsy boy approached the table cradling a duckling inside his shirt; its bright orange-yellow head peered out as the boy petted it. Mike handed him a hundred lire.

"He'll come back now with a friend," she said.

Mike watched the boy go around the corner. A minute later, he was back. This time a tall, Slavic-looking man was walking behind him. He bent on one knee to talk to them, and his breath reeked of alcohol.

"I'm from Bosnia. Please, do you have any money for food and a place to sleep?"

Juliet waved him away.

"He's not Bosnian; he's Polish," she said. "If you give him money, the gypsies won't let us alone."

It felt good to sit out in the air. It was dark now. The street was crowded with shoppers and tourists. She drank her coffee in silence. Having brought up the subject of what was going to happen to her husband, she no longer seemed to want to talk about it.

"You must have made a name for yourself by now," she said.

"I suppose."

"I know you wanted that."

"I prosecuted a big international drug ring a couple of years ago. The case was in the press for months. So what have you been up to?"

"I don't know as I can say. After all, I might be telling you something you don't know."

He was a little afraid of that too, afraid if he asked her anything about the present she might think he was trying to find out something he could use.

"It's amazing, you know, more than half the people on this street right now will go through their entire lives without seeing the inside of a jail, not even to visit one," she said after a while.

She looked away from him at the people passing by. "They'll never know the way a jail smells or the sallow look on every face, the endless hours and days of just logging time for time's sake. It wasn't until I got to Paris that I began to realize that you don't have to be sinking in human misery all the time. But maybe I should have known better than to think it could last."

Mike did not know what to say, but he felt as if he had to say something.

"I take it you're no longer practicing law," he offered.

"I thought we had a deal, we weren't going to talk about me." She was smiling for the first time.

"I'm sorry. I didn't mean to violate any agreement. You pretty much said so yourself," he said.

She played with her spoon for a moment, stirring it around in the dregs of her coffee.

"There are plenty of ambitious people without me," she said. "In the beginning I felt a little guilty—then I decided it's all right to be selfish. I'm someone's wife now, that's what I do. Besides, it's easy to waste time in Paris."

Mike kept looking at her; she was different now. Women are like that, he thought; they take on the personality of whatever city they're living in.

She was silent for a moment before turning to him and gazing at him with steady eyes.

"What are his options?" she asked.

It was like a door closing in his face, Mike thought, though he knew she was right; this was where they were now.

"You know what his options are. He can stay in jail and fight extradition or he can waive extradition and go to New York with no guarantees on bail. I might be willing to let him plead to fraud, but he'll have to cooperate." Mike lowered his eyes for a moment before lifting them again and looking straight at her. "I'd want you both to be clear, even if he cooperates, he's going to get time. A foreigner defrauding the U.S. banking system, loans to terrorist organizations, conspiracy to commit murder—it's not really in my control, they're going to insist that he get a jail sentence."

He was more comfortable talking professionally; then he felt sure of himself. He was no good at small talk.

She lowered her eyes again. When she looked back up, she was gazing straight at him.

"I want you to drop the extradition, Mike."

"You know I can't do that."

"What's ten million dollars to the U.S. government? Besides, there's a flaw in your case; if he was a nominee, then how are you going to prove he knew about the loans? He's not a terrorist, and without the terrorist angle your case has lost its jury appeal. So what if he played a little fast with the truth on a few forms? At worst, it's cheating, that's all. We've all cheated a little, Mike."

She was hitting a chord, and he was not going to let her get away with it. He grabbed her wrist. This time she did not pull away.

"Go ahead, try to water it down enough so you can swallow it. And while you're discounting coincidences, let's not forget your husband called his French lawyer before anyone told him what the charges were. Maybe you should be asking yourself how well you know your husband?"

She moved her arm away. "That's not your business," she said, sharply.

"Maybe not. But I know a lot of guys like him. You haven't been to a jail recently. Let me remind you, the jails are filled with guys like your husband. They always make the mistake of thinking there's someone they can buy to take the fall. But there never is. This isn't about cheating; people were killed. Do you know how much money a bank like this can put in the hands of terrorists?"

She stood up as if she were about to walk away. "You waited a long time for this, didn't you?" she said.

Without thinking, he reached over and grabbed her by the arm to prevent her from leaving. "I didn't do this, Juliet. Believe me."

"Maybe you're telling the truth, and the whole thing just fell in your lap. But if you go ahead, it doesn't make a difference, does it?"

He was glad it was dark because she was staring at him too intently.

"Let's get a cab," he said. "I'll drop you off at your hotel."

There was a taxi waiting at the taxi stand.

"Via Ludovisi, Hotel Eden," she told the driver.

Then she sat looking out the window. At the hotel she got out without saying good-bye.

He told the cab driver to wait until she was inside. He couldn't help noticing how good she looked from the back. She had a great walk, and her dress really showed it off. It occurred to him, the problem with seeing a woman naked is that afterwards, no matter what she's wearing, you can always picture her without any clothes on, that round ass of hers with the birthmark on one side that looked like a coffee stain, and the way the skin on her back was darker than the rest of her, probably the result of some tan she got as a kid.

By now it was almost eight o'clock, and he didn't have much hope that Richie would still be waiting for him. Unlike Juliet's hotel, the hotel where he was staying was dark, dusty, a three-star model; the government knew how to find those places in every city in the world. There was no lobby to speak of, only a front desk and two wooden chairs resting against the wall. When he went inside, the same woman who had been there in the morning sat behind the desk. She spoke some English, and Mike asked if he had any messages.

"*Sì, sì, Signore.*" She made a gesture, telling him to wait, and she took a note from his box.

Mike unfolded the little piece of white paper and read.

Got tired of waiting. I'm at Osteria Marcello, Via Aurora.

Richie

She was able to give him directions to Via Aurora, and he headed over to the restaurant.

9

When he arrived, he found Richie seated at a table near the back. The restaurant was crowded and noisy, the tables close together; it was a squeeze to get to the back. Richie was halfway through a bottle of red wine. The uneaten half of a roll sat in a pile of crumbs next to his plate. He seemed to be in a good mood. Mike reached for a roll, and poured himself a glass of wine. He suddenly felt famished. When he got the waiter's attention, he ordered a veal cutlet and potatoes.

"Sorry I'm late," he said.

"Did you decide to do some shopping?"

"Something like that."

They had a pleasant meal; Richie seemed to have gotten over the matter of the wiretap, and was now more interested in having fun for the night. He kept saying he wanted to meet an Italian girl.

"Don't you get enough Italian girls on Staten Island?" Mike asked.

A woman was sitting along the banquette at a table by herself. She was blonde, in her late twenties was a good guess.

Richie said, "Look, she has a guidebook in English. I bet she's American. We should invite her over."

"Go ahead," Mike said. "Don't let me stand in your way."

Richie smiled at her. She smiled back. Then he got the waiter's attention, and they had a conversation in Italian. The waiter went over to the woman. A few moments later the blonde was headed in their direction.

"You're a piece of work," Mike said.

Richie winked at him.

Mike was beginning to reel a little from the wine and the food. "I'm going to call it a night. I'll see you in the morning."

He left Richie at the table with the blonde tourist and walked back to the hotel. The night air was doing wonders for the wooziness he had felt in the restaurant. When he got back to the hotel the woman at the desk had gone. Instead a man sat reading a magazine. Mike asked for a wake-up call at six o'clock. Someone from the embassy would be taking them to the airport. That was one advantage to working for the government; there was always someone whose job it was to chauffeur him around.

He went up to his room, and went through the ritual of washing and brushing his teeth before collapsing onto the bed and turning off the light. The last time he'd slept had been almost two nights ago in New York; he thought it would only be a matter of a few seconds before he was asleep. He was not so lucky.

He turned the light back on. The tape recorder was on the nightstand. He thought about listening to the tape again, but he'd had enough for one day, a long day at that.

That guy, de Fournier, looked like a movie star in his jail fatigues, playing some kind of part. They're a pretty couple, he thought; I should have told her.

He had had too much wine to think about what he was going to do when he got back to New York, whether he would step down from the case and let someone else handle it. He was thinking of the past, and it was always better to think about the past with the lights off. So he turned off the light again and thought about the past.

He should have told her that he divorced his wife because he got tired of trying to pretend in the dark that his wife's body and hers were one and the same. Whoever said that all women's bodies are the same in the dark didn't know anything about women.

He had waited too long, three years too long to be exact—it was important to be exact when discussing the facts. Because he had waited, he'd lost his chance. That was the price of cowardice.

She wasn't at a loss for words. *We're only entitled to ruin someone once.* He hadn't intended to ruin her then; she should know that. Then he started thinking that he should pull out of the case, so that he would not be to blame for what happened to her husband. But women have a way of blaming you anyway, he thought.

10

Traffic was heavy along the Via Flaminia as they headed away from the center of Rome.

While they were stopped at a light, Alessandro reached into his jacket pocket and took out an envelope, which he handed to Juliet.

"I thought you might need money until you could make arrangements. It is not much, five hundred thousand lire for taxis and so forth."

"It's very kind of you. I have to notify the hotel."

"The hotel is not a problem; they are my client. I will negotiate a good rate for you, since it appears now you will be there for a while."

"Have you been involved in an extradition before?"

"Yes, once out of Great Britain."

"Do you mind my asking what the result was?'

"It was what you might call a mixed result. By mixed I mean the court refused to extradite, the client was released, and he left without paying my fee. Now I am making a lawsuit against him. *Bah.*" He threw his hand out into the air and smiled.

Alessandro made a quick exit off the Via Flaminia and onto a side street. He stopped suddenly at a large wrought iron gate overhung with trees. The gate was swung halfway open, and he got out to open it all the way so he could drive through; then he stopped the car again, ran back and closed the gate.

They drove up a long winding dirt road hidden from the main route by a grove of trees. "My house is at the top," he said. He pointed to a stone building built into the hill, "They keep sheep there. They graze alongside the hill during the day and make it impossible to drive down the road in the afternoon without waiting thirty minutes for them to pass. Thirty minutes. Can you imagine?"

At the entrance to the house, the gate was closed. He stopped the car and stepped out to open the gate.

"What does my family think? They know there are guests tonight, and they close the gate." He seemed as much amused as annoyed.

Large trees shaded and obscured the front of the house, and the short front lawn was mainly gravel. Several motor-cycles rested against the front of the house.

"Alessandro, you are late as usual," a matronly woman announced as they entered the vestibule. "You said you would be here by eight."

"Yes, well," Alessandro shrugged.

"I am Camilla, Alessandro's wife. You must be Juliet." She kissed Juliet on both cheeks and gave her a big motherly hug. "I am so sorry for you," she said.

Camilla looked elegant despite her matronly appearance. Juliet was struck by her eyes, a clear light blue like the aqua-marine she wore on her plump right hand or the amethyst clasp on her pearls. Amethyst, aquamarine, stones that were translucent—they suited Camilla.

"Come inside," she said, taking Juliet by the arm.

The guests were seated around the salon. The men stood when Juliet entered the room.

"This is Juliet de Fournier, visiting from Paris," Camilla said. "I leave it to you to introduce yourselves."

A dozen guests gathered around the pale blue couches in the center of the room. Despite the formal decor, large bouquets of sunflowers made the salon seem friendly and cheerful. Glass-paned doors opened onto a veranda filled with red geraniums, and the night breeze rippled along the edges of the drapes.

"Would you like a drink?" Alessandro asked.

"Scotch, no ice, thanks," Juliet said.

Alessandro returned with her drink and she had barely had a sip when Camilla opened the heavy mahogany doors to the dining room. Juliet glanced nervously around the room at the other guests who seemed to pay no special attention to her. She reassured herself; neither Alessandro nor Camilla would have been so indiscreet as to speak of François's situation.

Camilla directed the guests to their seats. Juliet was seated beside Alessandro, who was to her right at the head of the table; the man to her left introduced himself as Count Andrea Plotino. He pointed to his wife sitting across from Juliet. The contessa was at least fifteen years younger than the count.

Camilla, who sat at the opposite end of the table, made a toast in Italian. The count turned to Juliet.

"*Comprenez-vous?*"

Juliet shook her head.

"She said she is happy to be surrounded by her friends."

It seemed to Juliet that she had said something more. When the conversation took off in Italian she was relieved to be sitting with a weak yet polite smile on her face with no obligation to make small talk. She returned the smiles of the other guests and watched their faces as if she understood what was being said, though her thoughts strayed inevitably to François. She glanced over at Alessandro for reassurance, but he was in the midst of an animated conversation with the very attractive contessa and he did not notice.

"Do you not like your food?" the count asked, leaning flirtatiously close to Juliet. "The asparagus in Rome is the best in Italy."

She lifted some rice on her fork and stirred it back into her plate. The count seemed to be watching her so she forced herself to eat a little, though her stomach felt tied up in knots.

"I don't want to ruin my appetite for the second course," she said.

"A thin woman like yourself has no reason to worry about weight."

She noticed the count had already cleaned his plate.

"Juliet, more wine?" Alessandro interrupted.

"Alessandro, are you flirting with my wife?" the count asked.

"Hard to resist, I must say. We were just talking about Majorca."

Juliet smiled across the table at the contessa, who looked very proud. She did not smile back, but the two large diamonds in her ears gleamed when she moved her head, and had almost the same effect as if she had smiled.

"I hope you went some place other than Rome for the summer?" the count said, turning to Juliet once more.

"We have been in Tunisia."

"I know François," the count said.

This caught her off guard.

"Without being too indiscreet, let me say only that we once enjoyed the same circle of women," the count said as he

78

smiled flirtatiously. "When he arrives in Rome, you must both come to our house for dinner."

"I wasn't aware François knew so many people in Rome."

A woman named Antonella called to the count from the other side of the table and Juliet's thoughts could once more stray.

Alessandro's house reminded her of the sun-bleached villa in Mougins. She had always been happy with François in Mougins. The weather, the sunlight, a warm sea—every year they spent long weekends in June and most of July there. A domestic filled the glasses with red wine for the second course. Still lost in thought, she held the glass in her hand without drinking. François was never the type to talk about himself or his life before he met her. She had liked that about him. After all, she too had put the past behind her. It made their life together new; there were no ghosts, no shadows, just the life they made together.

"When we are old, we will have nothing to do, and then we will talk about the past," François had said, and it had seemed right to her. They had no need for the past. But she had been wrong. They were both wrong. The ghosts and the shadows were there all along, waiting for the right moment. Like Michael Chase.

She looked down at the delicately sautéed strip of veal, untouched on her plate, and cut it into neat pieces.

"You were saving yourself for the second course and you have eaten nothing," the count said, breaking her thoughts. "Are you not feeling well?"

Alessandro interrupted, "Andrea, are you tormenting my American guest?"

The count laughed, "I was merely hoping to eat what was left on her plate."

The count and Alessandro began to converse in Italian. Juliet's thoughts returned to the day's events. What had happened to François would soon be the subject of newspaper stories, the amount of attention depending on the size of the scandal, and the count and all of the people at the dinner would know. But no one seemed to know tonight; she was free for a little longer at least to pretend that nothing had happened, to answer questions with whatever lie or evasion suited her. Bad news had to be digested. One could not rush out and try to do something right away; that was always a mistake.

"A French dessert in your honor," Camilla said, turning to Juliet with a warm smile as she presented a tray of profiteroles with dark chocolate sauce. Afterwards the guests went into the salon for coffee. Alessandro handed Juliet a brandy. She drank in silence as the other guests talked. She had not been hungry, but the drink tasted good.

At Camilla's urging one of the women sat at the piano and began to play. The count seemed to have lost interest in Juliet.

"May I take you home, my dear?" Alessandro whispered.

"Was I asleep? I'm sorry. I didn't sleep well last night."

"Shall we?"

She got up and approached Camilla.

"Are you leaving?"

"Yes."

"You must be tired, I can imagine. So very tired, everything is so very, very hard. I am sorry that tonight with the other guests we did not have the chance to talk. I will invite you again and then we can talk.

"Alessandro, when will you be back?" Camilla's voice had a sharpness to it, a shrill note of distrust whenever she spoke to Alessandro.

He did not answer her.

"Because the guests will still be here," she said.

"Yes, but I must go to the office. What can I do?" he shrugged.

"Then you will not be back." She seemed annoyed.

"If I can finish, yes, then, of course. But I cannot say that the guests will still be here."

"Alessandro must go back to his office," she announced to the other guests.

"*Buona notte,*" Juliet called from the doorway.

Alessandro echoed her. "Goodnight my friends," he said in English. Before anyone could say anything more than goodnight in return, they were out the door.

The night air was cool and very black, the way the house in Mougins was on the nights when there was no moon.

"I know my wife will be angry at me, and I will pay for it tomorrow. These are her friends," Alessandro said.

"It's always difficult for people to understand when you have to work at night," she said, thinking of those years of practicing law when she had frequently worked late into the night. She had the impression Alessandro was relieved to be free of his guests.

"Our guests are rich. Work is something they do to amuse themselves. *Bah*—I too would not mind, but I am not in that position."

Juliet loved the way Alessandro slurred every "s" when he spoke; it was not the typical accent, but it had a lyrical sound.

There were very few cars out. Just before they turned onto Via Flaminia they saw three prostitutes standing around a fire burning in a large metal can.

"It's not cool enough for a fire," Juliet said.

"They use it to call attention to themselves."

As they drove along the Tiber with its beautifully illuminated bridges, marble and alabaster facades, she said wistfully, "Rome is extraordinary. Even if I should hate it right now, I can't."

"One night when you are feeling better, I will take you for a tour of Rome," Alessandro said.

For the remainder of the ride Alessandro seemed distracted by his own thoughts and they did not speak. As they approached the hotel she caught him looking at his watch with concern, and she could not help noticing that he seemed hurried as if someone might be waiting for him. She was barely out of the car when he sped off. Camilla's remarks as they were leaving took on new significance. Juliet no longer believed that he was returning to his office.

11

A different guard was on duty at the jail the next morning. He took Juliet's passport and let them through without anything further. It was another hot day. She took a seat beside the window. A faint breeze blew in the torpid September heat. She looked at her watch; it was half past eleven.

"Forgive me, I will speak to our friends to see if I cannot persuade them to expedite François's arrival. I have an appointment with the magistrate this afternoon unrelated to François's situation, and I promised my client I would meet with him at the lunch hour." Alessandro smiled an easy smile and shook his head, "Always the same dilemma, to be in one place while being obligated to be in another," he said.

"You don't mind if I see him alone for a few minutes, do you?" Juliet asked.

"My dear, I understand. I will use the time to telephone my secretary."

A few minutes later François came in with the guard. She found herself at a loss for words. His full dark hair was now nothing more than a stubble across his scalp; his suntan had faded. She did not say aloud what she was thinking: the haircut, the uniform, the pallid skin exaggerating his eyes as if he were a figure in a painting and the rest of his face were nothing more than a backdrop for his eyes. She was used to seeing him confident and powerful and handsome. She did not recognize the man sitting across from her.

Seeming to want to ease the tension, François spoke first. "I've been moved," he said.

"Where?"

"To a cell."

"And your haircut?"

"Hygiene."

"Is it worse where they've put you now?" she asked.

He shook his head. "I am still hopeful that I will succeed through contacts in Paris."

Her gaze fixed on his eyes. "*Tu me manqué*," she said.

His lips parted in the beginnings of a smile, but his eyes were lowered and he seemed somber.

"Where is Alessandro?" he asked.

"He's here. I asked to speak with you alone first." She paused for a moment, waiting for him to meet her gaze, for his eyes with their gold light to meet hers and reassure her in spite of everything. Yet when he looked at her, he seemed distant.

"Why didn't you tell me about Alain? You knew he was murdered. You knew when we were in Tunisia."

"It seemed easier," he said.

"That isn't much of an answer."

"Then I don't know what to tell you."

He lit a cigarette and smoked slowly.

She felt herself getting angry, but she knew when their visits were so short, it was a mistake to give in to anger.

"You need a lawyer in New York," she said. "The strategy on the American end is to drag out the proceedings here. The longer you're in jail in Rome, the more likely you are to plead guilty."

"If I am in Paris the American strategy fails."

She refrained from having to say Mike's name aloud, afraid that somehow he would see through her. "Regardless of whether you are here or in France, he also knows that in a foreign country he doesn't have the same control over what happens that he has in the States. That's why he'll offer you something to waive extradition."

François shrugged. *"Qu'est-ce que tu veux que je fasse?"*

"The right lawyer can work a deal that might make it worth waiving extradition. But you can't delay. I know some good lawyers in New York. It will be expensive."

She paused, waiting for his answer. He finished the cigarette and put it out. Lifting his eyes, he gazed steadily at her. "I want you to represent me."

What he was asking came as a shock, and for a moment she could only look at him, and she had only one thought—I want someone else to blame if things turn out badly—though she did not say it aloud.

"Why me? There are better lawyers. I ran away from that life. If it's money—"

He stopped her from finishing. "It isn't money," he said, shaking his head. "Hire anyone you wish to assist you."

She wanted to bang on something, to shout at him, to make him understand that he should not be asking her, but she was afraid that such an outburst would cause the guard to come in.

"Juliet, *écoute.* I do not want someone in New York. A stranger. I cannot right now. I am used to being in a position to pick up the telephone and get what I want. A telephone call. Here I have to wait days for permission to use the telephone. I call from jail; you said it first, no one will want to talk to me. They took my watch. I do not even know the time. *J'en ai marre.*"

She reached out and put her hand on his. "For God's sake, François, there's a saying that a lawyer who represents himself has a fool for a client."

She had heard that cliché a hundred times, but she had never seen the wisdom in it until now.

"I couldn't even bring myself to tell you why you were here. How am I supposed to insist you make hard choices? That's a lawyer's job. I love you. You don't know what you're asking of me. You don't understand the burden it is."

He let his gaze meet hers, steady and unwavering. "I want you to negotiate with Michael Chase. I watched him yesterday. He cares what you think of him."

She tried to hide the confusion she felt, but she wondered if he was testing her.

"What matters most in a negotiation is the person you negotiate against. He will want to prove to you he is fair."

"Fair? You think he cares whether he's fair?" she answered.

She felt herself on the verge of tears while he remained cool, and his coolness frustrated her further. Could she tell him there was another reason why what he was asking was impossible? She had been in love with the man who was prosecuting him. Was that what he had observed? Yes, he probably does care what I think of him, but I am not cold enough to tell you why, she thought. The other night I cut it off and let my feelings go no further, but what would happen if I had to see him over and over again?

"Give me the night to think about it," she said, and with her eyes she pleaded because she believed that maybe given the night the words might come to her and she could tell him.

He touched the ends of her hair with his fingers, looking at her with eyes that were dark and thoughtful, though he did not tell her what he was thinking.

"Juliet, don't let the night pass. I need you to say yes, now. I need to know."

He seemed strong, resolved and she felt his eyes on her face and his gaze unrelenting. An image of how his night would be passed came to her.

"Don't refuse me." He folded his hand over hers, warm and familiar to the touch.

"There's one thing I want you to tell me. Did you have anything to do with Alain's death, just that, tell me, please?"

A sadness passed over his face. "No," he said, quietly.

"You understand, don't you, you understand why I had to ask you?"

"You thought it might be true," he said. "I don't fault you. There are questions that have to be asked, just as there are answers that have to be given."

"I need to know you're not who they say you are."

His eyes met hers, steady and unabashed. "I did not know about the loans. I only knew they wanted the bank." He shook his head. "The rest of it, what kind of man I am, you will decide for yourself," he said.

He was right, she thought. And yet the starkness of it saddened her. Her gaze shifted to the window at the sparrows playing in the dirt. The midday sun was up and the light was white and too bright.

"What is this about?" she asked, turning back to face him. She felt a heaviness she could not disguise.

He glanced over at the door as if he wanted to be sure no one was listening. "It's no different than that wall," he said. "It used to be white. We start out with a clean slate, and after a while the dirt begins to collect."

He lit a cigarette. "It's an old story. There were difficulties when I took over Compagnie Financière. I never realized until after he died; my father had been living in another *époque*. If the company failed, my father's reputation and the family name would have been destroyed."

"What does Etienne Dufois have to do with this?"

"I was introduced to a group of Arab investors whose money was being managed by Etienne Dufois. They invested fifty million dollars, enough to save us from failing. A few years later, they doubled their investment. Since then they continue to increase their investment every year."

His gaze shifted nervously toward the door again as if he were afraid someone might be listening, but it was only the guard, who did not understand English.

"The Arabs make up seventy percent of my investment capital in Compagnie Financière. This was disclosed to the American banking authorities before I purchased the New York bank. I have a banking lawyer in New York, David Porter. Talk to him, and he will go through the details of the transaction."

He sat back in his chair and seemed to relax a little. Despite the haircut, he was beginning to seem more like himself, she thought.

"The concern is that the New York bank was being used to funnel money to terrorist fronts," she said.

"I sent Alain to New York to run the bank. I did not know what entities Alain loaned money to—that was the point of giving him discretion, to relieve me of having to be involved in those decisions. He was in New York. It was not practical for me to run things from Paris."

"François, it's not a question of practicalities. The allegation is that the bank was a conduit between the Middle East and terrorist organizations."

"My investors wanted a bank in the States. I bought it. *C'est tout.*" He met her gaze as if he wanted her to understand that she had to believe him, and she did believe him, but it was not enough.

"They're accusing you of being a nominee. The fact that you had nothing to do with the bank helps them," she said.

"I can't change that." He flicked the ash from the end of the cigarette before bringing the ashtray closer and stubbing it out. She had the impression he was thinking about something that he did not want to share with her.

"I need leads. People I can talk to."

"Talk to David Porter."

"What about Etienne Dufois?"

His eyes narrowed and made his gaze seem more intense. "Dufois will not talk to you."

"Who are his lawyers? They must be concerned about what's happening."

"Porter will give you the names."

She nodded. A moment passed in silence. "Did you know Alain was under investigation?" she asked.

"He is dead, so we do not need to think about him," he said.

His coldness struck her. "You sound like someone who's been here before," she said.

He shrugged off her remark with a slight smile. He seemed tired of answering her questions.

"Speak to Michael Chase. I understand yesterday he wanted to frighten me. Find out what he really wants."

Alessandro came into the room. Out of politeness and habit, Juliet thought, François started to get up out of his chair to greet him.

"Please, stay as you are," Alessandro stopped him. "I have had a message from my office that the application of the French Consulate to have the case transferred to France was submitted this morning to the Ministero di Grazia e Giustizia."

"*Ah bon.*"

Alessandro shook his head. "Impossible to predict how long it will take."

"I think it's to your advantage to approach the prosecutor now while he's unsure whether the case will move to Paris," Juliet said. She turned to Alessandro. "François has asked me to represent him in the proceedings in New York," she said.

Alessandro did not comment, but his eyes reflected his surprise.

"The Americans will want to offer you something to eliminate the possibility of the case being transferred to Paris. If you lose before the ministry and the case stays in Rome, the incentive is gone," she said.

"I take the risk." François turned to Alessandro. "Do you agree?"

"It seems early to negotiate. Provided of course, as only you can answer, that you can withstand the accommodations my countrymen offer you."

The guard stepped into the room and with his hand gestured for François to get up.

It was too soon, Juliet thought. She needed more time to persuade him that he should begin negotiating right away.

"We're not finished," she said to the guard who ignored her as he walked past her toward François.

It angered and upset her to see him handcuffed and she averted her eyes.

Alessandro seemed to understand without her saying anything.

"Wait here. Let them take him through the door. It is unpleasant for you," he said.

"When we're here talking around the table, it's easy to believe we're all going to get up and walk out at the end," she said, feeling sad and powerless.

"Did he say why he was moved from the infirmary?"

"I don't think he knows."

Alessandro seemed to have something on his mind. "I suppose he is more comfortable having you represent him," he said, though by the way he looked at her, he did not seem to agree with the sentiment he had just expressed. He seemed skeptical. And wasn't that the right reaction? She was skeptical herself.

"I would like to repay you for the money you loaned me last night," she said.

"Everything is taken care of, even that little amount," he said. "Dugommier called this morning to set up an account for you."

"I find it unsettling—these arrangements being made behind my back. Why did Dugommier need to speak with François alone?"

"I'm sure it had to do with Compagnie Financière. François trusts you. He would not have asked you to represent him if he did not. It's very hard, my dear, to say everything when the guards are watching and there is limited time."

She knew what Alessandro said was true, and yet it could not account for all that had happened. She thought about how François had not once put his hand to his hair, that gesture she associated with him; it must have felt so strange after they shaved his head that he stopped.

12

The summer heat had broken, and the temperature was pleasant. The breeze carried the scent of autumn leaves, and the sunlight slanted across the gray walls of the conference room. It had been two weeks since the arrest.

Nunzio, heavenly messenger in Italian, was the name of the guard who escorted François like an angel guiding him through purgatory. As time went on, Nunzio seemed more lax, and today he stepped away and left François to enter the room on his own.

"Juliet." He smiled at her from the doorway. He came into the room and quickly kissed her head and both her eyes before sitting down beside her. She felt the sudden stirring of a familiar desire interrupting her thoughts, until she heard the guard fidgeting in the corridor just outside the room and she looked at François and her heart ached.

"The Ministero di Grazia e Giustizia denied the request of the French Consulate to have the case transferred to Paris," she said.

She handed him the official decision decorated with ribbon and blood-red wax seal.

"It gives no reason," he said, after reading it.

"Alessandro is meeting with his friend, Melazzo, to find out more."

She saw through his efforts to remain calm that he was upset.

"Compagnie Financière is going to fail unless I can unwind investments. Juliet, I cannot do it from here. I have to meet with people."

"Even if you prevail, they can insist that you remain here through an appeal."

"What about Michael Chase?" he asked.

At the sound of Mike's name, she felt a nerve vibrating deep inside of her.

"I'm sure, like you, he was waiting to see whether we succeeded in transferring the case to Paris. He wants you to run out of moves. He believes every loss weakens your position more than the one before." She saw with her own eyes that he was right; the fatigue showed on François's face and told her of the sleepless nights he never spoke of.

"The government's case gets stronger over time." She reached over and rested her hand gently on his arm, "You wanted to wait until you found out whether you could go back to France. You have your answer. If you continue to wait you won't have anything to negotiate."

"A negotiation requires me to offer something," he said.

"Offer information about the people you were involved with. You are not of great interest to the Americans ultimately. You are a means to an end. They want to know who was laundering money and why."

His lips pulled together tightly and the muscles in his face became tense. "*Non, pas question.*"

"What choice do you have but to accept?"

He lit a cigarette and smoked in silence without answering her. She knew he was holding back. She felt a distance that had never existed between them before. During these visits they would never say anything to one another about how they felt. They would never find the words. Before this it had been unnecessary. They had their hands, their lips; they could make love. But all of that was impossible now, and they had only their silence.

"Sometimes I think you only want my visits so you can sit by the window and look at the sky while you smoke," she said, softly, smiling in spite of everything.

"My days are spent alone; not much happens. I try to read in Italian. What is there for me to tell you?"

He lowered his eyes and pulled the ashtray closer. He seemed to be thinking about something, and by lowering his eyes he sought to conceal his thoughts from her. But the way he had responded to the suggestion that he cooperate continued to trouble her.

"Is there something you're afraid is going to happen if you cooperate?"

He dismissed her question. "I don't know. And you? What are you going to say when Michael Chase tells you I'm guilty?"

She put her hand on his. "He's my adversary. You asked me to be your lawyer. The moment I agreed, questions of guilt or innocence are no longer my concern. Can the government prove that you did not own the bank? That's all that matters. A trial is not about the truth. It's about what the other side can prove."

He let his eyes meet hers. "What is your concern?"

She detected an irony in the question and the way he was looking at her. She felt defensive again.

"I'm concerned with what your options are," she said.

He merely nodded. "I am running out of options," he said quietly. Then he seemed to focus. "In New York I stay in jail?"

"I'd make an application for bail. If you're not a flight risk— I could vouch for you—with a few precautions, like giving up your passport, you'd be out on bail pending trial."

It was her own view that rushing to consent to jurisdiction in New York was a mistake without a plea agreement in place. Yet she knew that unless he was willing to cooperate, Mike was not going to agree to anything.

"The government hasn't even submitted formal charges to the Italians. It's going to be hard for them to present a case in Rome. I said you should negotiate, but unless you offer to provide evidence, if I were you, I wouldn't go to New York voluntarily. I'd make them prove the extradition here."

"Then I stay here? How long? Months?"

"I don't know. You're right. There aren't many options at the moment. Maybe you won't have to go to New York for bail. Maybe I can apply for bail for you in Rome from New York. It's not usually done, but that doesn't mean it's impossible."

He got up and went over to the window, resting his hand against the window frame as he looked out. After a moment, he turned toward her, "When could this happen?" It seemed that she had given him a reason to be optimistic.

"I need to go to New York to meet with David Porter. I could apply for your release before a federal judge in the Southern District of New York. If I persuade a judge to vacate the order of provisional arrest, it has the same effect as an order of bail from the Italian court. You would have to remain in Rome, but at least you could fight extradition without having to stay in jail."

Though she did not say it, it was also a way of initiating negotiations in New York. After the views Mike had expressed about François's guilt, it seemed that something more than a phone call was necessary to start negotiations.

Nunzio appeared in the doorway. "Ha finito, Signore," he announced impatiently.

François wrapped his hand around hers and held it. "I won't see you for a while," he said softly.

She wanted to say something encouraging, something to reassure him in her absence, but as she stumbled over the words in her mind, everything seemed so trite. Before she could answer, Nunzio pulled his arm away and fastened the handcuff around the hand that only a moment ago had been free to hold hers.

After François was gone, and she was alone, she started to think about what she needed to do in New York. Her conversation with Mike in the bar at the hotel played over in her mind. She blamed him for that too, for the way she felt when she was with him, for not having forgotten.

13

"Okay, Saed, I want you to tell me again. Where did the meeting take place?" Mike Chase addressed Saed Abdul Radwan with the veneer of indifference he used with government informants.

Since returning from Rome, Mike summoned Saed almost daily to the U. S. Attorney's Office, had him wait in the hall with Richie for an hour or two, then talked to him for half an hour before sending him back out in the hall for another hour or so under the pretext that something had come up that he had to take care of. Then he would tell him he could not get back to him today, and he would have to return tomorrow. It was his way of making Saed know that he was on the hook.

"Mr. Chase, why do you always ask me the same questions?"

"I want to make sure your answers haven't changed," Mike half-smiled. "Now let's continue."

"Plaza Athénée in Paris, in the bar. Dufois took me."

"Okay, go on."

"De Fournier had a woman with him. She seemed to know Dufois too."

"What did de Fournier say to Dufois?"

"He said he was—"

"Not in your words, in his."

"'It's not a request. It's a deal breaker.'"

"Did he ever say I want ten million dollars?"

Saed sighed. "No. I told you it was Dufois. He became very angry and blurted it out—'Ten million dollars!' He was furious."

"Dollars?" Mike scrutinized Saed, formulating an impression of how he might be perceived by a jury.

"Yes, I remember specifically, it was dollars."

"Did de Fournier say what he wanted the money for?"

"No. He called it a deal breaker—which I took to mean non-negotiable."

"How do you know it was for the purchase of the bank in New York?"

"Because they were talking about making arrangements with the lawyers in New York. Dufois expected something to be filed by lawyers in New York. François said the lawyers had not filed yet. Dufois became angry because he had already been to his investors and they were relying upon him to deliver. He was losing face in front of me." He shook his head and put his hand to his brow in exasperation. "I'm sorry, Mr. Chase, I was not taken into their confidence during this meeting or at any time. It was my *nahss*—as you would say, my misfortune—I was present when Dufois lost his temper, or he would not have spoken so openly in my presence. I wish very much it had not happened."

In the silence that followed, Saed began fidgeting nervously with a pen. "Put the pen down," Mike said. "What was the woman doing?'

"Nothing, listening with her eyes, you know, looking from one face to another."

"What was she wearing?"

"Something black—a dress maybe or a sweater and skirt. I only remember it was black."

A picture of Juliet sitting in the bar at the Hotel Eden came to Mike, her slim black dress, the pearls around her wrist, her diamond wedding ring sparkling across the table—"Was she wearing a wedding ring?"

"I think so. She was wearing diamond earrings. I remember because she took one off and put it on the table."

"Anything around her wrist?"

"I do not remember."

"Have you ever seen de Fournier's wife?"

"No."

Mike felt his own thoughts wandering back to Juliet, but he stopped himself. "Did de Fournier say anything else?"

Saed shook his head. "I keep telling you, Dufois knows everything. I know only this one part. Why do you make me come here to say the same thing? Someone is going to find out and they will kill me."

"Who is 'they'?"

"I am not sure."

"If you're worried for your safety, there are places I can put you." Maybe there was some danger, though for some reason, Mike had the impression he was exaggerating. "You have an agreement that creates certain obligations on your part. Your obligations will not be abated because they make you nervous. I want you to come up with the name of the woman at the Plaza Athénée meeting."

Saed sighed aloud and sunk back in his chair. "How?"

Mike studied him for a moment. He felt fairly confident that Saed was not at risk. "Do what you need to."

Saed rolled his eyes.

Mike leaned over the desk. "I want you to remember how lucky you are that you didn't run into me before you made your deal with the government. Because if you had, you'd be complaining about your meals instead."

That much was true; if he had been running the case from the outset, Saed would have been in jail.

A young assistant United States attorney stopped Mike in the hall and handed him a set of papers.

"We were just served with these in the de Fournier extradition."

As Mike took the papers his eye shifted reflexively to the bottom of the page to what he considered the most important piece of information—the name of the lawyer.

"*Attorney for defendant, Juliet Mason.*"

Mike stepped into his office and closed the door. For a few minutes he merely sat at his desk flipping through the pages without reading them. Why is she doing this? he thought.

14

"You're still here; it's after ten," Richie said.

Mike had his feet up on the desk as he read. "I lost track of the time."

"Yeah. I don't think so. You don't like going home."

"That could be. But de Fournier filed a bail motion to-day—if you can believe it—and I had to prepare a response."

"Bail? He's in Rome."

"You know, at first I thought it was a sure loser. Tell you the truth, now that I've thought about it, there is a way of reading the bail statute to allow for jurisdiction in the South-ern District of New York. And once the court has jurisdiction, the judge definitely has the power to order his release."

"Who's representing de Fournier?"

"According to the papers, his wife."

"Come on."

"I'm serious."

"Why? They don't want to pay a lawyer?"

"She's a good lawyer. I don't know why she would want to represent her husband."

"Maybe she's bored. All those massages and dinners."

"We'll see who shows up tomorrow. Conceivably she just signed the papers and someone else will show up to argue."

Mike had the impression Richie seemed uncomfortable and he attributed it to the disagreement they had over the wiretap.

"What's that?" Richie asked, pointing to the six neatly stacked sets of papers about two feet high lined up against the wall.

"What?" Mike asked.

"Those stacks of papers." Richie sat down as if he were planning to stay for a while.

"Nothing. Documents subpoenaed from Great American Bank."

"Anything good?"

"Not really. It's all pretty carefully drafted by lawyers to create the appearance of compliance with the law. The real issue is what's behind them. At this point I'm just familiarizing myself with the transaction. I need to know the steps that were involved."

"Today was about the fifth time you've met with Saed. I don't think the guy has that much to say."

"I'd like to shorten his leash. It would have been better if he were locked up somewhere."

Mike stood up to stretch; he felt tired all of a sudden; Richie had broken his concentration and he was ready to call it a night.

"How's the investigation going?" Richie asked.

"I'm not really sure I know where this case is going," Mike said. "It's going to be a while before the documents confiscated from Compagnie Financière are translated. Until then I've got to rely on what the French agents say is there, and I haven't gotten anything from them yet."

Mike had not told Richie, but he was planning to go to Paris at the end of next week. He wanted to speak to the Interpol agents himself and interview some of the people who worked for de Fournier at Compagnie Financière. For the first time he had not made up his mind whether he wanted Richie to come with him.

Richie took one of the documents off the top of a stack and began to read it. After a minute, he put it down, and looked across the table at Mike. "I still like Juliet Mason for the woman at the meeting in Plaza Athénée."

Mike said nothing.

"Have you considered that's why she's representing him?" Richie continued. "Attorney-client privilege makes it harder to question her."

Mike shook his head. "I'll move to disqualify her if I think she's hiding behind the privilege."

"It still gives her a two-week head start if she wants to skip town."

"I can detain her under a material witness warrant if I need to."

Mike took his keys out of his desk drawer, put them in his pants pocket, and got his jacket.

"Feel like getting something to eat?" he asked.

"Yeah, why not," Richie said.

It was brisk out, one of those chilly New York nights in early September when the humidity of summer has finally broken.

Richie had his car parked out front and they headed over to the Odeon. The bar was crowded, so they took a table. The waiter sauntered over and greeted them with a heavy foreign accent. They ordered beer. Fifteen minutes later, the waiter returned. Mike ordered a hamburger. Richie did not want anything to eat.

Mike took a few more sips of his beer. He was thirsty and the beer was cold.

"Don't you miss narcotics?" Richie began. "It's real cops and robbers. Not this fraud shit with all those fucking documents. You find the cash or the drugs, pick up a few diamond watches along the way and boom. The most you have to read is an address."

Mike laughed. "You know I've only fired a gun once in my life, and I burnt my hand."

"Are you going to eat those fries?" Richie asked.

"No, I'm finished."

Richie picked a few from Mike's plate. "Hamburgers and fries are funny. They're only good for the first few minutes when they're hot; then they get soggy."

Mike knew he could not avoid it anymore. "What's on your mind, Richie? You're not here for the fries."

"You want me to be honest?"

"Yeah, go ahead."

"Suppose she was involved. You gonna be able to prosecute her?"

Mike leaned over the table, and directed a steady gaze at Richie. "I've been a prosecutor for fifteen years. I prosecute anyone I have to. What I feel before and after has no effect on what I do."

"Yeah, we all say that. I can tell you, a few years ago I had to testify against a girl I'd been sleeping with. It's not easy."

Mike looked coldly at Richie, "But you did it."

"Let's just say I don't recommend it."

Mike signaled the waiter for the check. "I'm tired of the subject, Richie, drop it for good."

"What time is the hearing tomorrow?" Richie asked when they were out on the street.

"Two."

"Maybe I'll drop by."

"It's up to you."

Mike parted with Richie on the street and walked to his apartment only a few blocks away, one of those new, clean Tribeca buildings with low ceilings and white walls.

It takes a long time to get used to coming home to a dark apartment, he thought. He would call that the worst moment of the day, when he stepped inside and groped along the wall for the light.

15

New York always felt like home. She wondered how many years she'd have to live in Paris before that feeling stopped, the unmistakable relief to be paying with dollars and speaking English again. No matter how good her French got, she always had a vague uneasiness, a feeling that perhaps she had misunderstood or missed something.

She stopped at a newsstand and bought the *Wall Street Journal*, the *New York Times*, and the *Post*; there was nothing in any of the papers about François. Juliet was relieved. She remembered a client of hers once referring to "articles your mother won't clip." The less news coverage, the more room she had to negotiate.

She checked into the St. Regis Hotel in midtown. She did not have enough time to go up to her room. David Porter was expecting her. She left her suitcase with the concierge and took a taxi downtown to his office.

David Porter was a partner in a large New York law firm of five hundred lawyers in prime Wall Street real estate at One Chase Plaza. Juliet's office had been downtown. She stepped off the elevator on the fiftieth floor and took in the view of the harbor and the Statue of Liberty, the green slanted rooftops and winding streets; the sky was hazy and blue, but in her mind she pictured the fiery red and pink sunsets that so often she had watched until the last patch of light was gone from the sky.

Maybe I was wrong to leave New York, she thought. I could have stayed and continued practicing law. Instead I was hiding behind François or the person I thought he was. She no longer felt sure that François was to blame. Maybe it was as much her fault. Maybe the pieces were all there, and she never put them together.

"Good afternoon, Mrs. de Fournier. How was your flight?"

David Porter stood before her with outstretched hand, looking very much a corporate lawyer, head-to-toe boxy gray suit with vent, crisply pressed white shirt, striped tie and horn-rimmed glasses. Seeing him, she smiled to herself, I'm not in Paris anymore.

"Please, call me, Juliet," she said as she shook his hand.

As they walked down the hallway, he seemed a little reserved, a little too stiff. He did not mention François, as if the subject were taboo.

The files pertaining to the purchase of Great American Bank were laid out on his desk. A set had been made for Juliet; it was sitting in a large black binder at the end of the desk.

"I thought it would be a good idea for you to go through the files yourself," he said, handing her the binder. "I can explain the transaction in general terms, and the steps I took before the Fed."

He guided her through the transaction, pointing to certain documents in the binder, explaining at each turn the different Netherlands Antilles holding companies François had created for the purpose. Juliet was aware that these types of acquisitions always had lots of layers, and Porter seemed confident about the form the transaction took.

"The only cause for concern at the time was the fact that so much of Compagnie Financière investing capital comes from one group of investors, the Saudi investors, managed by Etienne Dufois," he said. "But the Fed was fully apprised of the situation and they approved the transaction."

"Did you have any dealings with Dufois or his lawyers?"

"No, it was unnecessary. All of that was handled through lawyers in Paris."

"Do you know who represents Dufois in the United States?"

"No idea."

Juliet was surprised, though she said nothing; François had told her to talk to David Porter, but it was Jean Dugommier who had the answers she needed.

"We've had no dealings with the bank since then; Alain Gilbert was using other law firms for the bank's routine legal matters; we were François's—I should say, Compagnie Financière's lawyers. I'm confident standing up for the decisions I made in the course of the transaction. You understand, however, that I was relying on the representations made by François."

"You probably have a document to that effect," Juliet said, smiling wryly. She could tell Porter was already distancing himself by claiming he was relying on the representations of his client. A lawyer had no choice but to protect himself in that way. In Porter' situation, she would have done the same. Yet she could not stop herself from resenting him for it. She also recognized his concern that this turn of events could ruin his reputation; just the association with a scandal like this could be enough, even if he did nothing wrong.

She opened the binder and began to flip through the pages. "I might have questions after I've read through the documents in the binder," she said. "I just want to double check that these are all your records. For example, if there are internal memos, I'd also want to see those."

"There's only one and I provided it. I had a paralegal search the files, but I'll double-check myself."

"Did anyone else at the firm work with François on this?"

"No one who had any contact with him. Research and the like, yes, but I was the person with the client contact."

"There would also be billing records. I know some firms are funny about that—I'm not interested in how much you billed, but the descriptions of what you did might be useful."

"I'll have a look; I have no problem showing you my own records," he said. "Do you think I'm going to have to testify?" he asked.

"I don't know how the proceedings will go in Rome."

He nodded thoughtfully. "Truthfully, I'm more concerned about what goes on here—whether the government will subpoena me."

The documents had been prepared for the Fed; and because the communications between client and attorney were made with the intent of disclosing them to a government agency, the privilege did not apply, as Porter must have known.

"If the extradition fails, the case never gets to New York," she said. His somber expression sufficed to tell her that he had not gotten the reassurance he sought.

She took the binder with her to read when she got back to the hotel, though she knew she was too spent to read anymore that night. Porter offered to call her a cab, but she said she would hail one on the street. She did not feel like going from the closed and airless office straight into a cab.

At One Forty Broadway she stopped to look up at the World Trade Center, lit up and looming into the starless night.

She could feel a chill in the wind coming off the buildings. She remembered it was always colder near the towers because of the wind. An empty cab stopped at the light and she got in and headed uptown.

At the St. Regis she went in the bar for a quick dinner, ordering a turkey sandwich and a glass of white wine. The bar had a name, the "Old King Cole Bar," though everyone she knew referred to it as the bar at the St. Regis. Little round tables were lined up in front of a banquette, each with a silver bowl filled with nuts. Two women were talking, a conversation without pauses or lulls. Women talked too much, Juliet thought. They kept too few secrets. She picked through the dish of nuts, looking for a cashew. She felt sad again, the way she had looking out the window in David Porter's office.

The last time she had been with Mike Chase in a courtroom the case ended with a guilty plea that was favorable to both sides. She had spent a lot of time negotiating with Mike and when the case was over he invited her out for a drink. They became lovers that night.

She let her eyes wander across the room to the Maxfield Parrish mural over the bar, Old King Cole sitting on his throne smirking; it was a mean smirk, *méchant*, the French would say. The nicest part of the mural was the patch of blue sky in the right-hand corner, she thought. She tried to recall the rhyme: *Old King Cole was a merry old soul, and a merry old soul was he; he called for his pipe and he called for his bowl and he called for his fiddlers three....* She couldn't remember the rest.

16

At St. Andrew's Plaza, the food vendors were set up. The outdoor tables were crowded. The sun was bright and warm and the leaves were beginning to turn colors. Juliet stopped for a moment, searching with her eyes, then she saw her, the old Chinese woman who came every day to collect the discarded bottles and soda cans. Nothing has changed, she thought.

The hearing was set for two o'clock. A long line had formed to go through the metal detector before entering the courthouse. She recognized the old faces of the courthouse guards, the impatient lawyers standing in line like a troupe of medieval monks, the backs of their heads bald and shining in the hazy light from the high windows, and the law clerks, fresh out of law school and self-important and knowing nothing about how justice operates, holding up their ID cards and breezing through. The last time she was in this courthouse she had identified with them, but now they seemed like children, and their job seemed little more than a dating opportunity. And then there were the others, the people for whom this was not just a place to work, the people whose rights were being decided. She could tell them by the expressions on their faces. It was a different place through their eyes, more foreboding than comical, more frightening than annoying. And she was in their place, so she knew, no longer did she have to imagine: courthouses were sad places.

The large wooden doors to Courtroom One creaked open at exactly two o'clock. A thin woman in her sixties with dyed brown hair and high heels, much higher than one was accustomed to seeing on a woman that age, peeked out into the corridor; she was Ellie, the judge's law secretary. Juliet remembered her once saying that she had worked in the courthouse for thirty-five years, which meant Ellie by now had reached her fortieth anniversary as a civil servant.

She flipped on the fluorescent desk lamp and slid a sheet of paper to the front of her desk, directly below the judge's bench. "Lawyers, please sign the sheet."

Juliet went up and signed the sheet using her maiden name, "Juliet Mason."

"I'm not sure if you remember me—"

Ellie looked up, pausing for a moment. "Oh yes, you're the girl with the pretty clothes. I remember you." She said it with the same exclamation that Juliet had once heard her greet an inmate. "Shlomo Cohen," she had said, "I haven't seen you since nineteen seventy-three." It was nineteen eighty-two when Ellie made this remark, and Shlomo Cohen had been in jail for nine years. Yet Juliet was sure Ellie did not hold it against him. On the other hand, she did not show any sympathy, either. It was Ellie's job to fill out the orders of commitment, orders of fines and restitution—all going to jail meant to her was a different kind of form.

"I was admiring your suit when you came in. I thought you looked familiar."

Juliet was wearing a black Chanel suit with small gold buttons.

"What matter are you here for?" she said as she took the sign-in sheet and read it, answering her own question. "*U.S. v. de Fournier*, that's a new matter, isn't it?"

"It's an extradition." Juliet glanced around the room. "You know, Ellie, the defendant is my husband."

This threw her, Juliet thought, judging by her loss for words, but she seemed to come back quickly. "Well, you tell him he's in good hands," she said.

Ellie looked at her watch. "It's already ten after two; no one's here from the government. The judge is ready to go on the bench."

Juliet took her seat at counsel's table. She knew how it went; the front table belonged to the prosecution, the rear table was for defense counsel and the judge's bench was raised, because justice must come from on high. To Juliet it seemed obvious, all of the players had their place; it just so happened the defendant's was last.

"Mr. Chase, you're here," Ellie cried out; "The judge has been waiting to take the bench; I couldn't stall much longer," she said in a friendly way.

Mike walked in with Richie Giordano, who took a seat in the back of the courtroom as Mike headed to the prosecution table.

"Sorry, Ellie; I was in a conference."

"Don't forget to sign in, Mr. Chase," Ellie said. "I'm going to tell Judge Stern everyone's here."

Mike turned to Juliet as if to say something. Before he had a chance, Judge Stern entered the courtroom.

"Ms. Mason. Mr. Chase—Sorry to be in this big courtroom, but I've got a jury out in mine. Well, Ms. Mason, I've read your papers. I'll tell you right now, I've never granted bail under these circumstances before. That may be because no one has ever asked me. However, I can't say that your reading of the statute is entirely wrong: I agree with you on the timing; an application for bail can be made at any time. But I'm not sure I have jurisdiction over someone who is in Rome. You've managed to intrigue me. So why don't you proceed."

Juliet stood up, pressing her palms flat against the table as if for support. She felt her voice quivering at first, but once she started to argue she was fine.

"Thank you, Your Honor. I think I should start by telling the court I am married to the defendant, Mr. de Fournier."

She paused, waiting for the judge's reaction, but there was none, so she continued.

"Your Honor, I'm not asking the court to exercise jurisdiction in a foreign country. I'm asking you to vacate the order for provisional arrest and proceed with the extradition, which is within the exercise of the court's supervisory powers. Provisional arrest is meant to safeguard against flight during the extradition process. There are many ways of securing the defendant's attendance short of incarceration; he can report daily to the American Embassy—even twice a day. He can wear a bracelet; the Italians have all of that technology. The government already has his passport. To detain someone pretrial, the government must show either a risk of flight or danger to the community. We are willing to fly someone from probation to Rome at our expense if your Honor wants a recommendation from probation. There is no risk of flight. I think I can speak to Mr. de Fournier's character as someone who will not flee. Mr. de Fournier is a businessman from a well-respected French family. He is not a threat to the community. I am willing to vouch for him to the extent of submitting myself to contempt proceedings if he misses a single appearance before the Italian tribunal. The extradition process is an extremely lengthy one—"

Judge Stern interrupted. "Forty-five days provisional arrest doesn't sound very long. We're about halfway through, anyway," he said, smiling thinly as if he were challenging her to refute him.

"Your Honor knows forty-five days is merely the period before the actual extradition proceeding commences. The proceedings themselves, conducted by an Italian tribunal, could take anywhere from six months to a year before a decision is reached." Judge Stern seemed to be listening with interest as she continued. "My adversary has offered no reason why Mr. de Fournier should be incarcerated during this time, when, if the arrest had taken place in France where he resides or in the United States, he would certainly be out on bail. I am simply asking the court to make the very same ruling on bail that would have been made if Mr. de Fournier were in New York."

"What is the position of the Italian government?" Judge Stern asked.

From the tone of his question, she had the impression that he was receptive to her argument, and she felt more confident as she continued. "Since he is currently incarcerated on the basis of a request emanating from the United States, the Italian government would just as happily release him on the same basis. If you would grant bail in New York, then I ask the Court to vacate the order of provisional arrest."

"All right, Ms. Mason, why don't you sit down?" Judge Stern turned to Mike. "Mr. Chase, what do you say I vacate the order on the condition Mr. de Fournier consents to house arrest in Rome?"

He sounded almost nonchalant, and Juliet had the impression that he wanted to rule in her favor.

"I don't see how the government would be prejudiced: Ms. Mason is trustworthy. She is a member of the bar here in New York." He turned to her and smiled. "It's always a pleasure to see her in my courtroom." Then, leaning back in his chair, he turned to Mike. "You can proceed with the extradition out of Rome."

Mike stood up slowly without raising his eyes from the table where his hands rested.

"Your Honor, I have no problem believing Ms. Mason is trustworthy, I just don't think it's relevant. With all due respect, the court has no authority to grant the relief the defendant is seeking."

Judge Stern leaned forward in his chair and threw out his hand. "If you think I'm acting outside my power, mandamus me. Frankly, I think I've got the power. Now what I want to hear from you is whether there is a good reason why I shouldn't exercise it. If you can't come up with one, then I just might grant her request," he said, sitting back in his chair again and folding his arms in front of him as he waited for a response.

Mike kept his head bowed as he read through the papers in his hand. He seemed to be looking for something. "If I may, Judge, this is the arrest report from the Italian authorities. I would like to have it marked as an exhibit," he said, looking up at the bench.

"By all means," Judge Stern said, reaching for his eyeglasses and adjusting the lamp on his desk.

Mike held the arrest report in his hand as he continued. "Since Your Honor is considering granting bail, the court should be aware that at the time of his arrest in Rome, in addition to his French passport, Mr. de Fournier was in possession of a Moroccan passport."

Mike paused momentarily. Judge Stern furrowed his brow, looking at Mike over the rim of his eyeglasses.

"The Moroccan passport is evidence that he had the means to become a fugitive. The government also has evidence that this was his intention," Mike said.

Juliet was too stunned to notice the judge's reaction. "Why don't we go off the record? I'll see you both at the bench," he said.

Judge Stern leaned forward and pointed his finger at her as if he were reprimanding a child. "Ms. Mason, you've appeared in my courtroom on enough occasions in the past so that I'm not willing to believe that you're so stupid as to have made this motion knowing this. I have too much confidence in your intellect and your integrity." He stopped shaking his finger and gazed hard at her. "I'm going to assume you didn't know about the passport," he said, his gaze unrelenting. "But I'm going to give you a little piece of advice, which is to go back to Rome and tell your client he should look for a new lawyer."

He turned to the court reporter and snapped, "Back on the record. Motion denied."

"Thank you, Judge," Juliet said in a soft, slightly hoarse voice.

She found Mike waiting for her in the corridor.

"You made me look like a liar," she said.

"He said he wasn't blaming you."

"He said my client should get a new lawyer; what does that sound like to you? Besides, what difference does it make what he said? You could have called me when you got the papers and told me."

"Your client could have told you too."

"The rules haven't changed. You're the one with the obligation; my client doesn't have to tell me anything."

Mike put his hands in his pockets and leaned back against the wall.

"Look, I was under no obligation to tell you, but maybe you're right, I should have told you. I thought you knew. Besides I was not sure you were going to be here today."

"You got my papers, didn't you?"

"I thought if you were going to argue the motion, you'd call first."

"We already had our private conversation in Rome."

She turned to walk away, and she felt his hand on her arm. "Juliet, wait."

"I've got to go to the airport."

"I saved you in there whether you want to admit it or not. Are you out of your mind agreeing to vouch for his appearance? You didn't lose anything today, unless you're so anxious to trade places with your husband. If that order had gone through, I promise you, that guy would have been gone. And don't think this judge would have thought twice about holding you in contempt for making him look like an idiot."

"You just love it, don't you? Standing there telling me how my husband is going to leave me. As far as I'm concerned, you're the one who set me up today. I'm not going to make the same mistake I made in the past of thinking there's anything behind what you say."

"I don't have to listen to this." He seemed angry; he raised his voice and narrowed his eyes as he looked at her. "You don't want to believe me, then go ahead, believe what you want. I'm happy to be your adversary. It'll make it a lot easier for me."

17

She had trouble finding a cab to take her to the airport. Traffic was slow as always because of construction on the Brooklyn-Queens Expressway. Though she had come to New York intending to open negotiations, after what happened in court it would have been futile. She tried to distract herself by looking out the window. Everything seemed dirty and awful, and everywhere she looked she saw a cemetery. If yesterday she had felt happy to be back, all she wanted now was to leave.

By the time she got her boarding pass it was less than an hour to takeoff. She ran to the check-in; the lines were moderate and they seemed to be moving fast.

After placing her baggage on the conveyor belt and handing her passport to the customs official, she noticed that the official picked up a portable telephone and made a call.

"What are you doing?" she asked. "Is there a problem? I'm going to miss my flight. The plane will be boarding in fifteen minutes."

"You're going to have to come with me," he said. "Is this all your baggage? Or did you check anything?

"No, this is it."

"And these bags have been in your possession the whole time?"

"For God's sake, yes. What's the problem?"

"We need to go through your bags."

"What do you mean you need to go through my bags? Open them up right here. I'm a lawyer. There's no contraband in these bags. I'm going to miss my flight."

"There's nothing I can do. Now either you come with me, or I call an officer and place you under arrest."

"Arrest?"

"Lady, I don't know what else to tell you. Are you coming or do I call the police?"

She saw that it was useless to argue and in the course of a moment her anger turned to a mixture of resignation and fear, the feeling she remembered from the night in the airport in Rome. She picked up her bag and her briefcase and followed him to a partitioned area about twenty-five feet from where they had been standing. The area was broken up into numerous small partitions, like the inside of a maze.

She was taken behind a partition where the walls were a sickly pale green.

A woman officer stepped forward.

"Is this all your luggage?"

"Yes."

"Put them down."

Juliet obeyed. Out of the corner of her eye she saw a second woman officer open one of the drawers.

"Raise your hands, spread your legs," the first woman said in a disinterested monotone.

She patted Juliet's sides.

"Okay, take off your clothes, shoes too, and drop them right there." She pointed to a spot on the floor just to Juliet's side.

Juliet took off her jacket. Her hand fumbled over the buttons on her blouse.

"That damn thing is complicated," the woman said in a lazy drawl.

One of the buttons fell to the floor, and Juliet bent to pick it up.

"Just leave it," the woman said.

Juliet slipped off her shoes. The other woman lifted the suitcase onto the table.

"What's the combination?"

"2-1-5-3." Her voice faltered. She realized that she was taking a long time, stopping with each layer of clothing. She had trouble with the hooks on her skirt. The floor felt unbearably cold against the bottoms of her feet. She lowered her head so her hair covered her breasts as she undid her bra. The second officer took a small flashlight out of her pocket and played with the on-off button. She spotted the tiny circle of light gleaming against the dirty gray linoleum floor as she slipped off her pink silk underpants and placed them with the rest of her clothes on the chair.

She heard the woman with the drawl. "Stand here and lean your hands against the wall."

Afterward she was told she could get dressed. Clutching her clothes, she glanced down at the floor for the button that had fallen from her blouse, but she did not see it. When she was dressed she was handed a cup.

"Urine sample."

"Why?"

"You have no choice."

A third woman took her down the hall to a row of open stalls and waited without lowering her eyes.

When she was brought back to the examination room a dog was sniffing through her suitcase. A customs officer she had not seen before was about to open the binder David Porter had given her.

"I'm a lawyer. Those are legal papers," she said. She felt herself on the verge of losing control. "I assert the attorney-client privilege as to each of the documents in that binder. You have no right to go through them."

The customs officer closed the binder and put it on the table as he began to search her belongings. No one had yet told her why this was happening or what they were looking for. At a certain point she began to wonder if they even knew.

"Am I free to go?" she asked.

The customs officer who had gone through her suitcase answered, "We have orders to detain you."

"Under what authority? You've found nothing. You have no grounds to detain me." She felt incapable of holding back her frustration any longer.

"We have orders to detain you. You're going to be placed in a holding cell. If you want to make a call first you have that right. Now are you going to be a good girl or do we have to put shackles on your ankles?" he said in a mocking voice.

She did not answer him. Her lips were dry and she kept biting them, tearing the skin into tiny bits. A guard escorted her through a back door, where she was handed over to the customs official at the desk. She noticed the telephone.

"I want to make a call," she said.

"Give me the number," the official at the desk said.

She gave him Mike's number. She was convinced that he had ordered the search and arrest.

He dialed and handed her the phone. After a few rings, Mike answered.

"I'm being detained by customs at the airport."

"What? What happened?"

"That's why I'm calling you. I was sure you knew."

"I don't. But I'll find out. Are you under arrest?"

"I'm being placed in a holding cell."

"Give me the name of the officer at the desk," Mike said.

She looked over at the officer's badge. "Fernandez," she said.

"Listen, I'll be there as soon as I can. Are you going to be okay?"

"Just come soon." Her voice began to break and she hung up.

Mike grabbed the first agent he saw in the hall, someone named Reilly, and told him to take him to Kennedy Airport.

From the car, Mike called customs and asked to speak to Fernandez to find out what was going on. Fernandez said an order had been issued by the Drug Enforcement Agency for a stop and search.

"Do you have the name of the agent at DEA?"

Fernandez read from a sheet. "Giordano."

For a moment Mike said nothing. His gaze shifted blankly out the window. Then he turned his attention back to the phone. "Look, where is she now?"

"We've got her in a cell."

"Let her out."

"I can't do that over the phone. If you want to come here and sign off on her release, that's one thing. But I can't release her until that happens. I have a detention order from DEA and I've got to abide by it. Nothing's going to happen to her in the meantime."

"Is she by herself or is she in a lock up?"

"Private room, first class."

"I should be there in half an hour. Have the paperwork ready for her release."

Mike sat holding the receiver in his lap, staring straight ahead. Reilly had just gone through a red light.

He thought about calling Richie, then decided against it. He was too angry. It was better to wait until he cooled down.

When they arrived at the airport, he told Reilly to wait in the car. Flashing his badge, he asked the first cop he saw to take him to Fernandez.

They walked through a revolving door and the cop indicated a short, balding man. "That's Fernandez," he said.

Mike approached him and shook his hand.

"So you're Mike Chase; you're a legend around here," Fernandez said. "You know, I was in on the Rivera bust ten years ago. Yeah, we all followed the trial every day in the papers."

Mike smiled graciously. "So what do I need to sign?"

"Here it is."

"Where is she?"

"In the back through those doors. Do you want me to send someone?"

"No, I'll go myself. Do you have her things ready?"

Fernandez reached beneath the desk. "These were the papers she had with her and her passport."

Mike took the black binder and flipped it open. "Did anyone go through this?" he said without looking up.

"Not yet."

"What about her luggage?'

"It's all here—one suitcase and a briefcase."

"Everything is there?"

"Yeah, as far as I know. Here's the report. There was no contraband."

Mike smiled to himself; customs was programmed to look for drugs, and he found the idea of their having treated Juliet like a drug dealer typical of government stupidity.

"She's in 312," Fernandez said as they walked down the aisle of painted blue iron doors.

Juliet was sitting on the bench with her knees up.

Fernandez opened the door. "Mr. Chase has signed for your release."

She looked over Fernandez to Mike. Then she got up. The three walked out in silence. When they got back to Fernandez's desk, she was handed her belongings.

Mike handed the binder back to her. "No one went though it," he said.

She was not in the mood to talk just yet.

"Can you tell me why this happened?" she asked.

"It wasn't me," he said.

"When I called you I was convinced you'd ordered it."

"No."

"I know that now." She lowered her eyes, "What were they expecting to find?"

"I think they were looking for drugs." He smiled. "Can I buy you a drink?"

"If it's still possible, I'd like to go back to Rome tonight."

It was after seven o'clock. They went over to a screen; the six-thirty Alitalia flight had been delayed.

"If I hurry, maybe I can get a seat," she said.

Mike took her bags and went with her to the ticket counter. Ignoring the line, he approached the desk, showed his badge and spoke with the ticket agent.

"There's a seat in first class," he said, turning to Juliet.

"I'll take it," she said.

He turned back to the ticket agent. "Tell them to hold the plane on orders of the United States government.

"Let me bring you to the gate to make sure there are no problems," he said.

The gate was far away and they had to run. As they approached, the boarding light was flashing and the waiting area was empty.

After handing her boarding pass to the stewardess, Juliet turned back to Mike. He put his hand on her shoulder. She brought her mouth to his and kissed him, and in the same instant she realized what she had done and pulled away. As she was about to enter the plane she turned back a last time. Seeing him standing at the entrance, she felt herself hesitating.

"Are you coming?" the stewardess called out to her.

The stewardess rushed to take her baggage and to usher her to her seat as the plane door was bolted.

Too many doors are closing and I'm always on the other side, she thought.

"Champagne?" The stewardess leaned toward her with a bright smile, holding a champagne bottle wrapped in a towel in one hand and a long-stemmed glass in the other.

18

On the way back from Kennedy Airport Mike called Richie and told him to meet him in half an hour at Kelly's on Leonard Street.

Richie was at the bar when Mike arrived. Though his back was to the door, Mike spotted his windbreaker. A baseball game was on the television above the bar. Richie seemed to be watching.

"Let's take a booth," Mike said.

Richie took his beer and followed Mike to the front booth.

"Anything to drink?" the waitress called to Mike.

"In a minute," Mike said.

"What's up?" Richie asked.

"I just got back from the airport. They had her in a holding cell. The supposed contraband was a binder filled with legal documents."

Richie did not answer.

"I could get you suspended for that stunt. Just remember that I didn't."

Mike got up and started to walk out.

"Is that all you're going to say?" Richie called after him. "Why didn't you subpoena her while she was here? Don't tell me, because she's a lawyer. That's bullshit. After what happened in court today Stern would have ordered her to testify. You're protecting her."

Mike turned back toward the table, but said nothing.

"I did it because it had to be done," Richie continued. "I wanted to detain her long enough to get a material witness warrant and keep her in New York, which is what you should have done. She goes back to Rome, we lose her. Now that she knows her husband was going to split, you think she's going to hang around?"

"I make those calls," Mike answered sharply. "I won't work with someone I can't trust."

19

His hair had begun to grow in and he seemed thinner, but it was his voice that had changed the most. He seemed cold and impassive.

"I take it the judge in New York did not agree to my release?" he said.

"You'll have to remain here," she said.

He nodded and said nothing, as if he had been expecting this result, and his reaction struck her.

Somewhere between New York and Rome she had decided that she was not going to confront him about the Moroccan passport. She did not want to hear his lie, the thing he would say to appease her. In her own mind she had reached the only conclusion there was to reach. Guilty people flee. The passport had been enough to convince her that his involvement was greater than he was admitting.

Yet she was not ready to confront him because she knew that more was at stake; when she did confront him, she knew it was not enough to say that she was not going to represent him. She had to be prepared to tell him she was leaving.

Among the few things she felt sure of was her decision that she would not speak about what had happened at the airport. Part of her wanted him to know his silence had consequences to others beyond himself. But by opening the subject, she would also have to tell him that she had turned to Mike, and she feared the power he would gain from that knowledge.

She had a new concern; it seemed obvious to her that she was being considered a suspect. Her mind drew a blank when she tried to come up with the reason. She wondered whether it was possible that she had unwittingly assisted François in a way that could be considered aiding and abetting. But what could they think she had done?

Despite what she did not say, she was angry; anger, confusion, frustration all mixed together, and she took it out on the one subject that she could discuss, her meeting with David Porter.

"David Porter has never met Etienne Dufois. He had no idea who represents him. He said Dufois's contacts were all in Paris."

"Dufois won't talk to you."

"If I can't talk to him, I'll go through his lawyers. Jean Dugommier must know who represents him."

"Juliet, listen to me, stay away from Dufois." He was emphatic and unyielding, which frustrated her further.

"What do you think you're accomplishing by sitting here? What am I supposed to do for you? It was a very lovely speech you made about how you needed me to represent you, but how can I when my hands are always tied? Is there someone you trust more? For God's sake, then let him represent you."

He lit a cigarette, gazing steadily at her across the blue wall of smoke.

"Did you talk to Michael Chase? What does he want?"

"He wants you to go to jail."

She realized this was cruel, and she stopped herself. "I'm sorry."

"*De rien,*" he shrugged.

He continued to smoke without talking. It occurred to her that neither of them had made any effort to sound optimistic.

She noticed he had a sore on his wrist. "Why hasn't this been treated?" she asked, wrapping her fingers around his wrist.

"I've asked for something to put on it. They haven't gotten around to it yet."

His breath had a bitter odor of nicotine and the tips of his fingers were stained. He was smoking a lot.

"François, you smoke too much," she said.

"Stop treating me like a child."

"What am I supposed to do?"

"Don't do anything. Do what I tell you," he shouted.

"So you can lie to me."

"I told you I was running out of options. You prefer to accuse me of lying. *Non.* I can't change things. It has to be this way."

"I won't accept being lied to."

"*Ecoute.*" Again he raised his voice as if no answer existed for what he was saying. "This is the way things are," he said.

"For you. Not for me," she said, though it sounded so cold that as soon as she said it, she regretted it.

She got up to leave. She knew if she went through the door, she could not turn back, and part of her wanted that.

He seemed to know it too.

"Juliet, I don't want to fight."

"Why are you angry at me?" she said quietly, the question giving away her desperation. "I have done nothing to hurt you."

She felt betrayed by every lie, frustrated by the position he had put her in. Everything she knew about him seemed nothing more than fragments, broken pieces of a larger picture. And yet she wanted to believe him. Resting her hands on his shoulders, she waited for him to draw her close against him, for the intimacy of a kiss to remind her of the man she loved, but he gently removed her hands.

"To be here I have to forget how your hands feel," he said.

He summoned the guard to take him back to his cell. From that moment she knew a transition had taken place and he no longer thought of himself as a free man.

But she felt the change in herself too. In the jail where he was stripped of everything, there was no disguise for the part of him she had closed her eyes to—"*Don't do anything. Do what I tell you.*" She felt a distance from him she had never felt before that had nothing to do with the doors and the walls that separated them, and she felt cold toward him; if she had let him stop her from leaving, it was because she still hoped that he could hold her and the coldness would melt away, but he did not hold her.

On her way out she stopped in the office and spoke to one of the secretaries at the desk about getting treatment for the sore on his wrist.

"*Sì, sì,*" the woman said, nodding her head, before turning back to whatever she had been typing. Juliet had the distinct impression that nothing would be done.

20

Alessandro invited Juliet to lunch the next day. They went upstairs to the restaurant at the hotel. It had rained heavily all morning, and though it had stopped, the sky was black over half the city. Juliet watched as the black cloud devoured the rest of the sky.

"From the look on your face, I gather the news from New York is not the news we would hope to hear," Alessandro said.

"The motion for bail was denied. Michael Chase did not seem interested in negotiating, and I was not in a strong position to open the discussion." She paused before continuing, "Were you aware François had a Moroccan passport?"

Alessandro shook his head; the news seemed to take him by surprise as well. "I had no idea."

"It was confiscated at Fiumicino. If I had known I would not have moved for bail, because no judge would grant it under those circumstances."

"What does François say?"

"I didn't ask him."

Alessandro furrowed his brow, seeming confused.

"I have my reasons for not saying anything now." She gazed earnestly at Alessandro. "Please don't tell him I know. I'm not ready to talk to him about it yet."

"As you wish, my dear," he said reassuringly. He seemed contemplative. "The news I have I will not say is the best news, because the best news in this situation is that the extradition has been denied. But it is more positive than not. I met again this morning with Melazzo. He told me the Americans have not made any communication, which is normal at this stage, since they are under no obligation until November, which is still a month away as we are in the beginning of October. Without the formal presentation of the Americans, Melazzo cannot say with precision what position the Ministry will take. Nevertheless he assured me that the Ministry is not eager to extradite François. They will most certainly give him every benefit."

"Will you tell François? He needs good news so that he can stay strong. He refuses to confide in me," she said. "Maybe he'll confide in you."

"I will do my best, my dear."

Alessandro picked up the menu. "Shall we order now? Perhaps today I will persuade you to share a risotto with me."

A bottle of white wine was brought to the table. Alessandro tasted it. Every step of the formal Italian lunch was observed—the four courses, melon and prosciutto, risotto with eggplant, fish, cheese and fruit, biscotti—it made her feel better to be lulled by food and wine into a slight intoxication that felt almost like well-being.

She sat sipping her espresso as Alessandro went off to use the phone.

When he returned, he said apologetically, "My dear, I am at fault. Our friend the count, Count Plotino, my wife's guest the night we had you to dinner, is expecting us for dinner tonight. The invitation came after you left for New York and I forgot to deliver it. He has a beautiful villa on the Appian Way and Camilla in particular would most enjoy to see you. Shall I come for you at half past eight? Dinner is at nine."

Alessandro finished his coffee, which must have been cold by then. "*Allora.* Unfortunately I must return to my office. I have a submission to prepare for the court tomorrow for a commercial client."

"You submit handwritten papers, don't you?"

"Ah, what can I say? It's true. But we Romans have very neat handwriting so no one complains."

21

"Madame de Fournier, *ravi de vous revoir*," Count Plotino said in a tone more appropriate for announcing the Queen of Sweden. He lowered his voice to a whisper and bent close to Juliet's ear. "I hope you're not too lonely while your husband is away," he said, as he took her hand and kissed it.

He was quite tall and he stood very straight, Juliet thought, as straight as an *I*, the French say. Tonight, especially, he looked like the perfect cross between Nostradamus and a headwaiter. His cigarette dangled elegantly between two fingers and he wore a silk ascot with a brown velvet jacket.

"I tell you, dear, who am I to talk, but François always had a bit of a bad streak, which is part of his charm. But the Americans are self-righteous, and too willing to engage in hypocrisy for the sake of preaching to others."

The guests were in the salon, a beautiful large room with blue settees and thick gold drapes.

Alessandro broke away from his conversation to come to Juliet's side. They exchanged kisses, and she clung to his hand for a moment, feeling more comfortable because he was there.

He pointed to the oil portraits in carved gilded frames on every wall.

"I take it they are the count's ancestors," she said.

"Not to seem an ungrateful guest, but beware these faces. You will see how quickly a story can emerge from one of these portraits to last through dinner," Alessandro said, smiling.

"I hope you are not discussing serious things," Camilla said as she approached. Juliet noticed her warm smile from across the room.

"You look so much better, my dear. Doesn't she, Alessandro? And your dress, the perfect little black dress. Chanel? You have to be tiny like you to wear Chanel. Ah, look at that little waist. " Camilla hugged her. "You're still so young, so very young."

To Juliet this seemed like Camilla's way of telling her not to worry.

The contessa approached. "Madame de Fournier, *bienvenue.*" She put her hand on Juliet's arm. Her heavy, sweet perfume wafted in the air around her and diamonds glittered across her slender neck. Her pretty brown hair was swept up, away from her face, and her blue eyes seemed to smile.

"You have such a beautiful home," Juliet said. "The gardens especially, they must be so pretty in spring."

"Oh yes," the contessa said. "It's too bad you came at evening, you can't really see."

The contessa continued to smile, like an actress waiting for applause, Juliet thought, before excusing herself and moving on to the next guest.

"They are nice to you now," Camilla said quietly in Juliet's ear, "but if François's name is removed from the *Almanach de Gotha* see if they invite you."

The contessa announced that dinner was ready to be served. As the guests went into the dining room, Juliet had the sudden desire to claim she was ill and head for the front door. Alessandro took her arm.

"François may need their help," he said.

The dining room table was covered in blue linens with a few dozen tiny white roses in the centerpiece. The windows were dark and reflected the sparkle of light from the chandelier. Candelabra burned on both ends of the table. A tapestry of dark fruit, plums, grapes and red pears and birds with long beaks hung from the far wall. And though the night was warm, to Juliet it seemed cold inside that room with its dark paneled walls and winter tapestry.

The contessa took her place at the head of the table. Juliet was seated next to Alessandro, and Camilla opposite them.

"Now I can keep my eye on you," Camilla remarked to Alessandro, only half-joking it seemed to Juliet, who recalled his odd behavior the night he had dropped her at the hotel after Camilla's dinner party.

Alessandro responded to Camilla's remark with a smile and a good-natured shrug.

Seeing the contessa scrutinizing her from the far end of the table, Juliet leaned close to Alessandro and whispered, "Tell the lovely contessa she will have no competition from me. In fact, tell her I think she's the most beautiful woman in Rome."

The conversation swelled amiably around Juliet in Italian, and she smiled pleasantly as she picked at her ravioli. She rested her eyes on the candles, which flickered gently as she pictured François, always so handsome and elegantly dressed, sitting across from her in the soft light, the way he used to smile at her across the table, or the gesture he made with his right hand when he spoke, an image so familiar on so many nights like this.

The candles seemed to grow longer as she gazed at the reflection of the light sparkling against the dark windows, and the image of François sitting across from her receded from her mind as her thoughts drifted to the child she wanted, the child they never had. No matter where the lie went, no matter what else it touched, that had been true between them.

"The *babba* is incredible," Alessandro said, delicately patting his mouth with his napkin after the first bite of rum-soaked pastry.

She had the impression he was encouraging her to eat. It was good, and she finished it.

A sudden burst of laughter and applause rang out from a corner of the salon where coffee was being served as the count, who was seated on a gold Louis XIV settee did his impersonation of Queen Victoria, consisting of putting a white handkerchief over his head, covering it with an upside-down ashtray and puffing out his cheeks.

Alessandro let his eyes smile for him. "Someone should tell the most beautiful woman in Rome to find a new man. She is pretty, but my God, poor her, married to him. If she isn't already, I imagine she will be lending her distinction to someone else before long."

Juliet noticed a somewhat lecherous expression linger briefly on Alessandro's face as he looked over at the contessa. And glancing back at Juliet, he raised his eyebrows and smiled.

22

He found her sitting along the banquette in the hotel bar reading through documents. The long-paned windows faced into a garden, and in the rain the light seemed black and foreboding.

"The concierge told me I could find you here," Mike said, and before Juliet could respond, he continued, "I have the extradition papers. As far as I'm aware you're still representing your husband. I thought the least I could do is deliver them to you myself."

She took the envelope and started to tear it open, but he put his hand on hers and stopped her. "No, don't. I wanted to talk to you first. Do you mind if I join you?"

"Scotch?"

"Sure."

"*Due scotch, per favore,*" she called to the bartender.

The bartender brought two scotches without ice.

"You didn't want ice, did you?" she asked.

"It's fine." He pulled up a chair and folded his hands on the table, "I couldn't—strike that, I didn't tell you last time I saw you, because after what you had been through I didn't see the point of upsetting you further. Outside the courtroom when I said those things, maybe it seemed like I was trying to hurt you. I know I lost control—"

"Why don't you spare us both the pretense that you're trying to help me?"

He shook his head. "Let's not get sidetracked. You can come to whatever conclusions you like about my intentions later. When he bought the tickets to Rome, he also bought a one-way ticket for himself from Rome to Morocco."

He paused to watch her face, which seemed too still. The rain was banging against the windows and it had gotten very dark.

"It's all in my submission to the court," he said. "I just thought I should tell you in person. We've known each other a long time. It seemed too cold the other way. Outside the courtroom when I said your husband was going to leave you, I wasn't going on a hunch."

After an awkward silence, he added, "I suppose going to Rome was your idea."

Something about the way she looked at him made her seem vulnerable and unsure of herself. He had to tell her, for her sake. He could not let her go on being lied to.

"Jean Dugommier is Dufois's lawyer. That's why he was at the jail that day. It wasn't the only time either; he's seen François since then."

She went pale and her lips parted as if she were about to say something, but no words came out. Mike could tell by her reaction that she had been unaware of the relationship between Dufois and Dugommier and that she was caught off guard. He felt sorry for her, but he kept on going. "You know what it means for Dugommier to visit your husband in jail— Dufois is telling him what to do, what to say—Juliet, listen to me. Dufois is the bigger fish, but right now I don't have a case against him. If you think you could persuade your husband to give up Dufois, it's his best shot."

"What kind of time would he get?" she asked. She seemed calmer; the lawyer had taken over from the wife, he thought.

"If he gives up Dufois, a couple of years at the most. Otherwise he's facing big time."

Mike watched her face as she moved her long white fingers across her forehead to brush back a few loose strands of hair.

"How long are you staying in Rome?" she asked.

"For the rest of the week. I'd like to schedule something with the magistrates here. There are some things I have to take care of at the embassy."

She took a sip of her drink. Her gaze drifted to the front of the bar and back. "What made you decide to file your papers early?"

"I was ready and I thought it would be easier on you if I filed early. You know I really don't—" He was going to say, "I don't want to hurt you," but she did not let him finish.

"No, don't say it, you'll only sound insincere," she said.

He smiled. "Have you ever met Dufois?" he asked.

She shrugged. "At parties, that's all." The corners of her mouth turned up in the beginning of a smile. "You don't really believe François had anything to do with Gilbert's murder. I can tell when you're bluffing. You think if you charge him with Gilbert's murder, he'll admit to the other things, because the murder charge will frighten him."

"He had the motive; I'm convinced he knew Gilbert was about to give him up. He was one of the last people Gilbert called before he was killed."

She gently shook her head. "He's not capable of murder."

"Put a high enough price on it and anybody is capable of murder. People kill for money all the time."

"In your world of cops and robbers maybe," she said. She bowed her eyes and looked away from him. Her expression seemed to become more pensive. "You come all the way to

Rome to tell me my husband was going to leave me and that he's an assassin. Then you go on to tell me how I can help him." Her eyes met his, her gaze steady and unrelenting. "Why would I want to help him if he's a murderer? And if I persuade him to cooperate, who is it I'm helping?"

He reached across the table and put his hand over hers.

"Juliet, you have to think about yourself. What's good for you?"

She pulled back her hand and did not answer.

He glanced over at the binder she was reading, "I've been through those documents myself. There's nothing there. Look, it's stopped raining. Why don't we go for a walk?" He thought it might do her good.

The sky was washed clean by the rain, and the light was very still and the air felt cool. Cars were speeding toward them as they walked along the curb of grass and dirt along-side the Viale Trinità dei Monti. At one point, he pulled her in and held her until a car passed, and he felt her flesh soften beneath his touch as if the memory of the nights they spent together still lived inside her, waiting to come to life again like the monuments and statues down every side street when the light shimmered across the cold stone.

"Rome is good at reducing all human achievement to something to decorate a garden," she said, as they passed the busts of famous men that lined the walk in the Borghese gardens.

They sat on a bench and he saw her looking at him expectantly.

"Who is your informant?" she asked.

"I'm sorry, Juliet, you know I can't tell you."

"At a hearing you're going to have to produce him."

"The hearing isn't for a while. Lean on François. I'll tell you this much, he knows who he is."

Two fat pigeons flew down in front of them.

"I hate pigeons," she said.

He smiled.

"Are you staying at the Hotel Sardinia? Will you walk me back to my hotel? You're only a few blocks away."

She seemed preoccupied as they walked, and he did not try to make conversation. As they were approaching the hotel, she said, "François has a sore on his wrist which looks like it's infected. I've mentioned it to one of the women in the office, but I'm sure no one has done anything. Do you think you could speak to someone about treating it?"

"I'll call the warden."

The clouds were gone and the sky was blue. The sunlight splashed warmly across the walls.

"It's the light I love the most in Rome," she said wistfully.

She turned and went inside and he was left standing like a statue in the beautiful light.

23

She went up to her room to read the government's papers. She wanted to be some place where she could be sure she was alone with no one watching her reaction. *Affidavit of Michael Chase in Support of the Application by the United States of America for Extradition of François de Fournier*, the caption stared back at her in all its brutal irony.

The government was accusing him of acting as a nominee—a pretense, a front, like the face he had presented to her in their marriage, she thought, and she blamed herself for being taken in and loving him back.

She did not want to admit it to Mike, but what he told her about Dugommier disturbed her. The reason why Dugommier had wanted to speak to François alone after Mike left seemed clear suddenly; he had to be sure François understood what was expected of him. At last she understood why François had turned to her to represent him; he was trapped and she was the only window out, the only person untainted by Dufois. If she turned her back on him, he was lost.

She believed Mike had told her everything until she read the paragraph describing a meeting in November 1985 at Plaza Athénée. It was on that occasion, according to the government's informant, that François had asked Dufois for the ten million dollars. All the government's proof that François purchased the bank as a nominee on behalf of the Saudi investors came from that single conversation. Even if it took place, the government had no proof that the money was paid. The informant claimed that Dufois brought him to the meeting, and that François was with a woman. But the informant could not give the woman's name. Who was she? Why had François believed he could speak freely in her presence?

She stopped reading and pressed her hands to her head. She was no longer thinking about François. Her heart beat fast and her thoughts were racing: suddenly it seemed clear; the government believed she was the woman at the Plaza Athénée meeting. This explained why she had been detained at the airport, why they had searched her bags. Mike said he was unaware of the stop-and-search order at the airport. Yet surely he had known this at the time, and if he knew, then he should have told her. But he was being careful never to give her the whole picture, just pieces, and he was using the pieces to control her.

She called Alessandro to tell him she had received the extradition papers.

"How did you get them? And isn't it soon?"

"Mike Chase is in Rome and he delivered the papers to my hotel. I would like to show them to François tomorrow."

"Yes, of course. I unfortunately will be before the Tribunale tomorrow. I am not able to accompany you."

"François doesn't realize it, but your friends at the jail are providing the U.S. government with the names of anyone who visits," Juliet added before hanging up.

24

Mike Chase was awakened from a deep sleep by a loud knock at the door of his hotel room and someone shouting in the room across the hall to keep the noise down. He fumbled for his robe and looked at his watch, the hands illuminated in the dark; it was almost one o'clock in the morning.

"I woke you—I'm sorry."

"Juliet?"

He opened the door to let her in. The man across the hall had stopped shouting. Her hair and black trench coat were wet. He took her coat.

"It's raining and I walked over from my hotel."

"Why don't you have a seat?" he said. But she remained with her back against the door as if she were undecided whether to leave or to stay. She seemed wanting and desperate, and she reached out to him with her eyes.

"I feel like I should say something," Mike began, "but to tell you the truth I don't know what to say."

"You think I was the woman at Plaza Athénée, don't you? That's what the search at the airport was about. Someone at Justice thought I was moving currency. Why didn't you tell me?"

"I told you I had nothing to do with that search."

"I wasn't at that meeting. I had no idea about any of this."

She bowed her head and her hair fell over her face. "As I was reading I kept thinking maybe none of it is true. The informant made it up. It isn't possible, is it?"

He rested his hands on her shoulders as if to embrace her, then he stopped himself and went no further.

"God," she uttered, raising her eyes and looking at him. "Why did this have to happen?" If only moments before she sounded angry and desperate, she now seemed wistful.

Without thinking he drew her to him, the heat of her body so sudden and warm against his. He lifted her face in his hands and felt the space between them close.

"I better go," she said, and she pulled away.

He felt exposed, empty, and he wanted to take her in his arms again, but he knew she did not want that.

"You don't have to go." He wanted to tell her to stay the night. She seemed to understand.

"You know we'd both hate ourselves in the morning," she said.

"You should have demanded that I leave my wife."

"It's too late for that. Besides, it wouldn't have made any difference."

"You're wrong about that."

"People are cowards. Now it's easy to say it could have been different, but at the time it wasn't that way."

He held her against the door; seeing her lovely lowered eyes, he caressed her face.

"Goodnight, Michael," she whispered, as she closed the door gently behind her.

25

The weather was hot again, and the air was stiff and heavy with the scent of dying leaves. François seemed lost in thought as he entered the room, offering a weak smile as he sat across from her.

"The bandage on your wrist—does that mean you were treated?" she asked.

"Yes, they gave me antibiotic."

"I'm glad."

"Alessandro said you have the application of extradition," François said.

"When did you see him? He told me he was busy today."

"He was on his way to the Tribunale."

She merely nodded as she handed him the affidavit. He seemed in no rush to read it.

"You did not come last week," he said.

"I had to go through the documents Porter gave me."

She fidgeted with the pen she had taken from her purse; he continued to look at her as though he expected her to say something more.

"I thought it was because we fought," he said.

He seemed contrite, and she felt the urge to open up. "I needed distance to think," she said. "It's hard for me to see you this way."

A look of despair flashed across his eyes which she caught before he could disguise it. "*Pour moi aussi,*" he said.

He took up the affidavit. When he had finished reading, he handed it back to her and lit a cigarette. She saw the strain of muscle in the corner of his mouth, his lips pressed tightly together.

"Dufois will go back to Jeddah soon," he said.

"How do you know?"

He shrugged.

"Did Jean Dugommier tell you?" She waited for his reaction, but he did not answer her.

"Is it Dufois who is paying my hotel?" she asked. "Alessandro's fee too? Is that the reason Dugommier set up the accounts?"

"Juliet—"

"The Moroccan passport? Dufois again? I know Dugommier is Dufois's lawyer."

"*C'est vrais*. But it is also true that I need him for Compagnie Financière, to keep investments there."

He leaned back in his chair, his hand with the cigarette resting on the table.

"What about the meeting at Plaza Athénée?" she continued, unwilling to relent.

"It is the informant's word against mine," he said flatly.

"Who is the informant?" she asked.

He shrugged. "I cannot remember his name. His family had a relationship to Dufois. I met him that once."

"Why did you talk in front of him?"

"I did not think—" he stopped himself from continuing.

"Go on," she said, straining to remain calm.

"I thought it was a business matter." He put the half-smoked cigarette out and pushed the ashtray to the other end of the table. "I made a mistake."

"You must remember the woman's name. After all, you brought her." She detected the trace of sarcasm in her own voice and she wished it were not there.

He shook his head. "They do not know who she is," he said.

"That was not my question," she said coldly.

"Silence has reasons." His eyes met hers as if to emphasize the importance of what he meant.

At last she gave way to the frustration she felt. "Why do you insist on being arrogant? The government won't give up because they don't know her name. They'll find her. If you don't do something to help yourself you are going to wind up taking the blame for everything."

His lips pulled together tightly. "I told you, there is nothing for me to do."

She banged her hands against the table. She could not hold back any longer.

"You don't understand, do you?" she said bitterly. "The government thinks I'm the woman at Plaza Athénée."

Until then he had seemed composed, and if the allegations in the affidavit had affected him, he had been able to conceal what he was feeling, but this seemed to shake him. His complexion flushed and his lips parted. "Impossible," he said, the surprise he felt showing in his eyes as he gazed at her. "You knew nothing. How can they accuse you?"

"They know a woman was at the meeting. I fit the description. By accusing me, the mystery is solved, and it's up to me to prove to the contrary. If I say nothing and they think I should say something, they accuse me of lying. That's how these things are," she said.

"What if I tell them you have nothing to do with this?" he offered earnestly.

She smiled at his naiveté. "It's not that simple. First of all, what makes you think they'd believe you? And if you talk about one thing, you have to talk about everything. You can't just say I wasn't at the meeting. You'll have to tell them who was there. Then you have to answer all the other questions."

He lowered his head and covered his face with his hands as if he were ashamed to face her. He seemed to acknowledge his own culpability, and for the first time she saw that his suffering came, not from the humiliation of jail or the loss of liberty, as she had believed. She had been wrong to call it arrogance. His silence had meant acceptance.

The sun disappeared behind a passing cloud and the walls were covered in shadow as if someone had turned off the lights. She took his hands and moved them away from his face. "You have to trust me," she said, gently. After a moment he lifted his eyes and let his gaze meet hers. "Tell me who she is and where I can find her."

"Her name is Mireille Vernon. Rue Jacob, 152. Tell her she should leave Paris. Tell her to go somewhere until this is over."

He put his hand over hers. "It will be all right," he said.

26

Mike slept late. It was a good sleep and when he woke up he felt optimistic. He opened the shutters. The street was crowded with traffic. It was overcast and it seemed that it had rained.

All things considered, he was feeling pretty good. He stopped at the outdoor café in front of the Hotel Excelsior for breakfast, reading the *Herald Tribune* as he ate. While he was sitting at the café the sun came out. He made a few notes for the scheduling conference before the magistrates. John Travers, the attaché for the Justice Department in Rome, would accompany him. He was unsure whether Juliet would be there, and if she were, whether she would feel awkward after the other night.

He was glad that it was all taking place in a foreign country. Somehow he knew when he got back to New York it would seem less real.

At the embassy he was escorted to John Travers's office and invited to take a seat. Travers was held up in a meeting.

He went to the window to look at the view of marble gods, curved walls and fountains trickling out of the pursed lips of cherubs.

"*Come stai?*" John Travers said.

"John, how have you been?" Mike extended his hand.

"I'm having a great time, Mike. I guess you're not doing too badly yourself if Justice sent you here."

Mike smiled. "I was enjoying the view from your window."

"Any window you look out of in Rome you see something beautiful."

Mike took a seat. "So what do you think of our chances for extradition?"

"Honestly?"

"Yeah, of course."

"Rome is a funny place. They won't extradite based on inference. It will be harder to persuade the panel of magistrates here than a jury in New York. They take pride in showing they are not the tool of American politics. And there is no way around it; they view a case like this as political."

"Have you spoken to anyone here?"

"Roberto Chiaro—you'll meet him at the hearing. He is the attorney for the Italian Ministry of Justice, the equivalent of one of our prosecutors, so he'll be at all the hearings. I showed him your papers. His view is you've got a witness, but they're going to want something hard—a document, some kind of physical corroboration."

"On the surface the documents are fine. This is a witness case."

"Then they'll want more than one witness."

Mike shifted in his chair. "This Roberto Chiaro—is he any good?"

"Yeah, I've worked with him a lot, mostly on the Italian side—organized crime, you know."

Mike nodded, "I want to do the questioning. Is that going to be a problem?"

"As far as he's concerned, this is your case."

"So far, so good. I'll need a translator. I might want use of an office while I'm here, too."

"Not a problem."

"But I want a good view," Mike said, smiling.

"No such thing as a bad view in Rome."

Mike looked at his watch. "We'd better get going if we're going to meet Chiaro first."

They drove to the courthouse in Travers's car.

"We can go in through the door off to the side," Travers said. "Believe me, you don't want to go through the main entrance if you don't have to; the place is a zoo."

"What's the Italian word for zoo?"

Travers smiled. "Zoo. Is there a reason you want to know?"

"Just curious."

Roberto Chiaro greeted them in the hall outside the chambers. He was a thin man with dark wavy hair and the characteristic black-rimmed eyeglasses that it seemed to Mike all Italian men wore.

"Roberto." Travers shook his hand warmly. "This is Mike Chase, a very famous prosecutor in New York."

Mike shrugged off the compliment, shaking his hand.

"Mike, you're lucky, because Roberto is the best."

Travers put his hand on Roberto's shoulder. "You understand, this is a very big case in the States, otherwise they wouldn't have sent Mike. They don't waste resources in the U.S. Attorney's Office."

"You're a prosecutor, I take it," Mike said, smiling.

Roberto answered thoughtfully, "Our system is somewhat more complicated than yours. How is it? The Italian mind has a craving for more gray than for black and white, but I will answer your question simply: yes, I am a prosecutor.

"Shall we go inside," Roberto said. "I believe our adversaries may already arrive."

"Listening to foreigners speak English is causing me to spend too much time thinking about verbs," Mike said quietly to Travers, who seemed amused.

Juliet was sitting beside Alessandro at a large conference table when Mike entered. He saw her lower her eyes as he walked in. She had on the trench coat she was wearing the night before. Roberto began to speak in Italian to Alessandro. Mike had the impression the two men knew one another. Travers joined in the conversation. Mike stood looking at Juliet, waiting for her to lift her eyes.

"Mr. Chase—"

"Mike. Please."

"Mike. We sit along this side," Roberto said.

"Hello Alessandro, Mrs. de Fournier," Mike said, turning toward them.

Alessandro reached across the table to shake his hand. Juliet looked up indolently.

Mike sat down and opened his briefcase. A few minutes later a heavily made-up woman came over and sat down next to him.

"Hello, I am here to translate for the defendant," she said in a pleasant voice.

Juliet looked up.

"I don't think we asked for a translator," Juliet said. "Alessandro?"

Alessandro turned toward the woman, "Since it is only a scheduling conference, Monsieur de Fournier will not be present."

"I requested a translator," Mike said. "English?"

"Yes, certainly." She opened her large black purse and took out a pad and a pencil.

The magistrates entered together, dressed alike in sports coats and gray flannel trousers.

Alessandro introduced himself and Juliet in English. From that point on the proceedings were conducted in Italian. The Italian lawyers took turns addressing the magistrates, speaking rapidly and throwing up their hands, their voices becoming impassioned and excited.

Mike turned to the translator. "What are they saying?"

"Sh, sh." She waved her hand as if she were brushing away a fly.

The magistrates answered in rapid and impassioned voices. They began speaking out of turn; it appeared to Mike that they were arguing amongst themselves; their voices rose and their hands gestured and the eyeglasses came on and off.

"What are they talking about?"

"Sh, sh—I'll tell you at the end," the translator said.

Mike felt growing impatience; he had the sinking feeling they were arguing over the substance of the case and he was annoyed as hell at John Travers for letting Roberto Chiaro handle it, too annoyed to look over at Juliet for her reaction. He had the impression the matter was not going well for his side.

Suddenly it was silent. The magistrates began folding their notebooks; Roberto Chiaro and Alessandro put papers back into their briefcases, which to Mike looked more like doctors' bags. Mike turned expectantly to the translator.

"The hearing will be scheduled for a week from this coming Tuesday," she said.

"They must have said more than that." Mike glanced at his watch. "They've been at it for forty-five minutes; that can't be all."

The woman shook her head and paused thoughtfully. "They speak very much and say very little," she said.

Mike went out in the hallway to wait for John Travers who appeared to be in the middle of an endless discussion in Italian with Roberto Chiaro.

Juliet approached him. "I'm going to Paris to meet with Dufois," she said.

It took Mike by surprise. "Your client wants that?"

"I haven't consulted my client," she answered curtly.

"I take it you don't want my advice," he said, not being able to help himself from matching her tone.

"You made an offer, didn't you? My client will get a break on jail time if he cooperates," she said.

"Yeah, that's true. Has Dufois agreed to meet with you?"

"Yes."

"Are you going to meet with him alone?"

She did not answer and he took it as a yes.

"I don't think he's a nice guy, and I really don't know if I like the idea of you meeting with him alone. Why doesn't Alessandro go with you?"

"I don't want to go into specifics," she said. Her voice had softened and she seemed vulnerable to him, the way she had the night before in his hotel room. He guessed that the reason she did not want Alessandro there was because she was afraid it would get back to François.

"I'll tell you what. I was planning on going to Paris to look at documents. I'll go with you. At least, you might feel safer knowing I was in town."

"I don't know, do I feel safe with you?"

He had the impression she was flirting.

"I'm leaving on a six-thirty Air France flight," she said. "We can go together. I'll pick you up at four."

"You know where I'm staying?" he smirked.

"I think I remember."

27

Juliet had observed Alessandro watching as she and Mike spoke. She knew that if he was going to trust her she could not meet with Dufois without at least telling him.

"I'm leaving for Paris this afternoon," she said.

Alessandro seemed surprised. " I hope it is the desire to be away from Rome, and not some crisis—"

"Etienne Dufois has agreed to meet with me tonight."

Alessandro frowned and seemed perplexed.

"I believe I have something to offer which will benefit him as well as François."

"Forgive me if I am unenthusiastic, but I do not think this is something François wants."

"François has asked me to represent him. I've given enough deference to his wishes. He has made it plain by his silence that he will not cooperate against Dufois. The longer we let it go, the more likely it is he will be the scapegoat for everything."

"What do you think will be gained by this meeting?"

"I want to persuade Dufois that both he and François should talk to the U.S. Attorney's Office."

Alessandro shook his head, but Juliet continued, "The issues are larger than just one bank. Who needed an American bank and why?"

"Why?" Alessandro shrugged. "*Ma*, laundering is laundering."

"No, money was being laundered for a reason. What is the reason? Where was the money going? To get a deal where they both walk, this information is critical. Who is behind it and what are they planning? Believe me, the government wants that information and they'll pay for it."

"*Allora*, what makes you think François knows the answers to these questions? In my opinion he does not."

"He may not, but Dufois does."

"Even so, my dear, he will never tell you." Alessandro folded his arms across his chest, a gesture Juliet read as signaling his unmistakable opposition.

"I don't think Dufois is going to want to spend the rest of his life in Saudi Arabia. He will welcome an arrangement that enables him to resolve this without going into exile."

"Yes, but the price is not one he is willing to pay, I am sure."

"I'm not going to ask you to come with me. I wouldn't want to compromise you in that way. I only ask as a personal favor that you keep from telling François."

"You are husband and wife," he said, shrugging his shoulders. "It is between you."

28

The sun was shining and the air was a golden haze. Mike waited for Juliet in front of his hotel. The sun against his face felt warm, as if it were summer. Yet the scent of autumn, of something slowly dying, was in the air.

"François received treatment for the infection on his wrist. I owe you a thank-you."

"Don't mention it."

She was looking straight ahead through the windshield, unwilling to make eye contact. "He doesn't complain, you know. He keeps it all inside. Sometimes I wish he would say something, tell me it's terrible, that he's going out of his mind, all the things I know must be true."

It made him uncomfortable to hear her speak of her husband, and he tried to change the subject. He told the story about the translator, which made her laugh, and the sound was like the golden sun and the warm breeze, he thought.

"I love your laugh," he said.

"Does any of it seem real to you?" she asked with lovely downcast eyes.

"I'm not a very deep person—I suppose," he said. "Strange things happen to people." He didn't tell her that he too had been counting on it remaining unreal. Yet his silence made his desire no less real, the way he felt sitting beside her, wanting to touch her, and holding back, that was real enough, he thought.

He leaned close to her and spoke quietly.

"If you're hoping Dufois will admit to anything, you won't succeed. Stay out of it."

"I have to do what I think is in his best interest," she said.

"Trust me, I know how these people operate. They make the mafia look like amateurs. They don't mind killing. Dufois is not going to talk," he said.

There was a long interval of silence after they boarded. He wondered what she was thinking. He fingered the glass of wine on his tray without drinking it. She had not wanted anything to drink.

"You're very quiet," he said at last.

"There are no safe subjects." Then she added, "I suppose it's safe to tell you I'm not looking forward to going back to my empty apartment."

"I know that feeling."

She seemed to fall asleep against his arm, though he had the impression she was not really asleep, just resting with her eyes closed to avoid having to talk.

The traffic was heavy on the way into Paris from the airport and the taxi driver stank of body odor. Mike rolled down his window. It was night and drastically colder than Rome, much colder than this time of year in New York.

"Is it always so cold this time of year?"

"Paris is pretty far north. It's cold."

He noticed she had slipped on the overcoat she had been carrying over her arm. At the Arc de Triomphe they got stuck in traffic for half an hour. Every few minutes, the driver would lunge forward, seeming to have succeeded only in embedding himself more deeply into the middle of it. The cars around them blew their horns, compounding the annoyance.

"It's remarkable that they don't have traffic lights," he said. "How can they function this way?"

"You're beginning to sound like the ugly American," she said. "We're not that far from the hotel."

She was meeting Dufois that night at Plaza Athénée. Not in the mood for the usual third-rate hotel that came with a government stipend, Mike had decided to take a room there; he would pay the difference himself. He usually did not feel inadequate over things like money, but if this was her world, he wanted to make a show of living in it.

He had another reason for staying there; the meeting Saed described had taken place in the bar, and he wanted to get a feel for the clientele and the rhythm of the place, the people who went in and out. He knew how important small details were to an effective cross-examination.

"Whose idea was it to meet at the Plaza Athénée?" he asked.

"Dufois," she replied. "Why?"

"No reason." Although he did not say it, he found it consistent with the meeting Saed described.

"I'm going to my apartment. Dufois likes to meet late. I'll call you when it's over." Then she added, "Please don't show up. There shouldn't be a problem; he's a businessman, for God's sake."

It had not occurred to him before whether she had any friends in Paris or whether she might be meeting someone for dinner.

He handed his suitcase to the woman at the desk after checking in. "Where is the bar?" he asked.

The young woman seemed surprised, *"Monsieur* has not been to his room?"

"I'll get there."

"*Donc.* Take the staircase at the end of the hall."

He walked through the sitting area where the afternoon tea was served. The long windows overlooked a courtyard, but it was already dark and the courtyard was not lit. After going down the stairs, he found nothing until he came to an open doorway at the end of the hall. The bar was there. No one who was not looking for it would just stumble upon it.

He stood at the entrance and took in the room, the red leather chairs, plaid rugs and paneled walls; it was meant to look like an English bar. The piano at the far end of the room was silent. Two men sat at the bar talking to the bartender. He thought back to everything Saed had told him as he tried to determine at which table the meeting had taken place. Under the arches at the back of the room near the piano the tables were all set up for two. It must have been the table for four in the far corner, he thought. He went over to the table and sat down.

"*Bonsoir,*" a voice behind him said. "*Vous desirez?*"

"A beer, please."

He drank his beer slowly as he looked around the room. De Fournier would have felt safe talking here, he thought.

On his way out he picked up a little card with a picture of the bar on the front. Inside it read, *Piano-Bar, Chansons francaises, Jazz, tous les soirs de 23 heures a 1 heure du matin.*

He found his room too feminine for his taste—everything, walls, bed, were a blush color, too pink to stop noticing. The air seemed to have been sprayed with perfume. He opened the shutters. The Tour Eiffel, illuminated in the dark, stood majestically in the window frame.

He had skipped lunch and was hungry, so he called down to room service, and ordered chicken, because he never liked the way the French prepared beef, and a bottle of white wine. The bill came to six hundred and fifty francs, more than a hundred dollars, the price of an airline ticket in the States, he thought. The food arrived hot and he ate it greedily, washing it down with several glasses of wine. Then he turned on the television and watched CNN while finishing off the bottle.

29

Juliet was to meet Etienne Dufois in the sitting area just off the lobby. She took a seat near enough to the dining room to hear the string quartet. Dufois arrived late. Dugommier was with him, which no longer surprised her.

Dufois's bodyguards broke away and began to pace up and down the lobby. Dugommier sat beside her on the settee, as if it were nothing more than a social encounter. "Is this your first trip back to Paris?" he asked. "It must be difficult." He seemed to be making an effort to appear sympathetic.

Dufois took her hand and kissed it before sitting in the chair to her right. It occurred to her that he had chosen that chair because he could see the entrance to the lobby from there. Everything about him was round, his head, his shoulders, his chest, even his eyes and his little mouth. Juliet noticed that his feet did not reach the floor unless he sat forward.

"We are all distressed to learn of François's situation. Such an extraordinary set of circumstances," he said, shaking his head. "One hates to hear of misfortune befalling one's friends. Be assured that our thoughts are with him, and that we are willing to do what we can to help him."

His voice was smooth as a lacquer surface. She noticed that he deliberately spoke to her in English. "I heard from *maître* that you will be representing François in the States.

He must have great confidence in your abilities to seek your representation."

She merely nodded, though to herself she wondered what Dugommier's reaction had been when François told him.

"You have a document for us," Dugommier said. He seemed anxious for the meeting to get underway.

"I brought a copy of the United States government's allegations in the extradition in Rome," she answered.

Dufois's manicured hand reached out to take the papers.

She noticed that he never made eye contact with Dugommier, and she assumed this was intentional.

"Who is Michael Chase?" Dufois asked.

Juliet had the impression he was studying her carefully. "He is the United States prosecutor," she said, looking over at Dugommier, who, she was certain, had already told him who Mike was.

"And he is in Rome?"

"He will be conducting the proceedings in Rome, yes, along with local Italian counsel for the government." Again she turned a hard, quick look at Dugommier, communicating with her eyes that she had not been fooled by the little exchange that had just taken place.

Dufois put on reading glasses and glanced at the pages. When he lowered his eyes to read, she observed his eyelashes, thick, black and curled; she thought he might be wearing mascara. After a few minutes he dropped the affidavit on the table.

"Madame, no such meeting took place. Do you think I or your husband are so stupid that if we were to have had such a conversation, we would have allowed witnesses to be present? Nothing of the sort took place."

She hesitated until she had gathered confidence, wanting to sound strong and sure of herself. "I don't think François's silence is going to change anything as far as you are concerned. If they succeed in prosecuting him, an indictment of you will follow regardless of whether he remains silent. I believe that if you and François came forward together with names of the people and organizations using the bank to launder money, the government's interest in prosecuting you would diminish drastically."

Dufois's round eyes, which moments before had seemed incapable of assuming any other shape, narrowed beneath the thick lashes. All the softness that money had brought to his face disappeared, and he looked hard and mean.

"Madame, I am not in the business of cooperating," he said coldly. "As to the difficulties befalling your husband, I have expressed my sympathy. He knows it is our hope that the matter will be resolved swiftly and to his advantage."

He threw a glance in the direction of one of his bodyguards, before turning back to Juliet.

"François knows his place," he continued, "and would not dare to permit so insulting and foolish an approach as you have made. It is the fact that you Americans never know your place that has allowed you to make such a mistake. Too often you confuse the strong with the weak."

He stood and nodded politely, the composure once again restored to his face. "I am sorry that our meeting, which up to this point had been so pleasant, has been spoiled," he said. Then he left.

Dugommier stayed behind. "I will try to calm the situation," he offered, though he seemed to reprimand her with his eyes.

"How can I believe you will help François?" she said.

"That's not true," he said, gently. "I do not want to see François hurt." He picked up the affidavit from the table and glanced toward the door where Dufois waited, flanked by two bodyguards. "I must go. I am sorry," he said.

Juliet felt naive and foolish. She could be sure that Dugommier would tell François about the meeting. But she had never intended to keep it secret for long. She had not wanted François to know beforehand because he would have stopped her. It was easy to say in hindsight that he would have been right. But it was the only chance of cutting a deal with the U. S. Attorney. No one was offering anything better. She was tired of blaming herself when all the choices were bad.

30

"Will you meet me in the lobby?"

"Juliet. Everything all right?" Mike had dozed off with the television on. He was glad she called.

"I'd just like to go out for a drink."

He was still dressed in the suit he had worn to court, except that he had taken off his tie.

"There's a Spanish bar open late not too far from here, Le Calvados. Are you up for it?"

"Sure."

He put his arm in hers as they walked in the cold, crisp air. The sound of their footsteps echoed down empty streets, and he could see her breath in clouds of vapor near her mouth. He had the feeling Paris was nothing more than a stage— the low sky, the white lights bouncing off the tops of gilded domes and monuments, the illuminated Tour Eiffel against the midnight blue night.

"Here we are," she said.

Le Calvados was a dark little place. The restaurant downstairs was closed; they climbed up a narrow flight of stairs to the bar, which was empty, and sat along the banquette, side by side at a table covered with a blue and white checkered tablecloth. The short candle burning in the center of the table provided the only light. A man in a white dinner jacket sang in Spanish, accompanying himself on an electric piano.

It was after midnight, late even by Paris standards, Mike thought as he glanced at his watch.

The Spanish singer asked if they had any requests.

"How about *Autumn Leaves*?" Mike said.

He claimed to know it. But the song he started playing was not *Autumn Leaves*.

Juliet laughed. "*Les Feuilles Mortes*," she said, repeating the name in French, and the singer immediately began playing the right song.

She ordered a brandy and Mike did the same.

"Let me see if I'm getting better at reading your expressions. Your meeting didn't go well and Dufois didn't admit anything."

"You were claiming to know that before I met with him. Suppose your informant is lying to you," she said. "That meeting never took place."

Mike took a long sip from his drink and smirked.

"Suppose I'm the King of Norway. Are we through with this? If Dufois is so good for you, let me talk to him. If I think he's telling the truth, that'll be the end of it."

"I don't believe you," she said without belligerence.

"Believing me may be the only thing you've got going for you."

"You're beginning to sound like a cop again. I wish you wouldn't."

She picked up the candle and tipping it to one side, let the hot wax spill out onto the blue and white checkered tablecloth.

"Another cognac?" the waiter asked.

Mike looked over at her empty glass. "Make it two." She did not object.

The Spanish singer had gone back to singing in Spanish. They sat in awkward silence for a few minutes, which she broke.

"It's funny how one runs out of things to say by the age of thirty," she said. "Oh, I know, people talk constantly anyway, men complain about their wives and women complain about their husbands and everyone complains at work. But if it's just that, it's better not to say anything."

She stopped playing with the spilt wax.

"You can't get in trouble for this, can you?" she asked.

"I'm not doing anything wrong right now. Leave me alone in a room with you, and I don't know if I'd be so good."

She smiled. "I was thinking of how angry I was with you a month ago."

"People have a way of complicating things for themselves."

"It was Pascal who said all the problems in the world happen because man can't sit quietly in his room," she said, smiling.

"I'm not really up on my French philosophy."

"Will you tell me something, honestly, is this prosecution personal on your part?"

"I've thought about it, yeah, it worries me sometimes. But I haven't treated François any less fairly. In fact, maybe in a few instances I've refrained from tactics I might have used on someone else."

He felt like he had to add something. "You know, I'm not afraid of going to trial," he said. "My own self-interest tells me I want a trial here; it's a good case, it'll attract a lot of attention and I think I can win. It's only for your sake that I've tried to come up with a solution."

"There isn't going to be an easy way out," she said.

"Let me guess. Dufois said nothing happened, which is what François is telling you."

She did not answer him.

He looked around the room and noticed the waiter looking back at him with the look waiters get when they want to go home. The Spanish singer had stopped singing and was packing up his equipment.

"It's been a long day," Mike said. "Why don't we get the check?"

He gestured to the waiter who seemed pleased.

"Is tip included?" he asked Juliet.

"Yes. See, here, gratuity," she said pointing to the check. Mike held a fold of francs in front of him as if it were a hand of cards.

She pulled out an hundred franc bill.

"This is good," she said; she was smiling again.

As they were walking, he put his arm around her and drew her close. She was cold; he could feel her shivering. The streets were empty and it was good that way because it meant the moment could pass with his arm around her and it wouldn't matter any more than if it were a dream. Then he thought to himself, when was the last time I dreamed.

"I'm going to go home," she said, at the entrance to Plaza Athénée.

"I understand," he said, though he was not convinced he had succeeded in concealing his disappointment. "Let me see you into a taxi."

A cab was waiting just outside and he waved it over.

The booze had not made her drunk; it had just given a languor to her features, to her eyes and her mouth, almost as if she were asleep.

"Why can't I hate you? If you knew how much I wanted to," she said.

He put his hand to her neck. "Don't hate me."

"I'm afraid, you know, afraid of my own weakness."

His hand moved from her neck to her cheek and caressed it gently. "Maybe he's not worth being a good wife for," he said.

She took his hand from her face and held it for a moment. "No, don't, please, don't say anything against him. My absolution isn't in his sins."

He watched the taxi speed off, the streetlights blurring through his half-drunk eyes. He knew what he felt, and that was real, all right.

When he got back to his room, he found a phone message from Richie. He held the message slip in his hand, considering whether to call him back. Then after a couple of minutes he figured why not; he was a little restless anyway.

"Hey, Mike, how ya doin'?"

"You called me."

"Yeah."

"What is it?"

"I understand we're no longer working together on this, but something came up and I thought you'd want to know. I'll get to the point. Saed called me. You were out of town and he wouldn't talk with the new agent because he didn't know him. Saed has the name of the woman at that meeting at Plaza Athénée."

"What's the name?"

"Miray, spelled M I R E I L L E, Vernon-V E R N O N, got it?"

"Who is she?"

"Some kind of girlfriend of de Fournier's. That's the fancy way of putting it. I got Interpol to run a check on her. She lives in Paris, Number 152 Rue Jacob, that's J A C O—

"Yeah, I know how to spell Jacob. Does she have a business address?"

"Who's the last prostitute you knew with a business address? Maybe our friend is off the hook after all."

Mike knew he meant Juliet.

"Okay, thanks." Mike wanted to end the conversation, but Richie continued. "I suppose you'll talk to her while you're in Paris," Richie said.

"Good bet."

"When?"

"What difference does it make?"

"I was just wondering how much longer you're gonna be in Europe."

"Depends."

"Well, listen, take care of yourself. I'm not tryin' to insinuate myself back in, but I thought this was important."

"No, you did the right thing. Thanks."

31

Juliet stood in the cold night air with her finger pressed to the bell, listening to the irritating buzz it was making inside. The café in the front of the building was closed, the chairs stacked on the tables, and the lights off. There was an entrance through a side gate. She pressed her ear to the door to try to hear whether anyone was coming, then she heard the lock turning on the other side.

The guardian, an old woman wrapped in a blue wool bathrobe, peered through the door, her thin white hair in a plait that ran halfway down her back.

"I'm here to see Mireille Vernon," Juliet said.

The old woman stared at her for a moment before unfastening the chain.

"Ringing the bell that way, you were going to wake up the whole house," the woman complained in a hoarse voice.

Juliet handed her a hundred francs.

"I'm sorry to disturb you. Is Madame Vernon in?"

The woman did not bother to check the wall where the keys to the rooms were hung. Clutching the hundred francs in her arthritic hand, she mumbled, "*Oui, oui, le deuxième étage.*"

The wallpaper in the hallway was worn and the stairs creaked loudly. There was a night light at the landing on the second floor and only one door. Juliet knocked, conscious of the way the sound was carrying through the building. The lid to the peephole slid open.

"I'm François's wife. There's something I have to talk to you about."

"I'll be home in the morning."

"It can't wait until then."

Mireille hesitated a moment before opening the door. The foyer was dark. A lamp was on in the salon. She had thrown on a white silk dressing gown with a print of red roses. Her dyed red hair was mussed as if she had been asleep. Her appearance took Juliet by surprise. She was older than Juliet by at least ten years, and her face, which had all the markings of a beautiful face in youth, had lost the freshness beauty requires.

"What do you want?" Mireille repeated.

They remained standing by the door, studying one another in the shadow.

"I don't know if you've heard—"

"Yes, I know," Mireille said.

"You've heard from François then?"

"No, someone told me." Mireille paused before adding coldly, "Are you sure this can't wait until morning?"

Juliet pleaded, "I know it's late, please—"

Mireille took a step back. "Come," she said. She led Juliet into the salon, inviting her to take a seat on one of two small Louis XV upholstered pale pink canapés. Juliet surveyed the room in the new light. A typically French apartment in many ways, and yet there was no mistaking that Mireille lived alone. Juliet noticed Mireille's eye go coldly to her wedding ring.

"So you are François's wife. You don't look American."

Juliet smiled. It was true she was neither blonde nor blue-eyed, small framed rather than tall and athletic, but all the same she was American.

"François has been in jail in Rome since August," Juliet said, realizing as she said it that it was already October.

"He surprised me," Mireille said. "I thought he would have taken precautions."

She sat on the *canapé* opposite Juliet and took a cigarette from the porcelain box on the table, offering one to Juliet, who declined.

In the light given off by the lamp, Juliet noticed the delicate blue vein beneath Mireille's right eye. The few lines near her mouth like *crêpe de Chine* made her face seem fragile rather than old. She was wearing no make-up. Juliet saw the true shape of her mouth, the color of her lips, the shape of her eyes—observations a woman allows only those with whom she is most intimate.

"Why did François tell you to see me?"

"He thinks you could help him when he presents his case to the Italian courts."

"If he wanted something from me, he would not send his wife. He has other ways of getting in touch."

A cloud of blue smoke drifted toward the lamp with each shallow drag of the cigarette. The antique bronze clock over the mantle struck two.

"I should have offered you something," Mireille said with cold politeness.

"A drink of water, please." Juliet suddenly felt her throat parched from nerves.

Mireille went to the kitchen, returning with a bottle of Vittel and two glasses.

Juliet took a few sips of water before beginning. "Do you read English?"

"No."

"Will you trust me?"

Mireille merely nodded, her eyes lowered.

"These papers contain the accusations of the American government against François. Someone told the prosecutors in New York about a meeting at Plaza Athénée in November 1985. You were at that meeting."

She watched Mireille's face contort with fear.

"Show me my name," she said.

"Your name is not mentioned. Chances are they don't know who you are yet. But they will find out."

"Because François will tell them." She seemed cold and hostile.

"François won't tell them."

Mireille looked down at her cigarette, smoked to the filter, before stubbing it out in the ashtray.

"What will happen to François? Will he have to go to jail in America?"

"The Italian courts will decide whether to send him to the United States. From there?" Juliet shrugged.

Mireille got up and crossed the room as if she were looking for something, but she stopped abruptly. Juliet watched as her shoulders began to shake, and the sound of sobbing, muffled at first, grew louder with each sob that broke through her attempts to suppress them. She went to her, placing her hand on her shoulder. "You're frightened, I know," she said, gently.

Mireille turned to face her. "You say you know. How could you know what I feel?" Her voice was high and shrill, and Juliet had the impression that she was no longer talking to her, but thinking aloud.

"After everything, this was going to be his way of taking care of me."

"They don't know who you are. François will never tell them."

"All men are cowards," Mireille said, wiping the tears with the back of her hand. Her face had changed again. The vulnerability was gone, replaced by a hardness and disdain that showed in the narrowing of the eyes and the tight pull at the corners of her sensuous mouth. "You are someone's wife. I do not envy you save for that. To be pretty, young, I had those things once. No, it is not that I miss. I am tired of love. Men bore me now. Do you understand? The opportunity to be deceived, to have someone come home to me every night out of a sense of obligation—for that alone I envy you. Even the Arabs have lost interest in me. There are women half my age who will do things for them I could not bring myself to do for any man, not even a man I loved."

She crossed her arms and lowered her eyes for an instant. When she looked over at Juliet again, she seemed to have undergone another transformation; the hardness was gone.

"Don't misunderstand. I never had any illusions about François. He was young. I taught him how to love. Because of this, with all the women after me, he could never completely forget me. If he loves you well, it is because of me."

She touched her lips and the gesture, anguished and sensual, struck Juliet.

"I got used to the way I knew it would turn out between us. When the time came I suffered by myself."

She gazed steadily at Juliet. "François never told you any of this, did he?"

She smiled, a slight smile with a hint of malice. "When I first saw you, I thought I should hate you. Now I find I feel almost sorry for you. François knows I cannot help him. You came here on your own. What do you expect of me?"

"I want you to tell me the truth," Juliet said. "No one else will."

"The truth." Mireille walked back to the *canapé* and sat down. "A nice way of putting it—you make it sound virtuous."

Juliet sat opposite her.

"Since I heard of the arrest I have been waiting for the knock on my door. I wasn't expecting François's wife, I admit. I thought maybe the police." Her eyes wandered a moment before she fixed her gaze intently on Juliet. "He told me you were a lawyer in New York," she said.

Juliet felt Mireille studying her again, the way she when she first came in.

"You think you can help me if I tell you?" Mireille said.

"I'll do whatever I can," she said sincerely, though she wondered what kind of help Mireille would expect from her.

Mireille was silent. She appeared lost in her own thoughts. She sipped from her glass of water and gazed vacantly at Juliet. Once she began to talk, her eyes shifted away from Juliet, as if she were alone in the room.

"Dufois was someone I met socially. When the sheiks came to town, the rich Saudi businessmen, Dufois would call me and I would entertain them. It was pleasant to go to restaurants and clubs. When François needed money for Compagnie Financière I introduced him. It seemed to go well. Then afterwards, there were favors, things they sought over the years. Dufois promised more money to invest. He took a long time living up to his promise and François was becoming frustrated. It seemed every few months there was something else they wanted from him. He would complain to me that he wanted to be free of them."

Her gaze shifted back in Juliet's direction and she became wistful as she spoke of François.

"He was meeting Dufois and he asked me to come with him. He knew Dufois always brought someone, a bodyguard, one of the people who works for him. They must have been talking about this New York bank before. It appeared François was reluctant; he said overseas investments were too much trouble. To entice him, Dufois offered to put more money in the fund run by Compagnie Financière. But François did not want that; he wanted money for himself, clear of the fund, which did not make Dufois happy."

"Do you remember who else was there?" Juliet interrupted.

Mireille hesitated before answering. "His name was Saed. A Syrian. I remember names; the faces I forget. Saed was related to one of the people whose money Dufois manages. I think Dufois was trying to help him get a job, which is why he brought him to meet François."

"Did they discuss the bank? What did François say about it?"

"They never referred to a bank by name. They were speaking in general terms. Dufois asked whether everything had been done in New York. François said he wanted more money. This made Dufois angry. By demanding more money I am sure François placed him in a difficult position with his investors. It is hard to entice the Arabs to commit, but once they commit they do not tolerate setbacks. Dufois could not go back to his investors and say that the deal had failed. They had agreed on five million dollars and François was insisting on ten. I assume Dufois paid the difference himself, which is why he was so angry. It was a lot of money to pay, even for Dufois"

"Who are the investors?" Juliet asked.

Mireille tilted her head to the side, her hair falling back and revealing her soft eyes and pale skin. "I imagine they are Yemeni. I doubt you know how it is in Saudi Arabia. The king disapproves of investment outside the country. The Yemeni do not feel accepted and they are afraid of the king. If they wanted to take money out of the country they would have to go to the king for permission. They are afraid the king does not allow it. They look for opportunities like this as a way of getting money out of Saudi Arabia without the king knowing. Dufois began as an arms dealer, an easy way to gain money and power in the Middle East."

Mireille's voice cracked. She refilled her glass from the bottle of Vittel and drank.

"Was anything agreed during the meeting at Plaza Athénée?" Juliet asked.

"When we left nothing had been concluded. Later François told me to go to Switzerland. I was the only person acceptable to Dufois that François believed he could trust." She lowered her eyes and looked away, and Juliet wondered if she had left something out.

"I went to Geneva and first met with a man; I was never told his name. I know he was not Syrian. Dufois would not trust a Syrian for something important. I am supposing he was from Abu Dhabi. I met him at the Hilton. François had given me an envelope that I was to give to him."

"What was inside the envelope?"

Mireille shrugged slightly and her mouth pulled together in a slight closed-lip smile. "I was not told. If what I say seems confused or vague it is because they wanted it that way." She paused to sip from her glass. "After the hotel, I went to the bank. It was a *banque privée* and the building overlooked the lake. DMMB—DMMB Group Bancaire, it was called."

"Do you remember who you met with at the bank? Doesn't it work so that someone high up, an official, knows you and connects you to the account?"

Mireille shook her head. "No one knew me. François gave me a ring, a red intaglio; you see the lion inside. He said I had to wear it when I went to the bank. It was too big for my left hand; I wore it on the index finger of my right hand. He gave me an envelope with the necessary information to present to the bank. I had to sign papers while I was there and I was given an account number."

She got up and disappeared into the back room. When she returned, she handed Juliet two small squares of paper, each with a series of numbers on it.

"I broke the number in half," she said. "I kept the first part in my drawer, the other in a purse. These numbers come first," she said, pointing to one of the pieces of paper. "François took the ring back. Without the ring, the numbers are nothing."

Juliet looked at the scraps of paper in her hand, wondering what Mireille had intended by keeping them.

"François felt he could press for the money. He must have known that Dufois was under pressure to deliver the bank. He thought by the end of the negotiation Dufois was weak and had no choice but to pay what he was demanding. I only know that they wanted him to do it for five years—two million a year—I imagine that is how François came up with ten million. Then after the five years they were going to find someone else."

Mireille sat back on the *canapé*, her face obscured by the shadow from the lamp.

"How was this his way of taking care of you? What does he owe you?"

"François?" Mireille smiled thinly. "We settled our accounts a long time ago. It was Dufois who owed me."

"Then why did you keep the numbers to the bank account?" Juliet asked, putting them together in her hand and glancing down at them before looking up at Mireille.

"I would not expect you to understand," she said, with a mixture of despair and contempt. "I knew when this was finished I was no longer of use to François. I might need him someday, and if I had the numbers he could not turn me down."

She sat looking at Juliet as if she had said everything there was to say.

"You haven't told me what happened to Alain Gilbert," Juliet said. "Why was he murdered and who murdered him?"

Mireille answered without hesitating, as if it were not worthy of further reflection. "Dufois, I assume. He had no choice. Gilbert knew the secrets of Dufois's clients; he knew where the money was going. Dufois learned he was going to talk, so he had him killed." She let out a little laugh. "You could not think François had Gilbert killed. Even if he wanted to, he does not have that kind of power. He probably thinks Gilbert deserved it for opening his mouth. Gilbert worked for Dufois. When the Arabs first invested in Compagnie Financière it was a condition that Gilbert enters the company to watch over the investment. Later Dufois wanted Gilbert in New York. François was not involved in their associations with the Middle East. But he knows enough for them to be concerned. Why do you think François is keeping his mouth shut? He knows if he talks, they will kill him."

Mireille sat back and rested her head against the back of the canapé, her face obscured by the shadow from the lamp. She seemed tired of talking.

"I don't think you should remain in Paris any longer," Juliet said. "It will be months before a decision is reached in Rome. That gives the government enough time to find you."

The fear returned to Mireille's eyes. "I have no place to go. Only a hotel, but it is easy to find someone in a hotel. A false name is no protection for long."

"I'll make arrangements for you to stay in the house in Mougins for now until we find a better arrangement. There is a caretaker; he will look after you. You're better off in France, so long as no one knows where you are."

Mireille brushed the hair from her face with a sweep of her hand, revealing a face as in one of those anguished portraits of the Virgin, Juliet thought, beautiful yet distraught.

"I am from the south. I moved to Paris from Marseilles when I was sixteen with aspirations of becoming an actress. Considering my chances, I was not so far off. The difference is my stage had four walls."

The clock rang for half past three. Juliet got up and Mireille accompanied her to the door. As Juliet was about to leave, she turned toward her. "I am willing to go to Rome and say what is necessary to help François," she said.

"They haven't found the money. That's why it's better if they never talk to you."

Mireille looked back at Juliet through sad eyes that once again seemed to scrutinize her. "He must be afraid he's going to lose you," she said.

The night sky was beginning to lighten when Juliet returned to her apartment. She took off her coat and went to the safe in François's closet where they kept cash and jewelry.

She found the ring in a box along with several pairs of cuf-flinks. He had not bothered to hide it. It was an oval shape with the profile of a lion standing on all fours, an antique of some kind. She wondered whose it had been as she slipped it over her finger. It was big on her and she had to close her hand to keep it from falling off. She put away the box and locked the safe. Afterwards she lay in bed, the ring still loose on her finger, listening to the silent street in the last hour of night.

32

It was almost ten o'clock in the morning. Mike rolled over one more time before getting up. He had had too much to drink the night before and he was paying for it. When he opened the shutters he saw the Tour Eiffel looking gray beneath a low ceiling of clouds. The air when he opened the window felt like snow; it was never this cold in New York until November at the earliest, he thought.

After he dressed, he went downstairs to the restaurant for coffee, which was served in a silver pot with a pitcher of hot milk and a basket of warm croissants. He lingered awhile, watching the parade of well-dressed people through the lobby.

When he had finished breakfast, he took a taxi to Mireille's address, thinking the odds were pretty good that he would find her home in the morning.

The guardian answered the door, a tan-striped cat stalking behind her and rubbing up against her leg.

"I'm looking for Mireille Vernon."

"*Elle est partie,*" the old woman answered gruffly.

"I don't speak French. Do you speak English?"

She looked blankly back at him.

"*Anglaise?* Is there someone who speaks English?"

The old woman seemed as if she were about to slam the door shut. Mike took out his United States Attorney's Office badge and pointed to the seal.

"Someone who speaks *Anglaise*?" he said again.

She nodded toward the sidewalk.

"*La-bas, la-bas*," she said, in a hoarse voice. She led him out front where the café was, and pointed to the man behind the counter.

Mike showed him his badge. "You speak English, I take it."

"Some."

"I'm looking for a woman who lives here named Mireille Vernon. Do you know her?"

"Yes," the man said.

"Is this woman the concierge?"

"Guardian."

The woman repeated the word in a loud voice while nodding her head.

"Would you ask her if Mireille Vernon is in? I'd like to see her."

The man spoke to the woman in rapid French. As she answered she made a gesture with her hands as if she were lifting something.

"She says she left this morning with her valises," the man said.

"Does she know where she was going or when she'll be back?"

The old woman shrugged and folded her arms across her chest.

"What time did she leave?" Mike asked.

"She says between eight-thirty and nine this morning."

Mike slipped a card from his wallet and handed it to the man. "This is my name and number. I work for the United States government. When Mireille Vernon returns, would you call me?"

He narrowed his eyes as if confused.

"It's for her sake," Mike explained. "She may be in some danger and I need to talk to her."

"*Telephoner les Etats-Unis?*"

Mike at last understood the nature of his confusion. "You can call collect. I just need to know as soon as she returns."

It was obvious to Mike that someone had gotten to Mireille Vernon. It could have come from Dufois after meeting with Juliet. But it was also possible that Juliet had spoken to her, and this thought troubled him. He had been hard on Richie; the airport stunt was stupid, but he could not blame Richie entirely; he had forced him to it by his own inaction.

It had begun to drizzle. He had Juliet's address on a piece of paper, Avenue Silvestre-de-Sacy, which he had in his jacket pocket. He walked along the Rue d' Université. A taxi pulled up to let out some tourists and he got in. In contrast to the gray light and the dense ceiling of clouds, his thoughts were clear for the first time in over a month. He was her adversary; he had to tell her that and walk away.

He had the taxi let him off on the corner at Avenue la Bourdonnais. Juliet's apartment was the first building on the left side of the street, one block from the Tour Eiffel. Without the building code, it was impossible to get inside the vestibule where the apartment buzzers were located. He waited fifteen minutes in the rain before someone came out of the building.

"*Qui est-il?*"

It was a woman's voice, but it was not Juliet who answered the intercom.

"Mike Chase."

"*Attendez.*"

It was less than a minute, but to Mike it felt like an eternity before he was let in.

Juliet lived on the fifth floor. There was an elevator, but he walked up the winding stairway, six flights to the fifth floor. An Algerian woman wearing a blue uniform answered the door; he assumed it was the same woman he had spoken to over the intercom. She had a plain face and short, coarse black hair, and for an instant he was amused by the thought of Juliet engaging in the most basic of feminine instincts by hiring an unattractive maid.

"*Attendez, s'il vous plait.*"

Mike found himself alone in the foyer, counting the black tiles in the white marble floor. There were two sets of French doors, one leading to a room that looked like a library and the other to a living room. The lights were off and the rooms seemed dark, though the windows went to the floor and the curtains were open. A chandelier hung like a branch coated with ice on a gray winter day.

He heard the woman returning.

"Come with me, please," she said with a heavy French accent.

She led him through a short hallway into the dining room. Juliet sat at the table, her head turned toward the window; she did not seem to hear him come in. The beauty of her whole figure—her head with its heavy frame of dark hair, her graceful neck—struck him with surprise as if he were seeing her for the first time, and he recalled the night before the way her body had molded to his touch like warm wax when he put his arm around her as they walked and the cloud of vapor near her lips, which he had longed to kiss.

"Why have you come?" Juliet asked. When she looked up he noticed her eyes seemed red, as if she might have been crying.

"I wanted to see you," he said.

He took a seat without her inviting him. There was a view of the Seine from the window; on a sunny day it must be quite lovely, he thought, but today the long windows facing the dark river made everything seem darker.

He began to say something, but she stopped him.

The woman who had answered the door came in carrying a tray with a cup and saucer and baguette with a small dish of apricot confiture.

Juliet poured coffee from a small porcelain pot. "Milk?" she asked before passing him the cup.

"Yes, thanks."

He ran his finger along the handle of his coffee cup.

"See the shafts of wheat around the outside of the cup?" she said. "The pattern is called Alexander. That's why I bought it. For a while I had an interest in Alexander the Great. It's easy to admire a man who has been dead for two thousand years."

Juliet got up from the table. "Will you excuse me?"

She followed the maid through the door into the kitchen. Mike could hear them speaking in French. Though he wasn't hungry, he buttered a piece of bread. He sipped from the coffee, took a bite of the bread, and, feeling awkward sitting at the table by himself, went to the window. Pedestrians rushed by in the cold. On the other side of the street, directly across from the window, he noticed a man in a tan coat with a scarf wrapped around his neck the way the French wore them, up high and tied in the front.

He heard the door swing open and he turned away from the window. Juliet stood for a moment tightening the belt of her robe and fastening it into a fresh knot. She seemed distracted and upset. "I told her she could leave for the day," she said.

"You look like you've been crying," he said gently.

"Can you understand how hard it is to be here?" she said. "I couldn't sleep. Every inch of the place reminds me—" But she did not finish.

She took a cigarette from the top drawer of the sideboard and lit it, and he suddenly remembered that during their affair she had smoked.

"You forgot I used to smoke," she said. "I stopped. But François smokes and so they're in the house and every now and then." She gazed softly back at him. "Your voice is so familiar—the way you say my name. Then I recognize myself and I'm no longer the person who wanted to forget who I was and become someone else. We only have one heart and when we give it away, we don't get it back."

He was not prepared for her to say that. To accuse him, to argue with him, these things yes, but not that. He wanted to take her in his arms, but remembering the resolve that had brought him there, instead he stood sheepishly a step or two away from her. Not knowing what to do with his hands, which were desperate to reach out to her, he put them in his pockets and took them out again.

"Do you know a woman named Mireille Vernon?" he asked.

He watched her face for her reaction. Though she did not answer him, her gaze which only moments before had been soft became hostile.

"Did you come here to ask me questions? There are things I will tell you this morning. Not that. Not the answers you came here hoping to get."

She seemed bitter and her voice quivered with anger. "I could have picked any door and I picked this one and inside there was a box. An empty box. And do you know what—

I can't even feel sorry for myself, because the minute I step outside, the first face I see tells me it's the same for everyone else."

She put the cigarette out and sat down at the table again. Her voice when she began again was cold and steady and full of venom.

"I told you I wasn't at that meeting at Plaza Athénée."

"I believe you. It wasn't just the meeting, Juliet—what about all the trips to Geneva?"

"There's a simple explanation."

"For God's sake, tell me."

"Why?" she snapped back at him. "Why can't you just trust me? Suppose I told you it was none of your fucking business? Why does my life have to be an open book for you to judge?"

"This isn't only between me and you. For me yes, you're right, maybe I should believe you and let it go at that. But I'm not here for myself and it's not me you have to satisfy. You took too many trips to Geneva for anyone to believe you were not going there for a reason."

"I see," she said quietly, seeming to respond to the change in his tone and the transformation it signified. Her steady eyes strained as she searched his face. And as he waited for what she might say, he had the feeling he did not want to hear it.

She looked at him in a way that seemed to defy consolation. "I was trying to have a child. François found a good doctor in Switzerland and I saw him. It went on for over a year. I kept making the trip to Switzerland every month, sometimes twice a month; I took drugs, submitted to every procedure the doctor recommended. And then I stopped. François didn't agree. He said I'd regret not having a child.

"I never told him why I stopped trying. It wasn't the kind of reason I could explain to someone. But I'll tell you anyway.

I was walking on the promenade beneath the Tour Eiffel and I saw a pretty little girl with soft brown curls falling against her shoulders, blue-gray eyes and pink lips like a porcelain doll. She was in a wheelchair and her neck was craned back in this awful position because she couldn't hold up her head. Our eyes met and I saw she was in pain, in constant physical pain, and that's when I gave up. Because it isn't a question of what we deserve or what we want. There are things we have to accept."

He saw the hot tears burning in the corners of her eyes like a screen that prevented their gaze from meeting.

"I walked out on two kids. I'm not exactly a model parent."

"Don't you see? It's all part of the same joke. Like you showing up in Rome. Or François trying to hide things from me. I want to have a child. I can't. I come to Paris to get away from you and make a new life for myself, and here you are. Even something as small as my insisting we go to Rome; I wanted to spend a few days more with him on holiday and he winds up separated from me in an Italian jail. It's all a joke, don't you see? Only no one is laughing. You asked me why I left you five years ago. I'm not a home wrecker, or at least I didn't want to see myself that way, and I wanted to give you a chance for the sake of your kids. But you left anyway because the damage was already done. We should just own up to the hardness in our hearts and admit that we don't give a damn about anyone."

Her voice had dissolved into a flat, steady monotone, as if she didn't have the strength to raise it or become excited. "What did you think? I was going to Switzerland to launder money? François told me nothing—that's the real joke of it."

"What about Mireille Vernon? Did you speak to her?" He waited for her reaction, scrutinizing her carefully, watching as she strained to keep her face still. She would not allow her gaze to meet his, though she was looking at him.

"What about her?"

"She's gone."

"What does that have to do with me?"

"Were you at her apartment last night? Did you tell her to go somewhere?"

He knew she would not answer him, and yet her silence told him everything. He also knew what he wanted to say; he knew that he had to say it before leaving; if he didn't say it now they would go on the way they had like a ship that's fallen off course.

"I'm going to prosecute your husband. I think he did something wrong, and he deserves to be punished. I'm not going to soft sell it or brush it under the carpet. I know what it's doing to you, and I'm sorry. "

"If you think I was leading you on last night, playing some kind of a game, you're wrong," she said.

"It has nothing to do with last night between us. We've known each other a long time. We don't have to apologize to one another."

But she seemed unwilling to drop it. "I thought you would understand without my having to say it," she said, her eyes fixed intently on his. "If the extradition fails, we're all free. But if he goes to jail, what choice do I have but to hate you."

"Juliet, you know it can't work that way." He softened his voice, and appealed to her, "Even if we want it." Then he kept on going because he was unsure of what he might do if he stopped. "If you had anything to do with Mireille Vernon's disappearance, tell me where I can find her, and this I can promise, you're out of it."

"I don't want your pass. I came to Paris so I could forget you. Nothing here could remind me of you." She clenched her hand into a fist and her eyes glistened with tears and malice. "You can put him in jail, if that's what you want—you'll win, I can tell you that now. And when it's over it will be just another case."

"I'm not on trial here. He goes to jail because of what he did. Not because of anything I did."

She pushed the hair from her face. "You let me down once. I don't know why I thought this time would be different. I was wrong last night when I said I couldn't hate you."

A long silence followed in which she refused to return his gaze. He turned from her and looked out the window. The man in the tan coat was still there, standing directly outside her window. He checked his watch; it had been three quarters of an hour.

"Please leave. You don't belong here." Her voice was cold and constant.

He looked back a last time at her face hardened by anger, before letting himself out.

33

Once on the street, he saw the man in the tan coat standing in the same spot as if he were waiting for something, and he began to walk over to him to get a closer look—the black hair and eyebrows, the broad dark face—but when the man saw him approaching, he turned and walked away.

He felt his heart beating fast, and he wanted to go back and warn her. Then he felt the same rush of unreality overwhelming him again, a feeling as if he had been dreaming, and as he saw the man in the tan coat heading up Avenue la Bourdonnais, he began to question himself.

He decided to walk back to Plaza Athénée. When he thought of the hotel he felt foolish. What was he doing there? He crossed the bridge beneath a light spray of rain. As he walked he made a mental list of the things he had to do; check out of Plaza Athénée and into a cheaper hotel; call New York and tell them to lock up Saed on Governor's Island for his protection; arrange with Interpol for a search of Mireille Vernon's apartment and tell them to begin looking for her.

Interpol sent over an investigator named Balducci, no doubt because they viewed it as an Italian case, Mike thought. All bureaucracies applied the same logic. He met Balducci at Mireille Vernon's apartment at Rue Jacob at four-thirty. Balducci wore a pullover and a navy blue jacket instead of a shirt and tie, the way an American FBI agent would have been dressed.

The old woman made no fuss this time; she just led them up the stairs and opened the door to the apartment.

"Ask the old lady if she saw anyone visit Mireille Vernon over the past few days," Mike told Balducci.

While Balducci was speaking to the old woman, Mike walked through the small rooms.

"She says last night a well-dressed woman rang the buzzer after midnight to see her."

Mike watched the old woman's face as she spoke. He did not need Balducci. Without understanding a word of what she was saying, he knew she was describing Juliet; it was as he had expected. Juliet had left him and gone to see Mireille Vernon.

Balducci lit a cigarette.

"What are we looking for?" he asked.

"I'm not sure," Mike said. It was true; he did not necessarily expect to find anything. From where he was standing he scanned the two slightly cluttered, yet clean front rooms.

"I'm going to start in the bedroom. Why don't you see if you find any bank statements," he said.

Mike walked down the short hallway to the little room at the end, with the wooden bed and its roll pillow. The bed was made as neatly as an envelope. The small cross hanging on the wall next to the bed made it seem austere. The drapes were closed. Inside the armoire the clothes were neatly hung on evenly spaced hangers. He could hear Balducci in the next room, the sound of drawers opening and closing. He sat down on the little bench in front of the dressing table and began going through the contents of the drawers—expired credit cards in a rubber band, a few blue plastic miraculous medals and a novena card, a wooden rosary, a package wrapped in colored tissue paper and tied with ribbon that contained photographs from childhood, slightly yellowed black and white film, the edges disturbed, the same handwriting on the back of each photo, Mireille's he assumed, done in the same blue fountain pen; it looked as if she had sat down one day and done them from memory.

The other photos were more recent; he glanced at them quickly, until he came to a picture of Mireille and François at an outdoor café, Mireille looking young and beautiful, her hair full and dark and hanging below her shoulders. She wore a black sweater with a revealing *découpage* and a sheer red scarf tied in a knot around her neck, probably the same scarf that he now saw folded into a square at the top of the drawer. François looked like a kid in his twenties. Mireille must have been in her thirties, he thought, an ephemeral perfection, when experience and physical beauty coincide, and confidence becomes a woman's greatest weapon. She was in control of her smile, of her expression, of the narrowing of her eyes and the slight tilt of her head, aware and in control of everything. He slid the photo into the outside pocket of his jacket.

The next drawer contained nothing but jars of make-up and skin cream, hair pins, discarded lipsticks, a few tiny porcelain trinkets; he stood them up and looked at them, a baker, a Dutch girl, a king and a queen, and a miniature birthday cake, the kind found on a table in a dollhouse. At the back of the drawer in a little paper box he found a gold wedding band with no inscription, a paper French flag and a key, which he thought at first might be a luggage key, but it seemed too big. He went out to show it to Balducci.

Balducci left the cigarette hanging between his lips as he took the key in his hand. "For the bank," he said.

"You mean a safe-deposit box?"

He took another drag of his cigarette, hunching his shoulders, "That's what it looks like to me," he said.

Balducci had laid out the bank statements across the dining room table.

"She has only one account," Balducci said. With his index finger he pointed to one of the statements.

"Look here, once a month there are small infusions of cash, probably to cover expenses—rent, utilities, groceries, nothing out of the ordinary."

"What makes you say it's to a safe-deposit box?"

"Give it to me." Balducci took the key and held it so the light hit it. "There should be a serial number on the top. You see," he said as he pointed to it. "This is it, here."

"Can it be traced?" Mike asked.

"Yes, it isn't a problem. We can get the name of the bank and they will have to tell us the rest. There's a lot of, what's your expression?" he thought for a moment. "Red tape?"

"Yeah."

Balducci nodded. "We have to make out the written requests for privacy reasons before the bank will provide us with the information. Once all the paperwork is in order, the bank doesn't care and they will release the information."

"Supposing there's a risk that someone may remove the contents in the meantime; can't the process be hurried?"

Balducci shrugged. "Here the woman has left; if she were going to remove anything she would have done so already."

Balducci was right, Mike thought.

"We can try her bank, since we have the information from the checks, but if it's anything she is trying to hide, it's unlikely she would hide it in her own bank." Balducci looked down at his watch, "It's too late today. I can run it through a check tomorrow and tell you the name of the bank at least. Then we can begin the paperwork."

"How long will it take?"

"To get the information from the bank, two weeks."

"If this woman had a Swiss bank account, how could we find it?"

Balducci smiled. "The whole point of a Swiss bank account is that it's difficult to find." He cleared his throat. "It could take a while to find her," he said, switching the subject.

"She might still be in Paris," Mike said. "There'll be credit card charges surfacing soon enough."

"A woman on her own," Balducci said, "she's probably staying with family or friends."

"Somebody wrote Marseilles on the back of some of the photographs. Maybe she's there. It's worth checking."

He glanced down at his watch for the time in New York. He decided to call Richie. He had said everything he needed to say to her at her apartment and his head felt clear; he had nothing left to answer for. He no longer had a reason to keep Richie out.

"Do you want these?" Balducci asked, pointing to the bank statements.

Mike looked at a few cancelled checks for Mireille's handwriting, which appeared to match the handwriting on the back of the photos.

"Yeah, take them all."

34

It was a little before six in the morning, and still dark and raining, a cold, steady rain. Juliet called for a *taxi bleu* to take her to the Gare de Lyons.

The TGV to Geneva was empty. She had purchased a first-class ticket, so she had the seat to herself. Someone came around with coffee and croissants. She looked out the window, the light nothing more than a black blur. The rain made a vapor against the glass. She thought of Mireille; she would have already arrived in Mougins.

She had not planned on going to Geneva. After Mike's visit, she knew she had no choice. She wanted to feel remorse for the things she had said yesterday, but she could not. She was too angry. All the memories in that apartment belonged to her life with François. When she stood in those rooms, everywhere she turned, it was François she expected to see across from her. Not Mike. He should not have come there to say those things.

As she handed her passport to the officer at Passport Control, she felt the knot in the pit of her stomach, half-expecting a repeat of what had happened in New York. But she went straight through.

It had been a little over two years. She hesitated before ringing the bell, feeling timid, as if the emotion she felt quivering inside of her would shoot up like the flame of a candle fanned by the breeze. If she never rang the bell, the flame would continue to quiver without bursting, as it had for so long. But she could no longer afford that.

The nurse opened the door and greeted her with a smile.

Juliet remembered the Chinese toile wallpaper, the design of the little man wearing his hat and sitting with his legs folded in the pagoda. A well-dressed woman sat with her well-dressed husband, both looking apprehensive, a look she recognized well.

"*Bonjour*, Carole," she said. "I happened to be in Geneva and I wanted to say hello. I might be moving to New York. I thought it was a good idea to bring my records with me."

She was called into the doctor's office. His immaculate hands rested on top of the folder. He spoke to her in English with a heavy German accent, his blue eyes luminous and kind behind his glasses. His handsome, slightly stern face showed a thin smile as he spoke.

The records were thick and they felt heavy in her hands. Every visit had its memory, a before and an after, the wave of expectation and disappointment, optimism and despair, each clinical recitation of facts, numbers and values little more than a code for a new heartache.

She opened the records and ran her fingers along the pages absently. During the procedures, she had wanted to be alone. She remembered passing the time by reading Pascal, as if somehow in the search for faith she could overcome the empty feeling she had alone in a sterile room, awaiting a conception, void of passion or lust or chance. Eliane had been the name of the nurse who administered the needle each time in the white examining room with the Venetian blind drawn. Sometimes they talked. Sometimes she closed her eyes.

Too many disappointments. Times when hope stretched out inside her womb, when a heartbeat pulsed briefly with life, only to extinguish and wither inside of her, until she gave up and the flame that burned high like fire shrunk again to a quiver between acceptance and regret.

The doctor reached out and put his hand on her shoulder in a reassuring way. "I was happy to learn you came for your records because it means you are considering trying again. You are still young, and from everything I saw you could have a child. The real heartache comes when a woman realizes that it is too late. When you no longer have a choice."

DMMB Group Bancaire was on the third floor. The name of the bank was inscribed on a brass plaque just above the bell. The heavy mahogany door was locked. She rang the bell and waited until a well-dressed man opened the door without asking her to identify herself. She had the impression that someone from inside had peered through a camera and, looking her over, had judged that she should be let in.

"I have a private account," she said.

He seemed to become more attentive as he invited her to take a seat on a couch in a reception area. With its chandeliers and floral arrangements, it seemed like a private floor at Cartier rather than a bank, she thought. A coffee was presented to her in a Limoges cup on a small silver tray. A few minutes later a handsome man came out dressed in a navy blue suit and Hermès tie and invited her to his office without introducing himself, lending the impression that he did not want her to identify herself.

She had taken the trouble to memorize the numbers and as she recited them he wrote them down in pencil on a blank piece of notepaper the size of a calling card. Then he looked up something in a Rolodex and, when he was finished, he sat quietly as if he were waiting.

She understood what he was waiting for, and she opened her purse and took out the intaglio and slid it onto the index finger of her right hand.

"Bien sûr," he said. Then he left the office. A few minutes later he presented her with a dossier.

She opened it and began to read. The first thing she noticed was that the account was dollar denominated, which was consistent with the statement of the informant that François had wanted dollars. The account had been at ten million dollars at the beginning of June, but the current balance was a little less than eight million. She saw deductions for fees in trifling amounts. As she read on, she came across a withdrawal of two million dollars at the beginning of summer. Yet the statement was without mention of where the money went or how it had been withdrawn. She read on. On the next page she saw a wire transfer to an account in Morocco. The account had no name; it was a number and a bank with an address in Rabat. The file contained no other information.

She looked across the desk at the bank officer.

"Is something the matter?" he asked.

"Can you confirm where the two million was wired? I can't tell from the sheet."

"Madame, excuse me for a moment," he said, taking the dossier and leaving the room.

He returned a few minutes later. "As you instructed us, it went to Company Import/Export."

The banality of the name made it obvious to her that it

had been created for the purpose of concealing ownership of the account. It was true, then. François had planned on leaving her from Rome; the passport and the airline ticket were only part of the story. He had intended to remain in Morocco, so he wired two million dollars into an account that no one could trace to him. A fresh anger broke like a wave across her thoughts.

"Will Madame have any instructions for us today?"

In that moment it occurred to her that nothing prevented her from taking whatever amount she wanted. François could not prevent her, and something inside of her, anger, the desire to hurt him back, made her feel that he deserved it for having deceived her. Why not take the money and leave him? She could remain in Switzerland until the Italian court made its decision.

She gazed out the window at the view of the lake. The rain had left a heavy mist on the water, a long gray cloud beneath which everything seemed to stand still in the gray morning light. She had run away once, when she moved to Paris, and the thing she had run away from caught up with her anyway. She would not run away this time.

"*Non, merci*," she said. "I was in Geneva and I wanted to check on the status of my account."

"If that is all, in the future Madame can do this by phone, and you need not trouble yourself to come in person," he said, seeming to assume that all she had needed was to know the amount of money in the account.

She smiled. "Sometimes one needs to see for oneself."

As she walked out onto the street she felt relieved that there was no longer any doubt about François's intentions. At the same time she felt sad. She thought of Mike. The lies we told each other were simpler. We were only lying to ourselves, she thought.

She returned to Paris that night. She decided to stay in Paris and not return to Rome until the hearing.

35

The conference room in the jail smelled of ammonia. The floor in the hallway had just been washed. Dugommier scribbled on a notepad as he waited. He was not looking forward to the conversation he was about to have. He heard François speaking in Italian to the guard. He got up from the table and greeted him warmly as he entered the conference room. "I am relieved to find you looking well," he said, though François looked thinner than the last time he had seen him.

"It must be all the rest one gets in jail," François said, grinning slightly. He sat and took out a cigarette, tapping the end against the table without lighting it.

"I brought you an orange," Dugommier said, reaching into his briefcase.

François nodded. "I thought oranges were given to people serving a sentence in France. I have yet to have a trial and I am still in Italy." He began to peel the orange with his thumbnail, turning it in his hand as the peel fell onto the table.

"You have come for a reason, *maître.*"

The *Affidavit in Support of Extradition* lay open on the table and François gestured toward it.

"It was a mistake to talk in front of the Syrian."

"It was not my only mistake," François said. He stopped peeling the orange and looked at Dugommier. "He cannot harm me without harming Dufois, and he will be afraid."

At first Dugommier did not answer, considering whether François's remark had been intended as a threat. He held up the affidavit. "He was not afraid here," he said.

François shrugged. "It was easy because it was paper, but in person it will be different."

The light in the room fell back into shadow as the sun disappeared beneath a passing cloud. Dugommier lit a cigarette. "It is a pity that to fight the extradition you must remain here given the arrangements we made and the trouble we took to avoid this," he said, moving the ashtray closer.

"Being here does not bother me as much as what happens afterwards," François said. He picked up the orange and began peeling it again.

Dugommier took a few drags on the cigarette and left it burning in the ashtray. "What about your wife? It appeared she might have some success in persuading Mr. Chase."

"*Rien.*" François's eyes met his briefly.

"I am surprised. They have been in Paris together," Dugommier said.

"*Qui?* Juliet?" The last peel fell onto the table. He held the fruit in the palm of his hand before breaking off a slice.

"Juliet met with Dufois," Dugommier said, reaching into the ashtray and stubbing out the cigarette.

"*Comment?*"

"You didn't know?"

"*Non.*" François furrowed his brow, seeming genuinely confused. Dugommier felt a pang of conscience, which caused him to hesitate before continuing. It was one thing to expect that François understood the risks when he agreed to the transaction, but he could not have foreseen what he was about to tell him.

"The American prosecutor, Michael Chase was staying at Plaza Athénée that night. Your wife left with him. The next morning a friend saw him leave your apartment."

The color drained from François's face, which became very still, though his eyes grew narrow. As he dropped the orange onto the table, Dugommier noticed that his hand remained clenched into a fist. He felt certain that François understood the liaison that was being insinuated. However unpleasant it had been to tell him, it was necessary for him to know that his wife had betrayed him.

"I am sorry," Dugommier said. "Her advice cannot be trusted."

François said nothing in response. He picked up the cigarette that he had left out on the table and lit it, turning slightly toward the window as he smoked.

Dugommier leaned toward him as he handed him the ashtray. "François, this is to be disposed of in Rome. Dufois has to be kept out of this matter entirely. He cannot be linked to these organizations."

It was a moment before he answered. "He has my silence."

"Silence is easy for him. He has Alain's silence too. He wants something more from you."

François looked back at him coldly. The cigarette poised between two fingers of his right hand partially obscured his face. "I am not concerned for my life at the moment. He is worried about the inquiry in New York; it will be nothing compared to my dying in a cell in Rome. It's too late for him to kill me," he said.

Dugommier shook his head. "No, François, you don't understand," he said, feeling compassion, and yet he could not change the message he had come to deliver. "It is no longer a matter of remaining silent. He trusts you not to incriminate him. It is the question itself he does not want asked. He wants the answers to be given by you so nothing points to him. The inquiry must stop with you, with Rome, *tu comprends?* Admit culpability for everything, the bank, the loans."

François looked steadily back at him. "I did not understand the risk I was taking. If I was wrong, let them punish me. Admit culpability for what I did not do—*non, je refuse.*" He banged his fist against the table. "I bought a bank. I stretched a few rules of the Americans—*mais, en France, c'est légitime.* Everything in France was legal. I can go back when this is over and know that I am forgiven. If I accept culpability for the loans, then I have no future in France."

"Yes, but it is New York we are talking about. No one will believe you did not know what they were doing in New York."

"No, *maître*," François smiled thinly. "There was no reason for me to know, since I could not have influenced anything that was done. I was never taken into their confidence. I had a simple arrangement."

Dugommier knew that he was right, but it made no difference. "Your wife's relationship with the American prosecutor has created a great deal of concern that you will be unwisely influenced. You are in no position to take the moral high ground."

Dugommier saw the look on François's face, like a drowning man who knows the current is about to pull him under, but continues to fight.

"I understand you need time to adjust to what is being asked of you," he said.

"*Moi, je comprend très bien, c'est toi qui ne comprends pas.*"

"Be assured pressure is continuing to be applied from Paris," Dugommier continued without responding. "Despite the refusal of the Italian court to send you to France, there is reason for optimism that the extradition will not succeed. Alessandro has told us that he hears from his friend at the Ministero di Grazia e Giustizia that the Magistrates have reviewed the presentation of the Americans and regard it as weak. Remain silent. Wait for the extradition to be decided. If you win, go to Morocco so this can die of its own."

François smoked the cigarette to the filter without another word.

Dugommier broke the silence. "We have known each other for years, and I consider you a friend. I never wanted to be in this position. I tried to protect your interests by setting up the account in Morocco and making the arrangements for you there. If you had not gone to Rome—"

"*Basta.*"

Dugommier understood; François was not going to listen to him appease his own conscience.

François summoned the guard and went out.

36

Juliet had a sick feeling as she stepped into the courthouse on the morning of the hearing. Though her mouth felt dry, she knew even a sip of water would make her sick to her stomach.

Alessandro had just had an argument with a guard in the parking lot who had insisted on seeing his identification and his pass. He was still annoyed.

"The idiot calls me back," he said. "You, for example, with no pass, he does not stop. Me, he decides to stop. Because we Italians have to be difficult with one another. To strangers we are perfectly obliging."

It was raining and water dripped from umbrellas onto the sawdust-covered floor. They took a crowded elevator to the fifth floor and entered the courtroom by a door at the end of the hall. A guard wearing military fatigues patrolled the hallway as another guard stood at the door.

David Porter had already arrived, looking tall and Anglican in horn-rimmed glasses and dark gray Brooks Brothers. Next to his Italian counterparts, he seemed an outsider. Juliet wondered how the magistrates would view him.

Porter was apologetic when he saw her.

"I understand, you have no choice," she said.

The courtroom itself was unlike any courtroom she had ever seen, more resembling an amphitheater or a law school lecture hall. The lawyers sat at two tables placed side by side. The magistrates' table was in the center. The prisoner's dock, where the defendant stood and watched the proceedings, was situated behind a long glass booth on the right side of the courtroom, approximately twelve feet above the floor. Two young, sheepish-looking men currently occupied it.

The seats toward the front of the courtroom were taken. She sat with Alessandro in the back waiting for François's case to be called; Mike Chase had not yet arrived. She had not heard from him since that morning in her apartment.

The proceeding continued for at least another three quarters of an hour. Upon its conclusion, two *carabinieri* stepped into the glass booth to escort the defendants out as the lawyers packed their briefcases and the magistrates stood up and left the bench. She had the impression that a piece of theater was drawing to a close.

Alessandro put on his black robe.

"Come, my dear," he whispered, taking hold of her hand for a moment as they approached the lawyers' bench.

She looked up at the empty glass booth. After a few minutes, François was led in. He was wearing the blue suit she had brought from Paris. She had not seen him in nearly two weeks. Apparently, the jail had allowed his hair to grow in for the court appearance, or maybe they simply had not gotten around to shaving it again; Italy was in her view a culture with too many rules and yet a place where everything was random.

When she first noticed Mike, he was already seated at counsel's table and writing on a yellow legal pad, his head bent and his right shoulder awkwardly raised. Then she remembered that he was left-handed.

News reporters from the French as well as Italian papers, and a young woman from AP, sat in the front row. Juliet saw Mike give a charming smile when they walked over to him, getting up and greeting each reporter with a friendly handshake. It seemed to please him, she thought. Tomorrow morning his name would appear in the Paris newspapers; the idea of international celebrity was attractive to him. Then she remembered how a trial was like a party for the lawyers and the press.

The magistrates took their places on the bench, the same men who had presided over the conference, though today they were wearing black robes. Everyone stood as the magistrates assumed their seats. The courtroom was silent and all eyes were fixed on the three robed men.

She bit against her lip until it ached. It seemed to her that when something like this happened to someone, there ought to be bells and sirens, the world around her should appear differently. Instead, as she looked around the room it seemed as if they were all waiting for the start of a university lecture. She ran her hand along the surface of the table, looked over at Alessandro who was adjusting the black robe across his shoulders, and then at her husband, remote and silent behind the glass pane. How was it that the blood pulsing against her temples and the dryness in her mouth were the things she felt most keenly and everything else only added to her numbness and her sense of disbelief?

Alessandro introduced himself to the court. The translator repeated what he had said in English. François had apparently agreed to forego a French translator. She heard the voice of the translator, the artificial female monotone, hearing the words repeat over again in her own mind, aware that because she was depending on the translator, she had no ability to judge the nuances for herself.

Roberto Chiaro, the prosecutor who had done all the talking at the conference, requested permission for Mike Chase to question the witness in English. The magistrates agreed.

Mike stood, holding his yellow pad in his left hand as he moved to the podium.

A small-framed Middle Eastern man, who Juliet guessed to be in his late twenties, took the witness stand.

"My name is Saed Radwan."

For a moment Juliet's thoughts returned to the night at Mireille's apartment. But Mike's voice, clear and resonant, caught her attention once more.

"Do you know the accused?"

"Yes."

"When did you meet him?"

"In the early part of November, 1985."

"Can you give us the day?"

"November 7."

"And where did you meet him?"

"For drinks in the bar at Plaza Athénée in Paris. I went there in the company of Etienne Dufois who brought me to meet Mr. de Fournier because I was looking for a job in Paris."

Saed seemed to be making an effort not to look around the courtroom.

"Do you know what Mr. de Fournier does for a living?"

"He is director of a merchant bank called Compagnie Financière de Fournier."

"And who is Etienne Dufois?"

"He is a Saudi businessman. He manages the money of wealthy Saudis looking to invest outside of Saudi Arabia."

"How do you know Mr. Dufois?'

"He is a friend of my family."

Juliet knew Mike's style on direct. He liked to keep the examination loose and never minded when the witness added things. He was like a child who takes his hands off the handle bars once the bike is up to speed.

"Describe your meeting on November 7 with Mr. de Fournier."

"It was at about six in the evening. I came with Mr. Dufois and we went to the bar downstairs from the lobby. Mr. de Fournier was sitting at a table for four in a corner with a woman whose name was Mireille Vernon." Saed paused, then added, "I had never met either of them before. Mr. Dufois told Mr. de Fournier my background and that I wanted to work in Paris. I said very little because it was not my place—"

"Was anyone drinking alcohol?"

"Maybe the woman; she had a drink which she took a sip of from time to time, but I don't remember what it was. Mr. de Fournier had a coffee, as did Mr. Dufois. I had a Coca-Cola." He stopped and glanced nervously up at François.

"Go on," Mike said.

"They talked about how it had rained all weekend and the ups and downs recently in the American stock market. After a while, Mr. Dufois said the filings had been prepared. He asked Mr. de Fournier whether he had spoken to the lawyers in New York, and whether they were ready to proceed. Mr. de Fournier said everything was prepared but there was one issue left."

Mike interrupted. "Did he explain what he meant when he said there was one issue left?"

"Mr. Dufois asked him. He said he had new terms; 'the price had doubled.' "

"Did you know what they were discussing?"

"I did not."

"What was Mr. de Fournier's demeanor?"

"He was very composed."

"What happened after that?"

"Mr. Dufois became angry and said his investors were relying on this and that the terms had already been presented. He said it was not possible for him to go back with a new request. Mr. de Fournier said that it was not a request, it was a deal breaker, and that the deal had gone too far not to meet his demands. Mr. Dufois seemed to become angrier at this point and threatened to withdraw his investors from Compagnie Financière. Mr. de Fournier said it was not going to make a difference."

"What tone of voice did he use?"

"A normal tone of voice."

"What about Etienne Dufois? Was he calm?"

"No, as I said, he was angry. He was not shouting, but his voice was raised, and he seemed to become more upset as the conversation progressed and Mr. de Fournier continued to insist."

Saed paused. Juliet caught the look he gave Mike, like a frightened bird, his dark, falcon eyes trembling without blinking.

"What happened after Mr. de Fournier continued to insist?"

"They went back and forth for a while and Mr. Dufois complained that the deal was set and it was too late to change the terms, but Mr. de Fournier persisted, saying that what he demanded was fair. He said something like, you have my price, take it or leave it, and it looked like he was about to get up, and Mr. Dufois got very angry and said, "'Ten million dollars! How dare you demand so much. You do not exist without me.'"

Saed paused.

"Did Mr. de Fournier respond?"

"Mr. de Fournier said it seemed to him it was the other way around."

Juliet felt a chill through her body. She caught François looking down at her with eyes of a broken god, and she turned away to hide the despair she felt. The conversation was more damaging than any of the accounts she had been given.

Saed took a deep breath that could be heard in the silence.

"Was anything else said on the subject?" Mike asked.

"No. Mr. de Fournier said he had to go and he paid the bill and we left."

For a while the examination fell into an uninterrupted cadence of question and answer.

"Did Mr. de Fournier lose his temper at any point during the conversation?"

"No. He was calm."

"Did you ever hear anything more about the ten million dollars?"

"No."

"Do you know whether it was paid?"

"No."

"Did you ever learn that the Great American Bank was bought?"

"Yes. Alain Gilbert hired me at Great American Bank in New York."

Mike showed something to Saed. "Could you identify the people in this photograph?"

Alessandro stood up. "I ask the prosecutor to provide the details of how he came into possession of the photograph."

"This photograph was seized on October four of this year from the bedroom of Mireille Vernon's Paris apartment in the course of an Interpol search," Mike said.

Juliet heard the note of triumph in his voice.

Saed seemed unsure about whether to continue. The magistrate in the center told him to go on.

"This is François de Fournier and this is the woman, Mireille Vernon, who was at Plaza Athénée."

Mike approached Alessandro and put the photograph on the table in front of Juliet. She felt his eyes on her as she examined it, and she could not say why, but he had never looked at her that way before, and something in his look frightened her.

"Do you recognize this?" His voice had a new ferocity. He held a piece of paper in his hand, brandishing it like a flag before presenting it to Saed.

"It is the agreement I signed with the United States government. If I am not telling the truth, then—"

Before Saed could finish his answer, she stood up and objected. "In the United States, a cooperation agreement is signed in every case and is not admissible unless the credibility of the witness has been attacked. For this reason I ask the court to refrain from considering it. There is an additional danger that too much meaning might be put on this agreement, when Mr. Chase knows that it is treated as a mere formality in the United States."

She waited for Mike to acknowledge her, but he continued to look straight ahead at the magistrates. "According to the terms of this agreement," he continued, without stopping to address her objection, "the witness will be prosecuted and the promises made to him revoked if it is determined at any point in his testimony that he is testifying falsely."

Mike had succeeded in giving the answer that she had sought to prevent Saed from giving. Frustrated, she sat down.

The magistrate in the center asked to be shown a copy of the document, appearing to read it quickly before passing it along to the other magistrates.

Mike had no more questions. Alessandro stood and began cross-examination.

"How long ago did the meeting you described at Plaza Athénée take place?"

"November 1985."

Alessandro smiled pleasantly. "What language was everyone speaking?"

"French."

"And even though the conversation took place in French, you used English to describe it today?"

"Yes."

He gestured with his hands to punctuate the question. "So, these are not the exact words, but rather you are making an interpretation?"

"Yes."

"And it is this interpretation, I might add, that is being translated into Italian for the benefit of the magistrates."

Alessandro put his eyeglasses on and took them off again as if to emphasize the point he had just made.

"You testified that the American stock market was discussed?"

"Yes."

"Would you tell us to the best of your recollection what was said."

Saed paused. "I do not recall," he said after a moment. His gaze flitted nervously to Mike, who sat with his arm slung over the back of his chair, listening with an inscrutable expression.

"How long were you sitting there?" Alessandro continued.

"Maybe half an hour, three quarters of an hour."

"You also testify there was a woman present?"

"Yes."

"What did she say during this time?"

"Hello. Nice to meet you."

"Do you remember if she said anything else?"

"She might have. I don't recall."

"In other words, you do not remember everything that was said during this meeting?"

"No." Saed shifted in his chair, seeming increasingly uncomfortable.

"And today, is it fair to say, you have selected certain portions of the conversation, and omitted others?"

"Yes."

Alessandro took a moment before continuing. "During the exchange you described at Plaza Athénée, did Mr. de Fournier or Mr. Dufois ever say that they were discussing the purchase of Great American Bank?"

"No."

"Were you aware at the time that Mr. Dufois and Mr. de Fournier are involved together in many different business investments?"

"No." Saed lowered his eyes.

"In exchange for your testimony, the American prosecutor, Mr. Chase, has agreed to drop all allegations against you, am I correct?"

"Yes."

"If you were not to give this testimony against Mr. de Fournier today, you would have faced prosecution in the United States, true?"

"I have been told that by Mr. Chase, yes," Saed said in a low voice.

Alessandro turned to the magistrates. "I have no other questions," he said, taking his seat.

Juliet felt satisfied that Alessandro had weakened Saed's testimony, and she thanked him with her eyes. She expected Mike to question Saed on redirect.

"The United States of America calls Richard Giordano," he announced.

This took her by surprise. She had not seen Giordano sitting in the back of the courtroom. After the incident at the airport, his presence made her uneasy.

"Mr. Giordano, in your capacity as a United States Drug Enforcement Agent, did you have the opportunity to investigate the death of Alain Gilbert?"

"Yes."

"How did Alain Gilbert die?"

"Alain Gilbert was shot to death in his apartment on West 66th Street in Manhattan on the twenty-fourth of August. The medical examiner's report places the time of death at approximately 8 o'clock the night before, on the twenty-third. Three shots were fired at close range with a .22 caliber handgun."

"Was Mr. Gilbert the subject of a criminal investigation at the time of his death?"

"In August, attorneys for Alain Gilbert reached an agreement with the United States Attorney's Office whereby Mr. Gilbert agreed to plead guilty to one felony count of wire fraud and pay a fine of five hundred thousand dollars with a promise of no jail time."

"Was Mr. Gilbert ever interviewed by the United States Attorney's Office?"

"No, he was killed within two days of entering into the agreement."

Mike presented him with a notepad, which he glanced at quickly, before continuing. "This was retrieved from a table next to the phone in Alain Gilbert's apartment. The paper, or notepad, has Great American Bank printed across the top and underneath it a handwritten phone number."

"Do you recognize the phone number?"

Giordano nodded, handing the paper back to Mike. "It is the telephone number of the villa in Tunisia where the defendant was staying during the two-week period leading up to and following Mr. Gilbert's murder."

Mike continued in a matter-of-fact tone. "Did Alain Gilbert speak with the defendant, Mr. de Fournier, at anytime during the two weeks prior to entering into the agreement with the United States Attorney's Office?"

"A tracer placed on Gilbert's home phone revealed three phone calls to the number written on the notepad, which as I said, turned out upon investigation to be the telephone number at the villa where the defendant was staying during this period."

Mike took the paper and handed it to Alessandro. As he approached, it seemed to Juliet that this time he was careful to avoid eye contact with her. She caught Giordano, however, looking straight at her with a look that made her anxious. Mike must have told him his suspicions about her visit to Mireille Vernon's apartment. What had Giordano found out since then?

Question and answer followed like a carefully choreographed dance, and Juliet felt her heart beating in the same relentless rhythm.

"How many phone calls were made from Alain Gilbert's home telephone to the number in Tunisia where the defendant was staying?"

"Three. The first took place on August eighteenth and lasted for six minutes and thirty seconds."

"Did Mr. Gilbert meet with the United States Attorney's Office on that date?"

"No."

"What about the second call?"

"There was a second phone call on August twentieth, which lasted four minutes."

"What is the date of Mr. Gilbert's agreement with the United States Attorney's Office?"

"The document is dated August twenty-first."

"When was the last time Mr. Gilbert called the number in Tunisia?"

"August twenty-first. The call lasted three minutes and twenty three seconds."

"Do you know whether the phone call took place before or after Mr. Gilbert entered into the agreement with the United States Attorney's Office?"

"Mr. Gilbert's attorney met with the U.S. Attorney's Office at nine a.m. The telephone call took place at eleven fourteen a.m."

Mike returned to counsel's table, and placed his notes face down on the table. It was the first break in questioning since Giordano began testifying, and it had the effect of emphasizing what was to come. "Are you familiar with the name, Mireille Vernon?"

"Yes. I have been trying to locate her in connection with this investigation."

Giordano shot a look at Juliet. She knew he was baiting her, and she gazed steadily back at him as he continued.

"Her whereabouts are unknown. Investigators of the United States government are working with Interpol to locate her. At the moment, every possibility is being considered, including that she is dead."

Mike stood, reading through his notes. "No further questions," he said after a moment. Juliet lowered her eyes to conceal her relief.

Alessandro adjusted his robe before he began. "Mr. Giordano, do you have evidence that Mr. de Fournier murdered Alain Gilbert?"

"I consider the phone calls evidence."

He furrowed his brow. "Mr. Gilbert was murdered in New York. According to your theory, Mr. de Fournier was in Tunisia?"

"Yes."

"If the phone calls establish anything, it is only that Mr. Gilbert called Mr. de Fournier in Tunisia, am I right?"

"Alain Gilbert's death has all the earmarks of a professional assassination. In other words the assailant was a professional assassin with no connection to Mr. Gilbert, but someone whose services are retained for the express purpose of killing someone."

Alessandro nodded. "You have no evidence that Mr. de Fournier hired a professional killer?"

"No."

"In fact, it is impossible to determine from these phone calls whether Mr. Gilbert spoke to Mr. de Fournier?"

"Correct. But the fact that there were three calls, and the duration of the calls, makes it hard to believe that they never spoke during this time." He turned toward Juliet. "We could ask Mrs. de Fournier whether she spoke to Gilbert."

"Thank you for your suggestion, Signor Giordano." Alessandro resumed his seat. "No further questions."

37

Mike waited at the front of the courtroom for the next witness to take the stand.

He saw Juliet look up at François, and he felt like a voyeur for watching, so he turned and looked out at the crowd. He liked to read the faces of the spectators; it was another gauge of how the case was going. The room had thinned out since the morning; he could see every face, the reporters from the morning, the three old men sitting up towards the front. It was then that he saw seated to one side of the courtroom a face that seemed familiar to him, though he had to think for a moment to place it. Dark tight hair, thick black eyebrows, the broad face with its dark complexion and dark eyes. After about a minute he recognized him as the man he had seen outside the window of Juliet's Paris apartment that morning; the longer he looked, the less doubt he had. The man noticed him looking at him, and bowed his head as if he were trying to conceal himself.

The arresting officer at the airport who had discovered the Moroccan passport and the ticket to Morocco took the stand. The examination was short, consisting of a simple identification of the passport and the arrest report.

At the end of the examination Mike looked back at the spectators. The man was gone.

David Porter took the stand. Mike was confident about Porter's testimony; lawyers always made good witnesses for the government, even when the defendant called them. It did not take much to make a lawyer nervous, and lawyers were willing to sell out a client if they thought their own reputation was being called into question.

Mike approached and handed him a document.

"Tell us for the record what this document is."

"It is the final request filed by Mr. de Fournier with the Federal Reserve Board in Washington, D.C."

"Who purchased the Great American Bank?"

"Windsor Holdings, a holding company of Compagnie Financière."

"Not Compagnie Financière?"

"No. It's typical in these situations to purchase through a holding company. In this case the company, Windsor Holdings, was a Netherlands Antilles corporation."

Mike nodded. Porter sounded like a college professor answering a student, rather than a witness in a criminal prosecution.

"The document you're holding in your hands was completed under penalties of perjury, wasn't it?" he asked.

"Yes."

He took the document for a moment and opened it to the last page, glancing at it first before handing it to Porter.

"And this, I take it, is Mr. de Fournier's signature?"

"Yes."

"And in this document, François de Fournier claims to be the sole shareholder of the holding company?"

Porter seemed very at ease. "There were no other shareholders."

"Windsor Holdings paid fifty million dollars for Great American Bank, isn't that correct?"

"Yes, I believe so."

"How did Mr. de Fournier finance the purchase of Great American Bank?"

"Compagnie Financière put seed money of twenty million dollars into Windsor, and the balance of thirty million dollars was financed with a loan from Banque Luxembourg d'Investissement."

Mike paused. "Do you know whether Compagnie Financière invests money for a group of Saudi Arabian investors managed by someone named Etienne Dufois?"

"Yes."

"What percentage of the total investment capital of Compagnie Financière does this group make up?"

"I think it's somewhere in the neighborhood of seventy percent."

"If an investor makes up seventy percent of an investment pool, would you say that they exercised *de facto* control of the company?"

"They might. Not in this case, however, since they were passive investors." Porter turned to the magistrates, again seeming like a professor in the midst of a lecture, helpful rather than partisan. "A passive investor is someone who has no say in the investment decisions, a limited partner, for example, which is the equivalent of what the Arab investors were by giving their money to Compagnie Financière to manage."

Porter's self-assurance went far toward creating the impression that the transaction was completely ordinary. Mike let it go on that way.

"A passive investor, once it gets big enough, say seventy percent, would be in a position to influence investment decisions, wouldn't you say?" he asked.

"It depends," Porter began, again turning to the magistrates. "In any case, I would like to point out that the Fed, I should say the Federal Reserve Board, was fully aware of the size of the foreign investment, and was in as good, if not a better position than I am now to make that judgment. They obviously were not troubled by it."

Mike nodded thoughtfully, letting Porter continue to play the part of professor. "Could a passive investor suggest a particular investment?" he asked, as if they were in the midst of an academic discussion.

"Suggest?" Porter reflected. "I suppose. Yes."

"So, for example, a passive investor, Mr. Dufois, for example, could call up and say, I think you should buy X,Y,Z company?"

"I don't see anything wrong with that."

"Your answer is yes, I take it," Mike said earnestly.

"Yes."

"How about insist? Could a passive investor insist on a specific investment?"

"I think I see what you're driving at," Porter smiled confidently. "Suggest is as far as I'd go. Insist, no—Mr. de Fournier had complete discretion; it was a condition of investing."

Mike persisted, continuing to draw him in. "Let's assume that I'm a passive investor in Compagnie Financière, and I don't like a particular investment decision. What can I do?"

Porter answered without hesitating. "You can withdraw your money at the end of a specified period."

"You say I could withdraw my money at the end of a specified period. What was that period?"

"Typically three to five years; it's specified in the investment contract."

Mike nodded. "So you say I would have to wait between three and five years and then I could take my money out?"

"Yes."

He went back to counsel's table for a document, which he handed to Porter.

"This is a contract between Compagnie Financière and the Dufois group," Porter said, after reading it and handing it back.

Mike held up the document. "It contains an amendment to the original contract between Compagnie Financière and the investors, doesn't it?"

Porter nodded. "According to the amendment the Dufois group could withdraw its investment at the end of any quarter by giving two weeks notice."

"Who made the decisions about whether to withdraw for the Dufois group?" Mike asked.

"According to the document, Etienne Dufois."

"So Dufois could have decided at the end of any quarter that he wasn't pleased, and he could have withdrawn the money?"

Porter frowned slightly. "It would appear that way from the contract." He seemed more tentative, and Mike could tell from the phrasing of his answer that he wanted to put distance between himself and firsthand knowledge of the document.

"Are you still willing to say that by holding the threat of withdrawing money over Mr. de Fournier every quarter, Etienne Dufois couldn't exercise control over his decisions?"

For the first time, Porter hesitated. "No," he said finally.

Mike paused to let the answer resonate.

"You testified that as far as you knew Mr. de Fournier owned all of the shares of Windsor Holdings, right?"

"It was represented to me that way," Porter said, again sounding tentative and seeming to want to create distance.

Mike needed one more answer to complete his examination. "As owner, would you agree that he could have disposed of those shares without anyone's approval?"

"I don't see why not. No one else had an equity interest."

Porter had given the testimony he needed, though he would have to wait until closing argument to tie it together. Mike smiled through closed-lips. "Thank you. I have no other questions."

Alessandro was about to begin questioning Porter when the magistrate on the far left interrupted. "Before we continue, I would like to address the American prosecutor."

Mike was struck by his having spoken to him in English.

"The important witnesses have not been called. Where is Etienne Dufois? Will he testify? We need to hear the account of the woman, Mireille Vernon, whom the witness claims was at the meeting at Plaza Athénée. The testimony of the deceased, Alain Gilbert will never be known. You have presented no evidence that Mr. de Fournier received a payment of ten million dollars."

The magistrate on the right looked over his eyeglasses. "The United States does not appear to have sufficient evidence to extradite the accused," he said, frowning.

"I would like an opportunity to address your Honor's concerns," Mike began, turning to the magistrate on the far left. "Mr. Dufois has made himself unavailable by returning to Saudi Arabia. We believe Mireille Vernon is still in France, however, and we, that is, Interpol and the United States government, feel confident that we will find her. To this end, I would ask the court to grant an adjournment."

As Mike expected, Alessandro stood up and began protesting. "Too much time has already passed. The hearing is today, and Mr. de Fournier's case should be judged according to the evidence presented today. If the prosecutor was satisfied to arrest my client before speaking to this woman, he should be satisfied that the case will proceed without her. It is unfair to Mr. de Fournier, who has already been in jail almost two months, to ask him to remain in jail any longer while the prosecution goes looking for additional witnesses."

The magistrate in the center nodded in silent agreement with Alessandro.

The magistrate on the right took off his glasses as if he had made up his mind. "Why should he remain in jail when the evidence is insufficient?" he asked impatiently.

"With the magistrates' permission, if I may continue, the United States believes that the defendant knows Mireille Vernon's whereabouts."

Mike paused, waiting for the reaction of the magistrates, who seemed to be paying close attention.

"That is an extraordinary allegation," the magistrate in the center said, throwing out his hand for emphasis. "What basis do you have for your belief?" He leaned forward expectantly.

"I appreciate the court's concern," Mike began. "According to the woman who is the guardian at 152 Rue Jacob where Mireille Vernon resides in Paris, on October fourth, sometime after midnight, Juliet de Fournier visited Vernon at that address. It was approximately three a.m. when Mrs. de Fournier left the premises. That following morning, at about eight-thirty, the guardian saw Mireille Vernon leave the building with a suitcase."

Mike studied the faces of the magistrates, who seemed poised and attentive. "The guardian can be brought to Rome to testify." Before the magistrates had a chance to respond, he continued; "The United States government believes that an inference can be drawn from her testimony that Mrs. de Fournier made arrangements for Mireille Vernon's departure."

The magistrate, who had first questioned Mike, put down his pen and looked annoyed. "Signora de Fournier, is it true that you called upon Mireille Vernon as the prosecutor asserts?"

"Yes," she answered.

"And what happened during this encounter?" the magistrate continued, leaning forward as if to listen more carefully.

"She said she would be willing to come to Rome to testify on the defendant's behalf."

The magistrate on the left put down his glasses. "Where is she?" he asked abruptly.

"I do not know," Juliet answered.

He seemed to frown. The other two magistrates looked skeptically at one another before conferring in low voices.

The magistrate in the center announced, "We will adjourn. Mr. de Fournier will remain at Rebibbia. We accord two weeks, until October thirty-first, to the United States government."

Mike saw Richie approach as the courtroom emptied.

"She's lying," Richie said.

Mike did not feel an answer was necessary. He finished putting away his notes. "I want you to go to Paris this afternoon and start working with Interpol to locate that woman."

He closed his briefcase and stood up to leave. "Let's go."

Richie stopped him. "You know, doing the right thing feels hard at the time; in the long run it's easier."

"I've been a prosecutor too long to still believe in good and evil," Mike said.

38

Juliet waited to leave until the courtroom was empty. She felt safe, for the time, at least, in answering as she had. Mike would view it as too risky to call her to testify. He had no way of countering what she might say to exonerate François. She also knew that the magistrates had regarded her answers with skepticism and that the chances were good that in two weeks time the government would have located Mireille.

"What has happened?" Alessandro asked, agitated. "They were going to release him. It was finished. He was free. Why didn't you prepare me?"

"I couldn't tell you," she said. Nothing more. Then after a moment, she added, "I should talk to François."

"I think you should," Alessandro said, sounding more emphatic than she had ever heard him sound. "He will remain here in the jail at the court all day and not be brought back to Rebibbia until the night. You can see him here."

The events of the morning seemed to have worn on him and, in addition to being angry, he seemed tired and concerned.

He took her to a crowded waiting room. "I make no representation of how long you will wait. I will try to use my influence to expedite things, but perhaps you should eat something first."

"I'm not hungry."

"Forgive me then for leaving you. Whatever the damage after today's hearing, nothing can be done now. I will make an appointment at the Ministry tomorrow."

She waited two hours before she heard François's name called. She was taken to a large room, long and narrow, divided down the middle by a grille that went to the ceiling, separating the prisoners from their visitors. A sparrow that must have flown in through the open window near the ceiling flew back and forth across the rafters.

She was directed to one of the wooden chairs along the visitors' side of the grille. A minute later François was led in. He had already changed back into the shirt and pants issued by the jail. She could tell from his expression that he was surprised to see her.

He leaned close to the grille. "I was told my lawyer was waiting to see me," he said.

"You were expecting Alessandro," she said, aware that she had not been to see him since she left for Paris.

"I am glad it's you."

She noticed the lines that were beginning to show around his eyes and near his mouth, the first of their kind. He looked older, yet handsome; he would always have that, she thought, no matter what he was wearing or where he was.

She felt she needed time before she could begin to talk to him. So much had happened so fast. But he did not wait. He leaned closer to the grille and pressed his hands to the metal as if to touch her.

"You met with Dufois. Why?" he whispered, with sudden intensity. When she did not answer, he said, "You understand, don't you, the gravity of the situation."

She thought she did, but what did he know that he was not telling her?

"Mireille is in Mougins," she said.

He seemed surprised, and his expression gave away that he understood the ramifications.

"She had no place else," she explained. "It was to be temporary, until other arrangements could be made. I can't take the risk of contacting her now."

Instead of the angry outburst she expected, he spoke quietly. "I see your face, I've seen it from the beginning," he said, "You're suffering and I can do nothing."

She let her fingers meet his inside the openings in the grille. "You were right. I should not have met with Dufois," she said. "But I thought it was your only chance to walk away from this, and I thought it was worth it."

"Let them blame me for Mireille," he said. "Tell them I made the arrangements."

"It's you who doesn't realize the gravity," she answered. "They will blame you. If they accuse me, it will only be to use it against you. They will blame you for Dufois too. They will say it was you who convinced him to go to Jeddah."

He lowered his gaze and became silent. He seemed absorbed in thought, though she had no idea what he was thinking. She glanced around the room at the faces of the other prisoners, each bearing some mark of defeat, in the bloodshot eyes, the yellowed complexions, but something else too. Then she realized it was hope that gave those faces their anxious look.

She saw one of the guards come to take the prisoner two seats down, and she was reminded that their time was limited.

"You could have insisted on a French translator," she said. Though it had annoyed her in the morning, it seemed trivial now, but it was the first thing she could think to say.

"It wasn't necessary."

"All the same, it might have been easier for you in French," she said, then she let the subject drop.

Streaks of sunlight slanted across the room in the last hour of afternoon light.

"When they read the charges, they used the word forfeiture. What does it mean?" he asked.

"If you're convicted they can take away the profits you made. It's more complicated. But forfeiture is not a concern until the case is proven."

"What do you mean, the profits?"

"They're accusing you of having received ten million dollars, so there's that. The profits from the New York bank. In the U.S. they can confiscate your assets until the outcome at a trial. If you're convicted, they keep the confiscated assets; that is referred to as forfeiture. If you're acquitted you have to sue to get the assets back; it's not automatic."

"There's no way around this forfeiture? " he asked.

"If you're convicted, they can take whatever they want so long as they claim you got it as a result of the illegal transaction. The judges don't care; it's a winner-take-all game, and the rules are stacked against you. There are ways of getting them to soften their position, but that would require you to cooperate, and you're unwilling to do that."

Though she knew well the importance of forfeiture, she did not want to talk about money then. The noise around them had begun to grow as more prisoners were brought in to confer with their lawyers. It became difficult to speak without raising their voices. For a moment she thought of the things she might say if they were ever alone, truly alone, with the door closed and no one watching. Then her heart sank at the thought that it might never happen again.

She looked nervously over to the guards stationed on the prisoner side of the room.

"Are you afraid the guard will take me back if he sees we're not talking?" François said, smiling slightly. "All that matters to them is time; minutes, days, years."

She looked back at him, "Don't talk that way."

"How should I talk to you?"

She detected something pointed in the question, though he did not seem to expect an answer.

"Why did you stay in Paris?" he asked.

"I wasn't ready to come back." She hesitated. "I suppose I couldn't face you," she said.

He nodded, and though he was silent, she had the impression he had something on his mind.

The guard pulled his shirt from the back and he got up. It was too soon, she thought. There was more they had to talk about. "François," she called out to him. He stopped and turned to look back at her. She wanted to tell him that she would see him the next day, but before she could get out the words the guard struck him with a baton in the back of the shoulder.

"You can't do that," she cried out.

François let his eyes meet hers. "It's nothing," he told her, submitting to the guard without anything further, and diffusing the tension of the moment.

The heavy iron door banged shut behind her as she left the visitors' room. The noise of everyone talking at once went away, and in its place there was only the sound of the guard's thick-soled boots as he walked her to the exit and the strained silence when she stepped outside.

39

Mike spent the remainder of the day at the American Embassy listening to agents from Interpol discuss Mireille Vernon's disappearance. Her bank accounts had been checked for withdrawals and there were none. He inferred from the fact that she had run up no credit card charges in the week since her disappearance that she either had cash with her or was traveling with someone. Her phone was being monitored for incoming calls; here too, they were coming up with nothing. He instructed the agents to contact everyone whose number appeared on her telephone bill for the past six months. They had begun locating relations in Marseilles. Mike concluded all of this was going to take time unless they got lucky.

An agent ran a check on Banque Luxembourg d'Investissement, which had loaned thirty million dollars to Windsor Holdings, de Fournier's holding company. The check revealed that Dufois was a large investor. Mike found it interesting, even suspect, yet it proved nothing. He went through the steps of the transaction in his head: Windsor Holdings bought Great American Bank; de Fournier maintained legal control and ownership of Windsor Holdings; though Dufois was also a large investor in Windsor Holdings, he had no legal power to make Windsor Holdings do anything. Despite what the documents said, it seemed suspicious. Dufois could withdraw his money at will from Compagnie Financière and inflict severe if not fatal damage. Why would he agree to a different arrangement with Windsor Holdings? He felt certain Dufois had the same agreement with Windsor Holdings that he had with Compagnie Financière—it was just hidden. If it had never been formalized, it was impossible to prove in a case where none of the principals were talking.

It was a little after five when Mike left the embassy. The air was still warm, and the light was a soft spray of gold, unlike any autumn day in New York, Mike thought as he walked back to the hotel. It struck him that Rome was made for walking, and he took his time looking in the shops along the Via Condotti.

He was still bothered by the man he had seen outside Juliet's apartment in Paris. Who was he? And why was he in the courtroom? Why didn't anyone else recognize him? He suspected a connection with Dufois. What was bothering him most was the feeling that he should say something to Juliet, warn her that she was being watched, but after what had happened in court, he knew he could not call her. Instead he decided he would arrange for Paris agents to begin talking to people in Dufois's organization, hoping that within a few days he would have more information. He had avoided the subject with Richie to spare himself having to explain why he had been at her apartment that morning. All that was in the past now, and he did not feel like bringing it up again.

It was after six o'clock when he got back to the hotel. The old lady was behind the desk, dressed in the same paisley dress as the day before.

"*Signore*," she said, her voice as deep as a man's.

Without his saying anything she held out the key to his room, at the same time handing him a neatly folded phone message.

Would like to meet with you,

de Fournier

He studied the note. The time was scrawled in the corner—17:00.

When he got back to his room he called the warden and learned that de Fournier was in transit from the courthouse and had not returned to Rebibbia. Mike was not surprised that after today's hearing he might have lost his nerve. By tomorrow, given the chance to calm down, or to consult with his lawyer, Mike also knew he might change his mind about wanting to meet, so he had to insist upon seeing him that night. The warden explained that, given the late hour, the meeting could only be arranged if he were willing to meet in de Fournier's cell. He agreed, and it was set for nine o'clock.

Mike called Travers at the American Embassy to let him know. Travers offered to accompany him, but he thought it would be better if he went alone.

He still had a couple of hours, so he went out again and walked a few blocks until he came to a *trattoria* where he ate a dish of pasta and drank a glass of red wine.

On his walk back to the hotel, he realized the temperature had dropped, but it was still pleasant. The air had an autumn smell that ten years ago would have made him wish he had his arm around a woman.

He was suspicious of de Fournier's wanting to meet, since he had come to the conclusion he was not going to cooperate. He couldn't; powerful people were preventing him. Mike was not sure he wanted him to cooperate anyway. Dufois was in Saudi Arabia. Even if he made a case against Dufois, he would not be able to bring Dufois into the United States to prosecute it.

Mike went back up to his room and shaved. He took a few sheets of hotel stationery and folded them inside his jacket pocket in case he wanted to take notes.

When he arrived at Rebibbia, he was escorted some distance from the main entrance to the cell. He followed the guard down the long, silent corridor. The paint had chipped and peeled and the iron doors to the cells were rusted along the edges. As the cell door opened, Mike caught a glimpse of François lying on his back in the dark. The guard shined his flashlight across the ceiling, beneath the cot and along the dark concrete floor and instructed François in Italian, gesturing for him to lift his arms. As the guard patted him down, François glanced over at Mike then lowered his eyes.

The guard stepped out and told Mike he could enter. The door banged closed behind him. François leaned against the sink, and offered Mike the cot. It was dark and Mike felt as if they were two passengers crammed into the same train compartment. Above him he saw the short piece of string connected to a light bulb covered with a metal grille. Mike pulled at the string and a dim light came on directly overhead, creating a shadow on the other side of the cell. François remained leaning against the sink with his arms crossed in front of his chest. His eyes were liquid and shining, though the rest of his face was hard to make out in the shadow. Mike was struck by how composed he seemed. He had a look that was hard to read, really cool; Mike had noticed that about him the first time he met him, and the weeks in jail had not changed anything.

"I got your message," Mike began. "You're entitled to have

a lawyer present, and I advise you, that is in your best interest."

"I do not want her to know about this," François answered. "It is the only condition."

Mike nodded. "You mean Juliet. All right. What about Alessandro Pucci?"

"A lawyer is not necessary."

"Why did you want to meet with me?"

"You appear to know my wife," François began, and then he stopped as if he were waiting for Mike's reaction before continuing. But Mike said nothing.

"Whatever money there is, I would like for her to keep it. Forfeiture, I think, is the term. She told me this is something in your control."

"She's right. But why should I do what you're asking?"

François shifted his weight from one leg to the other, dropping his arms to his side.

"I have no use for money in jail," François said. "She is the one you would be hurting."

"If I win without your help, why should I agree to what you're proposing?" Mike said.

"Decency." François fixed his eyes on Mike again. "I saw the way you looked at her that day when you first came to the jail. She has said nothing. She doesn't have to. A man can tell when another man is in love with his woman."

Mike felt a burst of anger, but he restrained himself. He knew he should say something, make some pretext of denying it.

"There is nothing between me and your wife."

François seemed unshaken. "If decency is not enough of a reason, I will give you another. If you let her keep the money, it will be you she is grateful to, not me. She is young. Once I go away she will forget me. She is the kind of woman who needs a man to love her."

"If you think she's going to walk out on you, why do you care whether she's comfortable?"

"I owe it to her." His gaze had a new intensity. "She had nothing to do with any of this."

The silence that followed seemed weighted by the proximity of the two men in the small cell. After a moment, François leaned back slightly on the sink and seemed to relax.

"If you let her keep the money, who knows, maybe someday it will be yours."

Mike felt another surge of anger, but he kept his cool, answering calmly, "If you're trying to bribe me, it's only going to make things worse for you."

But he knew there was no intent to bribe. François had succeeded in putting him on the defensive. He waited a moment for the fresh burst of anger to subside, formulating a response in his mind that would turn things around and remind the other man that he was in control.

"If you want me to drop the forfeiture, you're going to have to cooperate."

Something about what François was asking confused Mike. He had intended to leave Juliet to flee to Morocco. Now he claimed to be willing to give her his money and let her go her own way. Then too there was the relationship with the woman, Mireille, and Juliet's visit to the woman's apartment. François was too calm, and he suspected that he was trying to manipulate him into admitting his feelings for Juliet to use as a form of blackmail in the criminal proceeding.

"The only thing I can offer you—which turns on your giving up your buddy Dufois—you can't accept. I'm not so sure

I'd even advise you to talk under the circumstances. I could probably see to it that no harm came to you for as long as you are inside, but I can't make the same guarantees for your wife. You know these people better than I do, so you would know how to call that one."

Mike waited for a reaction. François said nothing.

"If you're counting on buying Mireille's testimony, you saw with Gilbert that kind of strategy doesn't work," Mike said.

François smiled, a slight, ironic smile. "I'm not naive enough to believe that a woman's loyalty can be bought. Women are not like men in that regard."

Mike took this as a reference to Juliet. François seemed to accept that there was no way of guaranteeing she would remain faithful to him.

"I don't think there is anything further," Mike said. He called to the guard on the other side of the door. He saw François look toward him as the cold, pitiless fluorescent light from the hall flooded the cell, and he had the impression that he was waiting for him to say something more. The sound of the bolt as it was fastened from outside answered above the silence that there was nothing more to say.

On his way out, Mike stopped at the office to see the night warden.

"He is to be allowed no visitors and no telephone until further notice. Can you see to that?"

He did not trust François and his motives confused him enough to cause him to suspect some kind of trap and that others might be involved. His mind went back to the man he had seen outside Juliet's apartment in Paris. What was he doing in the courtroom? By shutting out François's contact with the outside world, Mike could prevent events from unfolding until he uncovered his true intentions.

"*Il francese é un prigioniero americano, sei libero di fare come vuoi*," the warden said. "Do what you wish."

40

The morning after the hearing Juliet went to Rebibbia. After nearly an hour of waiting in the conference room, one of the women from the office came to look for her.

"I am sorry," she said, "I have been told that Signor de Fournier may not receive visitors."

"Why not?" Juliet demanded.

"*Non lo so.*"

"You don't know? You must have been given a reason."

She said something in Italian and remained with an awkward and regretful expression, until it occurred to Juliet that she did not speak English, and the fact that she had uttered a sentence or two was the extent of her abilities.

Juliet demanded to meet with the director of the prison. She seemed to understand this, and told her to take a seat. Another hour passed before the woman came back to her.

"*Signora, é proibito. Forse domani.* Tomorrow, please, I am sorry."

The woman called a taxi, and Juliet went straight to Alessandro's office. He had not taken lunch and was sitting at his desk writing a submission for court. When she told him, he seemed concerned.

"It worries me that this is the response of the Ministry to Mireille Vernon's disappearance," he said, letting on that he was still upset about the hearing.

These words hung ominously over the conversation and she waited for Alessandro to reproach her, though he did not. "I have arranged a meeting with Melazzo after lunch. Until then—" he shrugged.

"*Non lo so,*" Juliet answered somberly.

She found an open bar in one of the side streets along Piazza di Spagna, and took a table outdoors in the autumn light. The sun was hot. In New York it would have been called Indian summer. The tourist season was drawing to a close and the streets were empty except for the vendors selling fake Vuitton and Gucci handbags. The bar was only serving drinks and gelato. She ordered an aperitif. Wine would have made her drowsy. She never drank this early in the day, but drunk seemed better than drowsy at the moment.

She sipped slowly, letting the taste fill her mouth. The things Mireille said kept coming back to her. No piece of the puzzle was missing. She had all she believed she needed to know. Yet it seemed to matter less. She thought of François's offer to take responsibility. After all the lying and the deceit, she had not expected it, and it touched her in a place she did not think he could touch her anymore.

She took a few more sips of the drink. She remembered she had not had lunch, and it was not good to drink and feel sad on an empty stomach.

"*Un gelato, per favore, nocciola.*"

A man sat at a table across from her. He seemed to want to get her attention because he was gazing directly at her. A copy of *Oggi*, the Italian newspaper, lay folded in front of him. He was dark, nicely dressed; he did not seem Italian, though he could have been. The waiter brought him an espresso and he opened the paper and began to read.

When the gelato came she poured the last few sips of the aperitif over it. She knew that loneliness was partly to blame for the sadness she felt. She missed François and there were times when the separation was hard to bear. It had nothing to do with right or wrong or being lied to. She considered having a second drink and decided against it. Instead she called the waiter over and paid, and afterwards climbed the steps to the top. It was twilight and the piazza below seemed dark, but above her the sky was blue and light as a flock of evening birds with a shrill cry swirled above the tops of the buildings.

She saw the man who had been sitting across from her at the café head up the stairs. As he walked past her he seemed to stop, and she had the impression he was trying to get her attention. Was it chance that they had been at the café together, or had he followed her there?

Taxis were parked in front of the Hassler and she considered taking one back to the Hotel Eden. But the stranger's presence left her feeling vulnerable. If he were following her, several taxis were waiting outside the hotel, making it just as easy for him to follow her in a taxi. She went inside the Hassler and loitered near the front desk, hoping that he would give up when he saw she had no interest in speaking to him.

She let a quarter of an hour go by before going out, but as soon as she stepped outside she saw him again, staring boldly now with a look that was meant to intimidate her. François's reaction in the jail when she told him she had met with Dufois came back to her. *Do you know the gravity?* François had been visibly shaken, yet gentle rather than angry, as she would have expected. He was afraid of something. Yet his fear was not for himself, she was sure.

She went back inside the hotel and asked to use the phone at the desk. She called Alessandro, but he had not returned to his office.

The stranger seemed to want to engage her, to make eye contact and possibly speak to her. She had an ominous feeling, as if he were threatening her.

The concierge was looking in her direction. Her heart raced, and she glanced over her shoulder, expecting to find the strange man behind her. But he seemed reluctant to enter the hotel.

"*Signora*, may I help you?" the concierge asked.

She explained her fear that the man outside was following her.

"Would you like me to call the police?"

At every turn she had not known enough when she acted: her wanting to go to Rome, her decision to seek bail in New York or her meeting with Dufois—she would have done none of these things if François had confided in her. Hadn't she done enough harm by acting precipitously? It would be a mistake to call the police, she thought, not without knowing more.

"If there is a back door where a taxi could meet me that would be best."

The concierge called a taxi, and then told a bellman to accompany her to the laundry entrance. Her hands were trembling and she felt her heart beating in her chest. The bellman waited with her until the cab came through the alleyway.

The evening church bells were ringing when she returned to the Hotel Eden. A noisy little car sped by as she looked around to see if the man from the café was anywhere in sight, but he was not. She had no messages. She went straight to her room and left the curtains drawn.

A little after six o'clock Alessandro called.

"The order prohibiting François from receiving visitors has not come from the Ministry," he said.

Nothing further needed to be said. She knew at once it was Mike's way of getting back at her for what happened before the magistrates.

"Did Melazzo say anything about the hearing?" she asked.

"He was not pleased to learn of the circumstances surrounding Mireille Vernon's disappearance. On the other hand, Melazzo assured me that the position of the magistrates and the Ministry is inclined in François's favor. If Mireille Vernon is not present it is better than if she were to state before the magistrates facts that will make it difficult for them to deny the extradition."

After hanging up, she felt better. Maybe she had not ruined François's chances. She went to the window and pulled back the curtain, tentatively at first, until she was sure no one was watching. The man from the café seemed an apparition that had vanished with the coming of night. The connection she had been willing to make earlier to François and the people he was involved with began to fade from her thoughts in favor of more mundane explanations. She was a woman alone in a foreign city. Perhaps he had mistaken her for a different type of woman.

She opened the window. Noise from the street broke over the silence like a wave. The evening air was warm and balmy. Across the way a woman stepped out onto a terrace to water pots of pink chrysanthemums. A cat crawled out an open window and walked along the rail of an empty balcony three flights up. On the street below two taxi drivers were standing outside their cabs smoking. The street stretched before her in the darkness like a river of shadows. If tomorrow or the next day she asked François, who was this man? Why was he following me? Would he know? And if he did, would he tell her? The fear had subsided, but not the anxiety.

She closed the window and facing back into the dark room she thought of how François must feel, alone and no longer in control of what happened to him. He had hoped that she would be able to speak for him, shout into the void of silence, which was the only recourse left him. She had failed.

41

Balducci stood in the rain at the entrance to the closed bank, the collar of his trench coat pulled up over his neck. It was a soaking rain. Mike jumped over a few puddles and half ran across the street. He was late, but he never had any compunction about keeping people waiting. Somehow he felt that being late was his prerogative, borne out by the fact that in all his years as a prosecutor no one had ever left before he got there.

"How are you?" Mike smiled warmly as if he and Balducci were old friends.

"It's cold out here," Balducci grinned.

"Something came up at my office in New York and I had to take care of it," he offered by way of apology.

"Now that you are here it doesn't matter to me why you are late," Balducci answered with a smile.

"Where's the bank director?" Mike asked as he pushed against the locked bank door.

Balducci grinned again. "Inside, I imagine. If you don't mind my asking, why are you trying to open the door of a closed bank? If it were so simple, I would have been waiting in the dry lobby instead of on the wet street."

Balducci rang the bell off to the side.

"Tell me something," Mike said. "Maybe my blood is getting a little thin or is the rain colder in Paris than other places?"

"Stand out in it for as long as I have, you'll find it pretty cold most places," Balducci said.

The director was a meticulously dressed man with a neat moustache and thin straight hair parted on the side. He greeted them with several rounds of *s'il vous plait* until Mike told him that he did not speak French, and he switched to English, which he spoke without hesitation. Balducci took off his trench coat; the water dripped onto the rug. The director looked disgusted.

Before they went downstairs to the safe-deposit boxes, the director invited them into his office, saying there was something he wanted to show them.

A brown leather book was open on his desk.

"This is the log," he said, pointing to the book. "The box in question was rented on nine June, two years ago, under the name Agnes Desailley. The only entry in the log is also nine June. So you see the only visit Madame Desailley made to this box was on the day she rented it. To this I can add only that the rental payments are made in cash for twelve months at the beginning of every year."

"May I see?" Mike asked.

"Of course."

Mike looked at the signature; it was similar enough to Mireille's handwriting, but he was not a handwriting expert; it could have been someone else's.

"Do you require that a person verify his identity before taking a box?" Mike asked.

"No." The director folded his hands in front of him and looked earnestly at Mike.

"Why don't we have a look?" Mike said.

"Very well, I will take you."

They got up. Balducci looked at the director, "If you don't mind, I'll leave this here," he said, indicating his wet coat. Mike had absent-mindedly kept his own coat on until then. Following Balducci's lead, he took it off and hung it up on the coat rack.

"The people who bank here, are they wealthy, businesses, families?" Mike asked.

"*Oui, je comprend.* They are well-to-do individuals mostly."

"Isn't there a waiting list for one of these boxes?'

"It depends. There are openings when people die, when people move. It's possible that someone could come in and there would be one available."

Mike was only half-interested in the director's answers.

They went down a flight of narrow stairs into a room with a small dome ceiling and plaster flourishes. It was obvious to Mike that the director had gone to the box before they came because he knew exactly where it was. The director slipped the master key into the top lock. Balducci put his key in the bottom; it fit and the drawer slid out. The director set the drawer out on the counter. Balducci opened the lid. No cash, only a brown letter-size envelope. Mike took out the envelope and held it very close as he read it. When he was finished, he folded it back into the envelope and slipped the envelope into his pocket.

"I suppose we're finished," he said.

They went back to the director's office for their coats. The director walked them to the door, seeming content to be done with them.

Outside the rain had abated into a mild drizzle. Balducci and Mike stood on the street just in front of the bank.

Balducci surveyed the street with his eyes. " I take it you

don't view it as necessary for me to know what you found inside the drawer."

"I can handle it from here."

"Then I am relieved of any further involvement after today unless there is something you will need from me."

"No, that's it. It was good working with you. If you're ever in New York—," Mike began, extending his hand and giving off another warm smile, which Balducci reciprocated.

They shook hands and Balducci disappeared into the Metro.

The rain had turned into a mist and Mike enjoyed the cold air and the crowded streets as he walked along Boulevard Haussmann. He walked through the Tuileries and crossed the Pont des Arts. The Seine was choppy and green, and the wind blowing off the river was cold. He went to his room at the hotel across from l'Eglise St.-Germain-des-Pres, and sitting at the small writing table, he took out the document again. It was unnecessary for him to understand French to comprehend its significance. He had not wanted Balducci to see it; he distrusted Interpol and he knew that the French government had a habit of being disruptive in these situations. He was also afraid that the information might be leaked to de Fournier.

He took a dictionary and translated word by word as best he could, writing it out in English on a clean sheet of hotel stationery.

In conjunction with the loan to Windsor Holdings from Banque Luxembourg Investissement for the sum of U.S. $30,000,000, Banque

Luxembourg Investissement loans to Compagnie Financière *on a nonrecourse basis, the sum of U.S. $20,000,000, and accepts as collateral the shares of Windsor Holdings owned by the undersigned, François de Fournier, which, pursuant to this pledge have been delivered and are being held in escrow by Etienne Dufois as pledge agent.*

Given and executed in République Française as of the fourth day of June 1985.

de Fournier

There it was, Mike thought, the confirmation of all his suspicions. The transaction was a sham: Dufois had financed the acquisition of Great American Bank through his own bank; Compagnie Financière never put any equity into Windsor and had no liability for financing; Dufois had the stock.

It seemed clear to Mike; Dufois was no longer content with having the leverage of being able to destroy Compagnie Financière by withdrawing his investors' funds. He wanted a document signed by de Fournier—not because he ever intended to enforce it in court, but to blackmail him the next time he needed him to deliver. Once the ten million dollars was paid, without something like this de Fournier would have won his independence, so he conditioned payment of the ten million on his signing. And de Fournier had no choice but to go through with it. Having brought it to that point, if he had backed down from the ten million dollars, Dufois would have paid him nothing. The irony was that in trying to become independent, which Mike assumed to have been his motive—he must have calculated that at ten million he did not need Dufois anymore—he had instead made himself more beholden.

The document proved that de Fournier was a nominee. Mike no longer needed to find the ten million dollar payoff. This single sheet of paper was all he needed to extradite him and be certain of a conviction in New York. By insisting on this document, Dufois had brought about the downfall of the entire scheme.

Mike smiled to himself. It was obvious that Dufois had Mireille rent the safe deposit box to keep the document for him. So de Fournier was right that night in the jail, Mike thought, when he said he was not counting on Mireille's loyalty; by keeping the document for Dufois she had already double-crossed him.

He went across the street to Les Deux Magots and took a table facing St.-Germain-des-Pres. When the waiter came over he ordered a scotch. The church bells rang for six o'clock mass, long sonorous notes. It was beginning to clear and he could see the night sky showing between the low ceiling, navy and clear like his thoughts. He felt the piece of paper inside his jacket pocket and he took it out and looked at it again. Cases were won on documents, on scraps of paper. Paper was constant, people changed; there were too many risks with witnesses.

The waiter brought the scotch, slipping the tiny receipt face down under the ashtray.

The summation began to take shape in his head, the words flowing as smoothly as the first few sips of his drink. Over time Dufois had backed de Fournier into a corner; if he didn't do what Dufois's people wanted, they would pull their investment out of Compagnie Financière, and all of de

Fournier's investments would fail. That was how these things happened; people got pulled in before they realized what they were up against. They kept taking small steps, but it was all leading to the same precipice.

When he finished his drink, he ordered an omelet and a beer. The waiter lifted the little receipt from beneath the ashtray, made the addition, then slid it back face down. They were more polite about money here, Mike thought. He thought of something Juan Bastille, a drug dealer from Madrid whom he had prosecuted several years before, had said about the French. After the First World War the French chose love over money. "Big mistake," Bastille said; "Money never comes around to stab you in the back the way love does."

He ate, watching the sidewalk. The man sitting at the table next to his had his arm slung loosely across the back of the woman he was with and was smiling as she talked. It seemed to him that French men liked women. He had never thought about it before, but American men didn't really like women; they liked parts of their bodies.

When he got back to the Madison Hotel, he opened the window to let in the cold night air. The church garden was lit for night, and he could make out the mosaic on the garden wall more clearly than during the day. In the building across the way a woman with shoulder-length dark hair was smoking a cigarette beside the window. She must have noticed him watching her because she glanced at him for a moment before stepping back from the window.

There were only so many walks he could take, only so many drinks, before it all came back to loneliness, he thought. Maybe it was the little room, maybe it was being in a foreign place, but he was no longer feeling sure of himself. It was something he did not like to admit, but he was afraid of being alone.

He tossed the document on the writing table, undressed, got into bed and turned on CNN World Report, half-listening to a news story on sex education in elementary schools in Finland, which he had already heard two times before that day. Then it came to him: I'm holding all the cards, and I want her to come back to New York with me.

He was waiting for the other side of the argument to come to him the way it always did. Because he could always argue both sides with equal precision. But for the first time it was not coming to him, not even after the second fifty-franc scotch.

42

Since coming to François's house in Mougins, Mireille had awakened every morning at seven o'clock, gone downstairs to the kitchen, made coffee over the stove and sat for three quarters of an hour, her mind drifting pleasantly as she looked out the window over the long grounds laced with dew and the changing sky. Since she was a child, no matter what else, she had loved morning. And here the morning was open and fresh and flooded with light. Mornings were always a beginning, and the wonderful thing about beginnings, she thought, was that they came to one without a past.

Despite everything, it had been a pleasant week. In Paris her anxiety had become part of the surroundings, hidden in the walls and the furniture. With the change of scenery, she felt far removed from that world. In the afternoons she walked amid the crushed leaves and remnants of summer flowers, mulberry and chestnut trees and bougainvillea, and the open moody sky with its heavy white clouds seemed to reassure her. The groundskeeper, a hard-of-hearing old man with hair sticking out of his ears like fleece, ran errands for her, since she thought it imprudent to be seen in a town where after the first day everyone would know her.

The house had no television. On the days when the groundskeeper brought her groceries, he also brought a newspaper, but the news that she had seen thus far was ominously free of any mention of François.

At night she warmed a cup of red wine to help her sleep. She felt alone, but she had felt alone in Paris too, and here it felt good to be alone. At times she would despair when she thought of how long all of this would drag on, and she wondered when she would hear from François's wife.

She had been dreaming about the south recently, dreaming of going back to Marseilles, of the simplicity of that life which could not have satisfied her when she was young. There was something else which she did not want to admit to herself: for as long as she was in François's house, she felt as if she had stepped into the shoes of his wife. On the day she arrived, after an hour of listening to the half-deaf groundskeeper tell her about the various gardens, and his work to prevent the dessert grapes from dying with the first frost, she had gone through the rooms, the many bedrooms with their pretty beds and old marble-topped nightstands, choosing a room for herself. The room she decided upon had silk curtains on the windows and a small Chinese rug. It was a feminine room, and it seemed to have been left intact by its former occupant, who, judging from the photo on the wall, Mireille guessed to have been François's grandmother. After a few nights she began to feel that she did not need the man; his house would do.

It had become too late for certain things. She sometimes faulted herself for having wasted too much time with François. But at least she had loved him. There was the Englishman, just before she met François, who had wanted to marry her; she turned him down. She did not regret that either. Just as she had no regrets about not having children. It was the way things had turned out, and no opportunity to her liking had presented itself.

The first afternoon in Mougins, as she was going through the rooms, she thought to look for a gun. Houses like this always had a gun, and it was not a bad idea, she thought, to keep it at her bedside. She found what she was looking for in the top drawer of the nightstand in the room François and Juliet used as their bedroom. After checking to make sure it was loaded, she placed it on the nightstand alongside her bed where she kept the metal box with the money she had brought with her. She opened it and looked at the neat piles of bills. It was not to hurt François that she had saved the document in the safe-deposit box. It was simpler than that: Dufois paid her to do it. Somehow, she thought, François would understand.

Every day she felt a little safer, a little further away from the events she feared, until the morning when everything changed. The groundskeeper came to bring her a loaf of bread, some cheese and cold meat and a day-old copy of *Le Monde*. He put the package on the table and emptied the contents.

"Would you like tea?" she asked.

He usually sat with her for the better part of an hour before beginning his chores around the grounds.

"Not today. My wife is waiting."

Mireille surveyed his face for a moment. She asked him how much she owed him for the groceries.

"Seventy," he said.

She noticed that he was not looking at her when she handed him the money.

From the kitchen window, she could hear the red truck grumbling along the dirt road. Having come to depend on his hour of conversation for company, she felt disappointed he could not stay. She made a pot of tea and sat by the window to read the paper, getting only to page three when she saw the article about François's hearing in Rome. She was mentioned in the article, along with the fact that she had disappeared and that efforts were being made to locate her.

For the rest of the day her thoughts were clouded by anxiety until she was incapable of a single coherent thought. Everywhere she turned she felt trapped. She had no car, no means of leaving; yet she knew she had to leave. Even though she had never given her name to the groundskeeper, he could surmise that she was the woman in the article. She faulted herself for having trusted François's wife; how could she believe she would have her interest in mind? At other times, she felt that all of this was inevitable and that it had nothing to do with Juliet. She was worried that the groundskeeper might have already revealed her whereabouts before she had a chance to persuade him to help her.

Only Dufois was left. She made a desperate call to his office. Though she refused to leave her name, she left the number at the house with the message that it was urgent she speak with him. She knew Dufois would know it was she, and even from Saudi Arabia, he was powerful enough to help her.

She made soup for something to do, but her hand shook as she sliced the vegetables and she cut her thumb. With the coming of night, her anxiety increased. She had spent the day waiting for the phone to ring, that foreboding silence haunting her, driving her more than once to lift the receiver to check for a dial tone.

After closing the shutters, she lay in bed with the lights on, her eyes open wide and her body rigid and alert. She abandoned any attempt to read, since she would not have been able to concentrate. Instead she found herself staring into the light thinking about the past.

When she met Dufois, he was young and extravagant and his parties were the talk of Paris. Then over the years he began gaining weight and losing his hair. When his hair went gray he started using dye. He tried to compensate for age in other ways too, by wearing more gold so that women would know he was rich, manicuring his fingernails and using a stronger perfume, no longer trusting to the scent of his body. But that was all much later. In the beginning, he had kept her as his mistress. "You and I are the same, cut from the same mold," he used to say. Yes, they were both willing to sell themselves and not look back, she thought.

She heard a sound on the floor below, and her thoughts stopped abruptly. Her eyes focused on the door. All of her senses were directed toward that sound, until she became convinced someone was on the stairs. One eye was fixed on the drawer with the gun, the other on the doorway, but her limbs felt frozen and she was incapable of moving her arm. A seeming eternity of ten minutes passed that way before she was able to get up and gun in hand walk down the long hallway. She went through each room in the house, and finding things undisturbed, the sounds she had heard began to recede. The people who were looking for her would not come at night, they would be lawyers and police, who would not harm her; this was the first clear thought she had, and it put her mind at ease. She went down to the first floor. The doors were locked, the heavy metal shutters drawn closed in the front of the house. Nothing seemed disturbed. When she turned on the kitchen light, she saw a field mouse run into a corner, as frightened by the light as she had been by the darkness. The mouse remained still and she caught it, its tiny body trembling in her hand. She set him down again and he managed to make his way through a crack beneath the cabinet.

She slept until ten o'clock the next morning, feeling the desire to escape through sleep as strongly as the fear she had felt the night before. Yet the morning did not bring its usual peace. She had a great wish to be outdoors, and she wanted the old man to come back so that she could warn him not to say anything to anyone. After all, maybe there were other explanations for his odd behavior. Even if he had seen the story in the paper, it was hard to tell with that kind whether his reaction had been caused by something as simple as his concern that François would not pay him his wage.

She took a long walk during which she found herself talking aloud from time to time, the voice in her head leaking out into the desolate countryside. The walk, the air, the open fields helped to put her thoughts together. She had only to call Saed a liar. She was sure the man who met her in Switzerland had returned to the Middle East.

It was afternoon and she had calmed herself sufficiently to be able to eat lunch. As she was cutting a piece of yesterday's bread to warm in the oven, a sudden noise caused her to turn. Facing her as if he had been waiting for her to turn around was a tall, Slavic-looking man, who glared menacingly through dark, blood-shot eyes. Fear froze the scream inside her throat and she merely stared back at him in a way that might have been mistaken for composure. In that frozen stare she took in his chipped front tooth, which made him look older than he was, though from his hands she doubted whether he was twenty-five. Her soft brown eyes remained fixed on him, watchful. She knew that he had come for one of two reasons, to kill her or to take her with him. The gun was upstairs, another piece of bad luck. She did not run, as she did not scream; something made her sure that it was harder to kill someone who was not resisting. If she had tried to run his instinct would have taken over, as predator to prey, but by remaining still, her eyes warm like a soft flame, she might arouse the most primitive sympathy in him.

"Why are you here?" she asked.

He did not answer and she continued to stare at his coarse, hard face. She had given herself to the other kind of man, the pampered kind, who used creams for his face and hands.

"What do you want?" she asked.

She pushed back the heavy reddish-brown hair that had fallen across her face, and revealed her long pale neck, her beautifully shaped lips. Fear had transformed her face, the blood rushing through her racing heart had brought the blush back to her cheeks. She had the impression that he was moving closer; she could smell tobacco and coffee from his stale breath. She was buying time, but she did not know for what. Then she remembered the bread knife.

"You don't answer me," she said softly. Fear had deprived her of her full voice. She tried to talk, to engage him by her soft voice, going about it as she would have gone about seducing him, and as she spoke her hand moved slowly, gradually back toward the knife waiting on the counter. Yet she knew he was watching for any abrupt movement on her part.

"You are Russian?"

"Chechen," he smirked.

She took it as a good sign that he was answering her.

"You came all this way because Dufois sent you. I used to do the same for Dufois. The way he sold me out, he will sell you out too, only it will be quicker for you. With me at least he was never indifferent. Your life comes cheap."

She saw the confusion register on his face, and she took it to mean that he was considering what she had just said, so she continued. "I know all about Dufois," she went on, whispering, her breath racing inside her chest. "Dufois is not the only rich person." The sound of her voice seemed to be hypnotizing them both. "Only it is hard to undo all those years of being used. If it were not hard, I would have thought of it before now."

She smiled at him, her eyes lifting from their sleep-like trance as she gazed intently at him, and he too smiled and nodded his head.

"You like that idea," she said, and he nodded again. "Then yes, you agree for a price. Tell Dufois I was not here; he will never find out. Whatever he will pay you, I will give you twice the amount." She was thinking of the metal box that contained ten times the amount Dufois would have considered her life worth and of the gun beside it. "Come," she said quietly, and with her small feminine hand she waved him on, and it was that gesture at last that she believed he understood.

He nodded as he moved closer, so close now she could smell his breath on her face and his unwashed skin beneath his clothes. He touched her white shoulder, and the feel of his hand repulsed and horrified her, and in that moment, as his cracked lips pushed toward hers, she rested her hand on top of his as if to caress it, reaching back with her free hand for the knife. And he, seemingly unaware, began to caress her shoulder until with a wild swing she broke free and lashed at his body, madly, with a crazed strength. At the first shock, the first sting to his hard skin, he looked down to see the blood running along his arm from the open cut on his shoulder. Stunned, like a moth that has flown into the flame, he let go and in that moment she ran from him.

She got as far as the stairs when she felt the fire burning inside her. She could smell the seared flesh, as if she had caught on fire; she felt it before she heard the sound and when she heard the sound she knew. She raised her eyes, and saw his face, his menacing eyes glaring back at her, and she felt his coarse hands, still warm from the gun, as he wrapped them across her back and held her in the dirty net of a man's arms that before this had always broken her fall.

43

Dugommier was in the middle of reviewing a contract when his secretary interrupted him to tell him that François de Fournier was on the phone. He asked her to close the door.

"I was given a message to call you," François said. "I have not been permitted to use the phone and I have little time to speak."

The connection was bad, and Dugommier heard an echo after every word.

"You heard about Mireille?" Dugommier said.

"What about her?"

"Mireille was murdered at your house in Mougins."

A short silence followed.

"I see," François said quietly. Then after another silence, "Tell him I understand his position and I agree to his terms."

Dugommier heard the despair in his voice and he felt moved.

"François, c'est bien."

The phone went dead. The entire conversation had taken less than three minutes. Yet what had transpired would last a lifetime. Dugommier felt undeniably relieved that the whole affair would soon be over. He could be certain Dufois would be satisfied with the result. He could not say the same for himself. He remained for a minute or more with the dead phone receiver in his hands, overcome by his own failure to have prevented this result.

Though it was midday, he straightened a few papers on his desk and left for the day. He knew he would be back tomorrow; he would sit at his desk and work. Tomorrow he would already have begun to distance himself. Not today. The sound of despair in François's voice was too fresh in his mind.

He walked from his office in the 16th Arrondissement to his apartment in the 7th. His wife was surprised to see him home so early. His four-year-old daughter jumped up into his arms. His son was doing homework on the kitchen table. His eldest daughter was still at school. He sat down with the little one on his lap and at his son's request checked the page of subtraction and addition. He found two mistakes, simple mistakes, seven minus four was not two and nine minus five was not three—errors of inattention. His son corrected them as soon as he pointed them out.

"You see, your mind wandered, you stopped paying attention and you made a mistake," he said.

"*Je sais. Je sais.*"

Everything might have worked out differently if François had not gone to Rome, he thought. The arrangements they had made in Morocco, the influence they had bought in Paris—all of it was no guarantee against the power of life itself.

44

"I've woken you, I know."

"Michael," she said softly, half asleep.

The sound of her voice caught him off guard; she sounded like a girl, and he stopped for a moment.

"I don't know if you've heard—"

She did not wait for him to finish. "Has anything happened to François?"

"Mireille Vernon was found dead at your husband's villa in Mougins."

"When? When did it happen?"

She seemed confused.

"I don't have an answer yet. I got the call a little while ago," he said gently. "She was shot. The groundskeeper called the police."

She was silent, and after a moment he wondered whether she was still on the line.

"Juliet."

"What's going to happen?" she asked quietly.

"I'm not sure. There'll be an investigation. In terms of my case I don't have to tell you what it means." He heard the satisfaction in his own voice as he said it and it repulsed him. Then he heard a sound on the other end, a sob, which was stifled into silence. He waited before continuing.

"I'm going to have to question François. I'll be in Rome on Monday." He avoided telling her that he was already in Paris.

"I want to know why you're not allowing him to have visitors." Her voice sounded shrill and angry. "I haven't been permitted to see him. I know you're behind it, the same way you had him moved from the infirmary. I didn't think you'd be so small."

"I'm not doing anything any differently than in any other case," he said. The news about Mireille came as a shock, and she was upset. He was willing to let her remarks go at that. They were both silent. He wanted to tell her to watch out for herself. But he could hear in her voice that she was not going to take that from him.

"I'll arrange for you to see him on Monday," he said. "You can call me at the hotel—same hotel as last time." In the ensuing silence he began to dwell on how it was that she blamed him for everything that had happened thus far. He found himself getting angry, and a moment later it was already too late. "Just because you gave the old lady twenty bucks doesn't mean she wasn't going to tell me you had been there. Smart guy who said a woman's loyalty can't be bought."

"Go to hell." She hung up.

45

Juliet waited for Alessandro outside the Hotel Eden. It was a beautiful day, bright and warm and endlessly clear.

Alessandro suggested that they eat at the restaurant on the roof.

The windows were open. Fresh air and sunlight streamed through the room. They took a table off to the corner, away from the other patrons, the usual Japanese and German tourists, and the two large tables of Arabs, men and women sitting at segregated tables. Most people were already through with their second course.

"You seem tired," Juliet said.

"I had papers due in court this morning and I could not start them until the night, so as you might imagine I did not sleep."

Juliet gave a little smile, feeling more convinced than ever that Alessandro had a mistress.

Alessandro ordered a bottle of red wine. As the waiter performed the ritual of presenting the bottle and offering it to Alessandro to taste, Juliet looked out over the view of Rome, the gold crosses gleaming as if touched by heaven's ineffable light.

"When I called the jail this morning to confirm our visit I was able to find out that during these fourteen days François has not been moved from his cell," Alessandro said, wiping his mouth delicately with a corner of his napkin after the first few sips of wine.

"He's rotting in a cell while I'm drinking wine on a rooftop in Rome." She took a sip of wine. "Let it go to my head fast," she said, and Alessandro held out his glass to toast to that sentiment.

"We know at least that now we will be able to see him. It is unfortunate, the hearing is tomorrow and we will have so little time with him."

At the mention of tomorrow's hearing, she felt the pull of nerves in her stomach.

The waiter brought bread, the large, airy rolls with a hard pointy crust that seemed to be served in every good restaurant in Rome.

"You agree, don't you? There's nothing to be gained by letting Mike Chase question him about Mireille?" she asked, breaking a corner of a roll.

"I think we should wait to hear what he says," Alessandro said. Seeing from her expression that she did not want that, he added, "But I am sure you are right."

The waiter brought two plates of mozzarella, tomato and basil. Juliet said, "The colors of the Italian flag."

Alessandro looked down at his plate. "So you are right. Here in Italy we show our patriotism through our stomachs."

Alessandro cut neat little pieces of cheese and tomato and put them together onto his fork.

"How do you survive on how little you eat?" he asked, directing a look at her undisturbed plate.

Her eye kept shifting to the two tables of Arabs seated on the other side of the room. The men seemed to be enjoying themselves; the women were enjoying themselves too, but in a different way, like a table of well-behaved girls on a boarding school outing. Then she thought of Mireille, the frightened look on her face. *"You are someone's wife; for that I envy you."* She looked down at the wedding ring on her hand, the empty sparkle of diamond and gold.

Alessandro leaned over the table and took her hand.

"We won't be able to do anything," he said in a hushed voice. "I spent the morning at the office of one of the magistrates trying to persuade him that the tribunal should withhold decision until an investigation into Mireille Vernon's death has been conducted and a suspect identified. What can I say? Their minds were already made up and they just want to be rid of the matter before further complications arise."

His soft brown eyes were looking into hers, the corners drooping; the look she had mistaken for fatigue had been something else, the burden of what he had to tell her.

"They are afraid because of this latest development, and they are going to extradite."

"Yes, justice," Juliet let out a little cry that almost sounded like a laugh.

"My dear, the woman was found murdered in François's villa."

She wrapped her fingers around the stem of her wine glass so tightly it seemed it might break. "How does it go? *'He shall separate them one from another, the just on His right hand, the guilty ones on His left.'*" Her voice trembled. She pressed her hand to her forehead and shut her eyes.

Alessandro reached over to put his hand on hers again.

"There is an appeal," he said quietly.

"What makes you think the result will be any different? More delay, more waiting. A new hope, and in the end it will be nothing more than this." She knocked her wine glass on its side and the last drops of red wine spilled onto the white linen.

"Maybe by then they will have found whoever killed this woman," he said softly.

"If they haven't already, they never will. If they conclude Dufois did it, it's as good as saying François did it himself."

"I'm so sorry I was able to do so little for you," he offered.

"It isn't your fault," she said.

Alessandro stroked her hand. He had never asked her whether it was her idea to send Mireille to Mougins. Yet she had the feeling that he blamed her. "If its anyone's fault, it's mine," she said.

He did not contradict her.

46

When François entered the conference room, she was struck by how withdrawn he seemed; the look in his eyes was so distant, yet contemplative and serene.

"When you did not come, I thought you had left Rome," he said quietly.

"I did come. They wouldn't let me see you."

"I know that now."

The same secretary who had called a taxi for her last time came into the conference room carrying two coffees. "Mr. Pucci thought you might like coffee, and there was extra. I didn't see the harm."

François smiled. *"Grazie, sei gentile."*

"We all missed seeing you," she said to François, then she blushed. "And the *signora*," she added.

"Thank you," Juliet said. After so much coldness and distrust, it felt awkward to be treated with kindness.

"She has a crush on you," Juliet said after she left.

François smiled slightly. She noticed how he drank the coffee thirstily, sucking on a cube of sugar between sips, his other concerns seeming remote compared to his enjoyment of the boiling coffee.

She reached across the table and took his hand in hers. He no longer seemed to have the resolve to push her away.

"Mireille was murdered in Mougins," she said.

"I know."

"François, I'm sorry."

The weeks of isolation had broken something inside of him, and he no longer tried to disguise what he felt.

"She was nothing to them. It was more convenient to kill her," he said.

"Michael Chase wants to talk to you this afternoon about what happened to Mireille."

He leaned close to her, looking at her intently, seeming to convey with his eyes that he had made certain decisions. "I don't want you to have anything to do with this. As far as anyone is concerned, I made the arrangements for Mireille."

She started to say something, but he put his finger to her mouth.

"Let them blame me. One more thing, it will not make any difference now."

She saw him look toward the door at Nunzio, the guard, who, after François caught his eye, got up and walked down the hall.

"He's your friend now?" Juliet asked.

"I wanted a chance to be alone with you. I do not know when I will see you again after tomorrow. They may send me straight to New York."

She knew he was right, but she wondered why he was saying these things, whether someone had already told him.

He took her hands and, folding them together, drew them to his lips before letting go. There was urgency in his gaze and his voice, his words coming out in a hurry.

"There is an account in Switzerland. You have to memorize the instructions. Dugommier will arrange when this is finished—"

"No," she said, "Don't talk this way." He seemed to her a condemned man—the way he had drunk the coffee, his giving her instructions.

He grabbed her wrists, and his voice, though hushed, was excited. "We have run out of time. The truth doesn't matter to lawyers, but you are my wife."

"I know enough about the truth," she said, her voice high and thin as she pulled her hand away. "I've been to Switzerland. I know you transferred two million dollars to Morocco. They all talked to me—you're the only one who is silent. I never wanted to represent you. Remember that."

A cool breeze wafted through the open window. The nervous twitter of sparrows and the sound of brittle leaves blowing along the pavement filled the silence between them.

"I'm sorry," he said at last. He spoke softly. "This is my last chance to be alone with you. There are things I want to say before it's too late. Dufois thinks you are too close with the American prosecutor."

He watched her face for a moment, as if looking for some acknowledgment that what he said was true.

"Because of that he no longer trusts me. He is afraid you will persuade me to do what the Americans want. Dufois has had someone watching you in Rome." Then he stopped as if considering whether to tell her. "In Paris."

She felt sick suddenly. Her first impulse was to try to explain, but as she started to speak, he put his finger to her lips.

"It was my fault for insisting that you act as my lawyer. I have told Dufois I will do as he wishes. So long as I keep my word, he will leave you alone." He looked at her gently before continuing. "Whatever else you might have heard, it was not because I wanted to leave you that I was going to go to

Morocco without you. I wanted to go without telling you—this way no one could ever say you had anything to do with any of it. I did not want you to come with me out of obligation. I would have gotten in touch with you somehow. And when it was safe I was hoping we could be together again."

He touched the ends of her hair and his voice was wistful. "When I learned of Alain's death, I thought I had time. I was not ready to leave you. I thought it could wait a few more days. In Rome I was going to tell you I had to go to the Middle East on business."

"Why didn't you tell me the truth? I could have helped you."

"Tell you I was a fraud? I was afraid. Afraid you would leave."

"You're wrong," she said as she caressed his face.

He pulled away and the wistfulness and the softness left his voice. "I do not want you to follow me to New York," he said firmly.

"Let's not talk about it before it's happened. It's bad luck."

"Luck?" He let out a little laugh. "I intend to resolve it quietly. Our life together is finished. You think that ten years from now I can walk out and we will pick up where we left off. We will be too different. And if you wait for me I will have taken those years from you. When it was finished, you would hate me."

She saw him looking at her, waiting for her answer.

"Why don't you leave what I do up to me?" she said.

"Because if you stayed with me it would be out of pity. I don't want your pity."

He took her hand again. "You wanted to have a child."

"So did you," she said quietly.

She got up and walked to the other side of the room. Her back was to him as she began. "It isn't just you who's been holding back. I should have told you. But it was a long time ago and I thought it would make everything worse for you if you knew."

She put her hand to her brow and rested her shoulder against the window frame, trying to find the courage to say it. He came up behind her, and taking her by the shoulders, turned her around gently, facing him.

"It's better if you never tell me," he said.

He took her face in his hands and lifted her mouth to his, kissing her, her lips, her hair, her neck, each kiss carrying within it the seeds of its own oblivion. Then something inside of him seemed to break, and he stopped and simply held her.

She heard a crash in the hallway as Nunzio kicked the chair before sitting down. Those few minutes of intimacy were gone.

"Call Alessandro so I can say hello," François told her. She understood; he no longer wanted to be alone with her.

Alessandro put his arms around François and embraced him.

"I hear from the secretary that they are expecting Michael Chase," he said.

"François, it's better if you're not here when he arrives," Juliet said.

François turned to Nunzio. "*Per favore.*"

Nunzio stepped back from the doorway.

François turned to Juliet a last time, and placed his lips to her ear. "*Je t'aime,*" he said quietly, with lowered eyes.

47

"Hello, Alessandro, Madame de Fournier," Mike smiled at Juliet. "Where is the defendant?" he asked as he laid his briefcase flat on the table.

"François is not going to talk to you," Juliet said. "I'm sorry you came all the way to Rome."

"I had to be here for the hearing." He gazed directly at Juliet. "I have to talk to you too, Juliet. You've probably been expecting it."

She did not answer.

"You're entitled to be represented by counsel."

She turned to Alessandro, "Will you stay?"

"Of course."

Mike noticed her playing with the empty cup.

"Do you mind, Alessandro, before we start, could you arrange for coffee?" Mike said.

The coffee had been a pretext; he wanted the chance to talk to her alone.

"Justice is going to pressure me to indict you for your role in Mireille Vernon's disappearance," he began as soon as Alessandro left the room. "Witness tampering, obstruction—conspiracy to commit murder. You are as implicated in her death as your husband. The Justice Department is bigger than I am. I won't be able to help you if it gets to that. Tell me your husband was the one who told you to arrange for her to go to Mougins and I will make it go away against you."

"It wasn't François."

He took the brown envelope from his pocket, and, taking out the share pledge of Windsor Holdings stock, handed it to her. "Mireille Vernon was keeping this in a safe-deposit box," he said, studying her face as she read it.

"I don't have to explain to you what that piece of paper represents. Juliet, he's already going down. You know that, don't you? You can't save him."

She handed the paper back to him without a word. He put it in the envelope and slipped it into the inside pocket of his suit jacket. He could see from her expression she was not going to talk.

"What are you waiting for?" he said, slamming his hand on the table. "He was cheating on you. He lied to you. He was going to leave you. When are you going to get smart?"

But she would not answer.

Alessandro returned with the coffee. "I hope no one minds if I am the one with the honor of serving you as opposed to the girl at the desk."

"Who made the arrangements for Mireille Vernon to stay at your husband's villa in Mougins?" Mike asked abruptly, wanting to make a show of getting straight to business.

"François had nothing to do with it. If you have any other questions—I'm not going to answer them today. You'll have to get a subpoena," she answered.

"We're in Rome. You know I can do better than that."

"You mean a material witness warrant? Is that what you're talking about? You're the tactician. I can't stop you from trying to extradite me."

"I'll do what I have to, Mrs. de Fournier."

"I know," she said quietly.

"Are we finished?" Those words had a double meaning for him, which she seemed to understand from the way she looked at him.

"Yes," she answered. Then she bowed her head just enough to obscure her face behind her long dark hair.

48

Alessandro sat with her for what seemed a long time. There was nothing to say, and after a while he offered to take her back to her hotel. She wanted to walk, and she asked him to drop her off in the Old City. It was a long walk to the hotel, but she wanted that.

She came upon the church where she had stopped when everything began and went inside. The candle she lit that afternoon had extinguished and been relit more than a hundred times since then she thought. Somehow she knew François would not want her prayers, just as he had not wanted her pity. She lit a candle for Mireille, and then she sat in a pew. She believed Mike when he said Justice would pursue her involvement in Mireille's disappearance. Yet she felt at peace with her decision.

A nun came out from behind the altar to lock the church. Until then Juliet did not realize how late it was. She had lost track of time, though as she walked through the dark streets back to the hotel, along the Corso and through the side streets off Piazza di Spagna, it seemed that time, which she felt with every step, was all that remained between the night and the inevitable events that would take place in the morning.

At the hotel she retrieved her key from the front desk and went straight to her room. A figure presented itself to her, giving her a feeling that she was being watched as she stepped into the narrow elevator. Her thoughts were so heavy inside of her that she felt alone in spite of it. But the man who stood beside her seemed to defy her refusal to look over in his direction by the sheer insistence of his stare. She caught him watching her in the antique mirror, which made him appear closer. It was then she noticed that only one stop had been pressed, and this seemed to grab her attention as the elevator bounced to a halt with a loud, habitual sound. She pulled back the gate and pushed the door open and for a lingering instant as she stepped into the hallway she believed she was free of him, until the space seemed to close again, and without looking up, she heard his footsteps keeping pace behind hers.

The hallway seemed a narrow cul-de-sac. Her only chance was to get to her room at the end of the hall, and close the door. She placed the key in the lock and, as she began to turn it, she was suddenly and forcefully knocked against the door. The violent thrust at last gave form to the anxiety she had felt building inside of her since August, and she let out a scream, a desperate outburst of fear and rage, until her assailant covered her mouth and in a hushed tone threatened, "Tell your husband he is expected to keep his word." She had caused enough of a disturbance for someone along the hall to open a door and look out to see what was going on. At that, her assailant let go and stepped back, and she escaped into her room.

She was shivering in the warm room and her hands shook as she felt the door to make sure it was locked. Then she fell against the inside of the door, exhausted, not by her efforts to break away, but from everything up to that point.

49

When Mike got back to the hotel, he felt tired, the kind of tired that made every bone in his body feel like lead. He had gone out to dinner with John Travers and Roberto Chiaro. Before he knew it, it was eleven o'clock.

He unbuttoned his shirt, took off his shoes and collapsed onto the bed. The weight in his legs started to lift and he felt better. He did not want to think about Juliet. Instead, he tried thinking of what he was going to do when the case was over.

All night Travers had been saying that he could count on a promotion for winning the extradition. At this stage, he was more interested in private practice than he was in a government promotion, though a promotion certainly would not hurt. Everyone always said it was best to begin talking to law firms as soon as a big case was over, while your name was still in the papers. He was unsure what kind of money he should be holding out for; Travers said a friend of his, a partner at one of the big firms, was pulling in three quarters of a million dollars a year.

The phone rang. Because of the hour he assumed it was someone in the States. Instead, he heard Juliet's voice, thin and frightened.

"Somebody was here waiting for me."

"Where? Where are you?"

"In my room at the hotel."

"What's your room number?"

"316."

"I'll be right over."

He did not want to waste time calling Interpol. He thought it was better to call once he got there.

"I need a taxi," Mike said to the man at the desk.

"No taxis," he said, pointing to the clock.

Mike glanced down the deserted street stretching out before him, the dim lights scattered like small stars in a black sky. He began walking at a fast pace before breaking into a run. Someone sped by on a Vespa going too fast to notice him.

When he got to the Hotel Eden, he stopped long enough to catch his breath, standing in the cold night air, looking around him, waiting for the sound of footsteps, a voice perhaps, but there was no one, not even the sound of a distant car.

The man at the concierge desk did not stop him as he crossed the lobby and got into the narrow elevator. He glimpsed himself in the old mirror. His broken image through the stains and marks beneath the surface of the glass struck him more as a reflection of his soul than of his face.

She was standing just on the other side of the door to the room, waiting for him. She seemed shaken and he held her tight against his chest.

"He's gone," he said.

"He was here when I got back. He followed me up in the elevator."

"He wanted to scare you. They don't want your husband to cooperate, that's all." He hesitated for a moment. "I should have warned you. I saw someone, first in Paris, then at the hearing. You can add it to the list of reasons to hate me."

"It wasn't because I hated you that I left New York."

"Maybe if I had done things right then, we wouldn't be here now," he said, feeling the struggle gaining within himself as she remained in his arms and he heard the words repeat in his head, *Do not let this happen.*

"I can make a few calls and have someone stay outside your room tonight," he said.

"Tonight? What about tomorrow night, and the night after? Don't go," she whispered, as if she had read his thoughts. "Please, don't leave me. Do you love me?"

"I've loved you from the moment I saw you. I've always loved you."

She put her mouth against his and he felt the heat of her breast beneath his hand. The robe fell from her shoulders and he pressed her body against his. Desire possessed him as if a nerve had been laid bare. Desperate, he caressed her mouth, her eyes, holding her, he knew this was his night in the garden, his agony, and he felt the weight of it on his shoulders, and he said yes, give in to weakness, and through weakness discover strength. He was willing to stake everything.

He lifted her in his arms and carried her to the bed. Her head was bowed and he lifted her chin in his hands and saw her beautiful face covered with fresh tears. He knew that he was hurting her, that even his lips were too rough against her breast. Her sobs broke through the silence; the sweat that covered him mixed with her tears, and he saw the anguish in her face as she bore his agony inside of her. She opened her eyes, and through the darkness, she seemed to beg.

When it was finished, he felt her slip away. She was lying with her eyes open, not looking at him. In the dark her face took on the appearance of a marble statue, and part of him wanted to reach for the light next to the bed. He saw the brutish red marks on her breasts left by his hands. He touched her face, and her eyes turned to meet his, and something in her look recalled François looking at him with a steady gaze and those shining eyes from across the cell, and he believed himself the lesser man. From the bed he heard a car drive by on the street below and he looked toward the window where the drapes were drawn closed. His eyes began to dart around the room and he felt a rising sense of uneasiness.

"There was no one here. That's not why you called me," he said.

But she did not answer, only the murmur of her breath in the silence.

"There was no one, was there?"

She would not look up.

He felt something snap inside of him. "Answer me. You made it up, didn't you? You wanted to set me up." She tried to turn away but he grabbed her shoulders. "Why didn't you call the police? Why me?"

"I knew you'd come."

"You were lying."

"No."

But he no longer cared what her answer was. "Say it." He slapped her, repeating, "Say it, " and he felt the sting of his hand hitting her soft cheek and the stain of her tears as he shook her hard and shouted, "Say there was no one there. Say it."

His hands gripped her shoulders as she tried to pull away.

"I want you to say it."

She did not answer him and he let go.

She lay there like a dead woman. He sat motionless at

the edge of the bed. He had no idea how much time passed that way. Suddenly he felt a draft in the room, and he realized it was cold. He turned his head to look at her. She had not moved. He reached over to cover her with the sheet, gently pushing the hair from her face.

"Juliet," he whispered.

Her eyes met his. "I love him. I love François."

He fumbled in the dark for his clothes. At the door, he hesitated before going out. He was waiting for her to stop him, but she was silent.

50

The courtroom was crowded, and everyone had to wait for the magistrates to take the bench. By chance Juliet and Mike both arrived at the same time. She did not lift her eyes, but she could tell he walked past her as if he had not seen her. She took her place in silence. Alessandro filled a paper cup with water and set it in front of her. She was aware of most of what was going on. She noticed when the lawyers put on their black robes. She saw the briefcases being placed on the table and dossiers taken out. The calendar on the bailiff's desk said October thirty-first. It had all taken a little over two months. She saw Alessandro look up toward the prisoner's dock, and she assumed François had just been brought in. It was too painful for her to look.

The bailiff asked whether all the parties were present. Then the magistrates were summoned. A few minutes later they filed in wearing their robes and everyone in the courtroom stood until they were told to sit. To Juliet it had taken on the dimensions of a ritual, as if everyone present were acting out something that had already taken place.

The magistrates said they would like to hear first from the attorney for the Ministry of Justice. He stood up and sought permission to defer to the attorney from the United States government. Mike stood. Juliet grasped the edge of the table, bracing herself.

Mike spoke quietly, not his usual courtroom voice.

"The United States of America wishes to withdraw its application for extradition of the defendant."

The translator repeated it in Italian as if she were reading.

The magistrates seemed surprised, and one of them asked on what basis the United States wished to withdraw.

"It is our opinion that without the testimony of Mireille Vernon or Etienne Dufois, the evidence is insufficient to proceed to trial in the United States," Mike answered.

After that things started happening too quickly for Juliet to follow. The magistrates conferred with one another for some time before summoning the parties to the bench to discuss the things that would have to happen before François could be released. Then the magistrates announced that they would comply with the decision of the United States government. Court was dismissed. A crowd of reporters surrounded Mike. Alessandro was being congratulated for his brilliant performance.

Juliet waited in the hallway for Mike to come out. When she saw him, she tried to go over to him.

"Save it for your husband," he said curtly. Then he walked away.

As with everything else in the Italian justice system, numerous steps had to be performed before François could be released from Rebibbia. The following day was a legal holiday and nothing could be done. Two days passed before Juliet got the call telling her he had been officially released and she could pick him up.

The street was covered with a thin stream of fresh rain. All morning it stormed, and the sky was black over the hills around Rome. They were only at the beginning of the Via del Corso when it thundered and began to pour again, dense, vertical rain. The driver pulled over to the curb, and remained with the engine idling. She looked out the window and saw only the sheet of rain. She wanted to feel happy, yet she could not. The rain and the clamor of church bells all morning fit her mood. Church bells rang from Santa Maria in Montesanto and Santa Maria dei Miracoli, and through the rain it was a sad sound.

The driver saw her face through the rear-view mirror.

"It's All Souls' Day," the driver said, "the saddest day of the year."

Part Two

"If you can put the past aside, so will I," François said before we left Rome.

He came and took my hand. "I am leaving for Rabat in the morning. Will you come with me?" He gently traced the shape of my eye with his finger, then removed his hand and stepped away as if he had accepted the distance that he must have believed was inevitable between us.

"It's better I go somewhere where I cannot be arrested. It isn't over."

"Rabat for a year or two, then maybe, Geneva." I smiled, ironically, "It will never be over."

He surveyed the room like a ghost coming back to a place and trying to discern what had gone on in his absence. "I meant what I said the last time we spoke. You are free if that is what you want," he said. Then, "You look so unhappy."

"No more than you," I said. "We have both been unhappy."

There was a difference. He was no longer afraid. He was stronger than I was.

He became pensive again, the way he had been so often in the jail. "Part of me believes it would have been better if things had taken their course," he said quietly, pressing his lips to my ear. He held my head in his hands, and though he was gentle, I felt his desperation, and with it, the hint of violence. "I didn't want that from you," he said.

Without my having to say anything, he seemed to understand why the extradition was dropped. Maybe he had seen my shame on my face. I had gone too long wearing a mask, and I made no effort to hide it.

I watched as he gathered his things into the black carry-on case that he had with him when we first arrived in Rome.

"Where are you going?" I asked.

"If I stay the night it will only make it harder." He kissed me on the tops of my eyes, a kiss filled with sadness.

He was right. How could either of us be sure after a night of silent recrimination and unspoken regrets? Counting, minutes at first, then hours, the way we had sat across from one another in the jail until the only thing we were waiting for was the moment to pass.

"I will be in front of the hotel tomorrow morning at seven if you decide you want to come with me." He covered my hand in his.

In the morning I found him outside the hotel lobby. A car was waiting to take him to the airport. The wind was cold and it was raining, a cold, thin rain. I slid my hand inside his and leaned my face against his chest. I was shivering. His hands rested lightly against my shoulders. His lips pressed against the top of my brow. It seemed neither of us knew what to say. I heard the engine of the Mercedes filling up the silence, another reminder of time passing, like the white cloud of vapor trailing off into the cold morning air. *Say the words. You are wasting time, and it will be too late. My husband. My love.*

"I couldn't bear to leave you," I said.

We kissed. The way it is meant as a beginning when it comes at the end.

Rabat is flat, as flat as my open hand, open and waiting, for the rain to fall, for a coin, a piece of bread, like a woman with nothing left but to beg along the road lined with palm trees that leads to the sea.

The house in Rabat was spread out over two floors, a white house with blue painted parapets north of the Kasbah des Oudaias with a view of the phosphorescent autumn sea, and the town and the harbor across the way. When we arrived, a damp wind was blowing and the sky was a low cover of clouds. The spray of rain left a wet trace on the sand. In the front of the house there was a large cactus tree, so old its trunk had hardened into bark. The shutters were closed. The tall arched doorway opened onto a silent courtyard with tiled floors. It was intended to create a sense of openness to the long narrow rooms, yet it left me feeling that someone was watching. The vines that grew up the walls and cascaded from the second-floor balustrade made it seem dark and confined.

"You will see, it will all look better in the sun," François said.

A mosquito net was draped over the four-poster bed, which was neatly made with fresh white sheets as in a hotel. Everything about the last few weeks had exhausted me.

"Why don't you sleep for a while?" he said.

I did sleep, long and deep as the darkest hour of night, but it did not last. Afterwards, when I first woke I seemed to have lost my bearings. The unfamiliar room appeared to me through the haze of the mosquito net, the terra cotta-colored walls with elaborate blue, white and black tiles across the floor, intricate patterns, without a face or an image, no tree or flower, no point where the eye could rest. It was dark, already night, though I had no idea of the time. I opened the shutters. The sea was a vast, haunting emptiness. To the south, in the distance, I could see the lights from the harbor.

François was sitting in the courtyard. That too seemed strange; I had gotten used to his absence. A candle was burning on the table. He was unaware that I was watching. I felt as if I were intruding, yet I lingered watching him before going downstairs.

When he heard me approach, he too seemed uncomfortable. "I am not myself yet," he said, apologetically.

There was little furniture, a wrought iron table with four chairs. The sparsely furnished house was a mixture of French and Arabic tastes that seemed to have been brought together at random. The fountain was trickling in the corner. White jasmine grew against the wall, but the scent of the sea in the heavy air was stronger than anything else.

The rain had stopped and the moon was up. It was damp, and I felt a chill.

"Aren't you cold?" I said. He was wearing only a thin sweater and cotton shirt.

He half smiled. "It feels good to be outdoors. In the jail the day had no dawn, night came without dusk—like death." He poured some brandy and handed the glass to me. "To safety," he said, holding his glass to mine.

I had the impression he had been drinking for some time, though he seemed brooding rather than drunk. "To safety," I said. I filled my mouth with the warm taste of the brandy before swallowing. Not happiness. Neither of us believed we had the right to happiness. His eyes met mine intently. I reached across the table and caressed his hand. The candle flared, and I saw the hollows under his eyes and the strained expression. The image came to my mind of his face obscured behind the shadow made by the screen in the jail, which was worse than his sad eyes. I felt a wave of longing wash over me. "We must forget everything until now," I said.

"If you wish." The corners of his mouth turned up and his eyes narrowed as if he questioned what I said.

"And not you?" I said. "How can we start over if we don't forget?"

He reached for his empty glass and filled it with the last of the brandy. "More than forgetting, I want the dreamless sleep I used to take for granted." He smiled bitterly.

An owl was hooting in a nearby tree, an annoying, insistent sound. I watched a small lizard race sideways across the wall. It is a lonely place, I thought. But there are lonelier places still.

"You are hurt and you have been alone. It is behind you now," I said gently.

"I can put the past aside, but that is not the same as forgetting," he said.

I reached out my hand for him to take it. He pressed it to his mouth before letting go. A fleeting look of severity passed across his face, and it frightened me. His voice after a cruel minute of silence was filled with anger and despair.

"At a certain hour at night the lights went off until morning. It was pitch dark. I'd wake up in a sweat or sometimes shivering from the cold. In the dark I pictured your body, the way your hair falls over your shoulders, and your eyes looking back at me from the closeness of a kiss. I knew what it was to want to kill another man."

He folded his hands on the table and looked at me intently before lowering his eyes. "I never want to speak of it again," he said quietly.

"We won't have to. I promise."

It was very late when we went back into the house. The sconce on the wall beside the bed gave off a dim light. I slipped the nightgown from my shoulder and it fell to the floor at my feet. We were alone for the first night in many nights. I waited for a tender word, a caress, a kiss, for him to take me in his arms. Nothing. Before this he would not have hesitated. It cannot be the way it was, I thought; we are both broken.

It was his turn to sleep. I lay awake, watching the night evaporate through the haze of the mosquito net. Before long the sun pressed against the wooden shutters. I lightly placed a kiss at the back of his shoulder. He seemed brooding even in sleep. As I gazed at him, I had a feeling of loss, a premonition that we did not have much time together. It came to me so strongly that I got up from bed to push it from my mind.

I went downstairs into the courtyard. The empty glasses and decanter on the table, the charred wick sticking up from the burnt out candle were sad reminders of the night. A large black ant crawled across the spilled wax. The morning blossoms had opened, and the red hibiscus tree was full of flowers. Honeysuckle seemed to grow wild everywhere. The jasmine gave off a strong scent, stronger than the sea air. I thought, this will be the difference between days, when the jasmine is strong, there will be those days, and the night will belong to the damp breeze from the sea and the sour smell of algae and salt. I was overcome by how still it seemed in the shadowless light of morning. And then last night, when the moon at last broke through the clouds, I remembered that it was also a place of shadows.

I went back into the house. The kitchen was large and whitewashed, with long cabinets and glass-paned doors. The pantry had been filled for our arrival. I made coffee in the small pot on the stove and carried it on a tray to the bedroom.

He was awake when I returned, lying with his back propped up against the pillows and the sheet drawn to his waist. Sleep had restored him and he seemed like a different person. I set the tray down on the nightstand and sat on the bed beside him. He drank the coffee and put the cup back on the tray. He brushed the hair from my face and kissed my lips. It seemed he had discarded the silence and coldness that had protected him for so long. He must have sensed my despair.

"We don't have to stay in this house. We can go somewhere else," he said.

"The house is fine," I said. "It isn't the house or the place."

"What is it then?" He spoke gently.

"They will always own you," I said.

"I will dissolve Compagnie Financière, then they will leave us alone," he said. He held my hands in his as if to reassure me. "When it's finished I promise we will go back to Paris. It means everything to me," he said. I know he wanted me to believe him because he wanted to believe it himself. Yet the feeling I had earlier was stronger than anything he might have said.

We hired a housekeeper named Fatima. She was young, not yet twenty, but already a woman with a woman's body and a long heart-shaped face framed by thick, black, wavy hair. She spoke French and did not understand a word of English. The houseboy, Ahmed, came to us through Fatima. He seemed quiet and shy at first, though he was neither, and he had an annoying habit of lowering his eyes whenever anyone addressed him.

"He is hiding something," I said.

"He is a boy. You are a woman and you frighten him," François said. "Let him be. He does what is asked of him."

François gave me a bottle of Jasmal, the perfume I wore in Paris. It was his way of alluding to the past without having to speak of it. The outbursts, the tears, had stopped long ago, and all that remained was the quiet relentless spray of rain from the sea, like a whisper, a drizzle just light enough to get stuck in one's hair and on one's skin. The rainy season did not last, and when it passed, it was pleasant to sit outdoors at night. The evening meal was eaten late. Then we were alone. The reluctance of those first nights passed and his desire matched mine, though sometimes he seemed low, even after loving. It is something in this place, I thought. Why else the call to prayer, the mournful lament unto the sun and the darkness?

He took a room at the end of the hall for his study. During the mornings while he worked I often walked along the narrow winding streets of whitewashed walls that made up the Kasbah, basket *souks*, textile shops with large urns filled with blue dye and shops for tourists with Moorish scarves and caftans, rug stores, the smell of oranges and myrrh and crushed almonds, colorful spices piled high into bowls. "Saffron, the king of spices," the merchant would say, then he would invite me to smell it, cup out a spoonful and hold it up to my nose.

I walked along the Rue Jamaa where the old mosque was at the center of the medina. The noon prayer came through the loudspeaker. A hot wind was blowing, the scirocco from Algeria or the chergui from the southeast. Beneath an archway of carved wood near the end of the Rue des Consuls a pair of black eyes was looking straight at me, an Arab boy, black hair and brown skin, distrusting and resentful, his black eyes watched me without appearing to look from beneath lids at half mast. I continued walking, but he followed me until I turned and held out a few coins. He shook his head, refusing the money and remained obstinately before me as if to prevent me from passing, his dark eyes lowered, yet his voice insistent and familiar sounding.

"Monsieur sent me to look for you."

I stared for a moment at the tilted face, the eyes that would not look up. It was Ahmed, our houseboy.

He did not make eye contact as he led the way down the winding streets, walking with his eyes down, a servant not a child. I had a feeling as if he were mocking me, mocked, spied upon, often this is how I felt. "I am as much a stranger here as you," François said when I complained.

He was waiting for me at the Café Maure. The table had a view of the Mediterranean. I could see a copy of *Le Figaro* open in front of him. It might have been early spring in the south of France; it was a good feeling, though it did not last.

François looked to me. "What would you like?" I saw that he had already had a coffee.

"A tea for now."

He summoned the waiter and ordered the tea and a large bottle of mineral water.

"Jean Dugommier is coming to Rabat," he said.

I could not hide how I felt. "If he is coming here it is to make demands of you." I was angry and upset.

"I cannot put my head in the sand," he said, reaching for my hand, but I stiffened and withdrew it.

"Don't you see? It was never the intention for things to end in Rome," I said.

The waiter brought the water and poured out two glasses. I swallowed a few sips before I began to feel nauseous.

"What is it?" he said, imploringly. He reached over and

clasped his hand tightly over mine, unwilling to let go this time.

I wanted to tell him, to say the words aloud and watch his reaction. Yet the words died in my throat.

A few minutes passed in silence, each of us absorbed in our different thoughts. I caught him watching me, imploring me with his eyes. I wrapped my hand around the glass of cool water.

"Why does Dugommier want to see you?"

"There is a new investigation in New York of Etienne Dufois that possibly involves Compagnie Financière." He paused, then said in a low voice, "I am here because I believed something like this could happen."

The waiter brought the tea and it sat for a minute or more before François poured it into the glass for me. The smell of the mint was so strong I could not drink it.

I saw him scrutinizing me, a look of concern flashed across his face. "*Tu es malade?*"

"It's nothing," I said. " I shouldn't have ordered the tea."

He called the waiter and paid the check.

When we returned to the house, Fatima was hanging the sheets to dry in the sun. White powder had been sprinkled on the floor to keep the ants away. I went to the courtyard and sat on the low cushioned sofa against the wall with a book. I often read there after lunch. Fatima brought a bowl of fresh figs from the fig tree in back of the house. A little yellow bird, the same bird that was there in the mornings, alighted briefly on the edge of the fountain and flew away. I could hear dogs barking nearby and the sound of a car and always the wild cries of seabirds. The daylight was too stark, the walls too white, the tiles too blue and too many shadows at night. François pretended to himself—If he sold Compagnie Financière, if he waited long enough. After today he could no longer close his eyes.

I had wanted to tell him at Café Maure. Instead I remained without speaking as in a dream where everyone is silent, and only his words echoing in my head, *I knew what it was to want to kill another man.*

It was to be my secret a while longer.

It was my exile, not hers. Yet she had agreed to share it with me. The doubts, the hesitation, the uncertainty, that much at least seemed to be behind us. We were alone for the first night in many nights, my wife, Juliet, and I.

The house had been arranged for us by Jean Dugommier, beautiful, if not triste, with sad leaning palm trees, the sea creeping up along the gray beach, and the thin film of water left by the rain on the balustrade, a mirror of the despair we both felt.

My wife could not hide what she felt. The first night we were there I saw the bruise on her breast, faded by then, but still visible. But that had all taken place beforehand. "To forgetting," she said, as she brought the glass to her beautiful lips the night we arrived. The oblivion of dark nights, the afternoons with the shutters closed, I did not want what the light might reveal. The afternoon shadows faded against the white wall, white, the color of the sun in the desert, giving way to blindness. In the evening the light was tinged with blue. I filled my longing with the taste of her kiss and the feel of her breath against my cheek, the warmth of her naked body, the perfumed scent of her soft hair, for a time it was everything.

"Tell Fatima not to come tomorrow. I want to stay in bed all day," she said. She was smiling. For too long her smile had merely served as the mask for tears. Despair gave way to desire, and then sleep, dreamless sleep, and before too long despair again.

I followed her into the kitchen and found her crying silently. Her head was bent and she leaned against the sink. When I spoke to her she did not turn around to face me.

"You can't just dissolve Compagnie Financière and believe it is finished. You have to walk away from everything," she said.

"I am not so free." I heard the calm in my voice as something apart from me and unrecognizable. From the window I looked out on the moribund landscape of palm trees like columns with only an empty blue sky above them. I knew what it was to be stripped naked and left standing like a shell of something that had been.

"I am afraid of what will happen," she said. "I cannot help what I feel."

I smiled, incapable of disguising the irony I felt. "You believe that what is happening to Dufois is a bad omen." I stroked her hair. "There are no omens, only consequences."

At last she turned and looked at me. The expression in her eyes seemed childlike and angelic. I ran my finger down the side of her face to her chin.

"Will you meet with Dugommier?" she said.

"I cannot afford to turn him away," I said. The things Dugommier had said about her in Rome were fresh in my mind. I knew her secret, the secret I refused to hear from her lips. There are some things better left unsaid. Even so, she has been good to me, I thought. She does not have to be here,

and yet she is. These thoughts seemed to occur simultane-
ously with the anger I felt.

"Were you asked why the extradition was dropped?"

I felt myself growing more agitated. "I told Dugommier I
paid the Italians."

"A bribe? Will anyone believe you?"

I listened to her voice coming to me through the darkness of my own thoughts.

"A bribe is something easy to understand. I am uncertain
myself of the precise circumstances that led to my release,
though I have no illusions."

She turned her face away. I had a growing feeling of op-
pression as if the walls were closing in.

"What is it that you want to know? And what makes
you think I have the answer? Fear? Regret? Yes, there is that.
Haven't I humbled myself enough to satisfy you that my face
is against the wall, and I am scraping the floor with my knees?
You talk about trust and betrayal. You are the woman I loved."

My lip started to quiver, and I attributed it to anger. So it
was done. The words were spoken. She was crying and she
covered her face with her hands. A kind of delirium clouded
my thoughts. And I knew only that I wanted to be gone from
there, though I had no idea where.

The low sun cast a light like a flame across the swollen
and rough water. It was the hour of blinding sun, more unbearable than the midday heat. The wind that came up from
the sea was growling and the air smelt of salt. A stray dog
crossed the beach and went for a swim. I saw a goat to remind
me of how far away I was from anything I had ever known. It
was cream colored with reddish-brown spots and large shining yellow eyes that stared back at me when I looked at it. A

boy came running down the path and tethered it. The sound of the goat bleating cut through the monotonous back and forth of the waves.

I lost track of how far I had walked or how much time had passed. When I came back to the house, Fatima told me she had not left the bedroom all afternoon. The door was shut and I went inside without knocking. The lights were off and the shutters were drawn, the room was dark as if she had been sleeping. I reached out my hand and placed it over hers. Her eyes were shining as if minutes before she might have been crying.

"I haven't made it easy for you," I said after a silence.

"We are letting ourselves be destroyed by ghosts," she said.

I slipped the dress from her shoulder and ran my hand across her swollen breast.

"I am pregnant," she said. She lowered her eyes, and bit down against her lower lip.

"Why have you said nothing?" I stroked her face gently. For an instant all that had happened that day seemed unimportant. A moment later, it seemed all one.

"I was afraid," she said without lifting her head or looking at me.

"Afraid? Of what?" I did not voice my doubts about whether the child was mine. Yet the bitterness I felt showed through.

She too sounded bitter. "Before today I believed it was possible for us to start anew."

"And now?"

Her gaze hardened and all the vulnerability went from her expression. "Isn't that the point of this new indictment? To tell you that nothing has changed." She lowered her eyes and looked away, pulling the dress back over her shoulder. "What are you going to do?" she said in a low voice.

"I will swallow it with everything else," I said.

I got up and walked across the room to the open window. The night air was gray rather than blue, cool and thick with mist. The palms seemed to shiver in the breeze from the sea and the white oleanders looked like snow in the night, and I wondered if I would ever see France again.

I went back over to the bed and sat beside her. How faint her features looked suddenly. I had the feeling of looking up at the afternoon sky and seeing the ghost of a white moon. I pressed my lips to her palm and felt the weight of her hand against my face.

"After today the old wounds are open," she said.

"It will all pass," I said, lifting her chin in my hand. I rested my lips between her closed eyes. I could see from her face that she felt ill, though she did not complain. She lay back down on the bed. After a moment, I reached out my hand, placed it over hers, and laying my head on the pillow, closed my eyes.

In the mornings it rained, a heavy, tropical shower. I could see the cloud from the bed, and I listened to the musical sound of the rain above the silence. The windows were open to let in the cool air and the damp breeze and whatever else was lurking. I had the feeling of being watched, and worse, a feeling of malice in the void left by the dark sea. Juliet was asleep. I closed the windows and went to my study to dress before going downstairs to the kitchen. The girl, Fatima, had prepared coffee on the stove. I waited for it to boil over before drinking it hot and black with sugar.

The front door was open and the girl was sweeping the entrance. When I walked by she did not lift her eyes. I had called a *grand taxi*. It was waiting on the road in front of the house. Small white clouds passed slowly across the sky on the way to the sea. The air was scented with the odor of hibiscus and orange peel. By then the rain had stopped and the light was soft as a whisper and there was a chill in the morning air. I turned to the girl, "Tell Madame I will not be back for lunch."

It was after ten at night when I returned. Juliet was sitting at the kitchen table. I had the impression she was waiting for me. There was a dish containing a half eaten peach in front of her. She pushed it to the other end of the table. Her face had taken on an air of tragedy, the sad expression in her eyes eclipsed by her eyelids, which covered over half her eyes.

"Where were you?" she asked. She sounded cold and accusatory.

I went no closer to her, but her gaze met mine. "I was at the embassy. The papers are signed. The dissolution of Compagnie Financière is complete."

Beneath my cold expression feelings of failure burned inside of me. She seemed to be searching for the right words. The corners of her mouth turned down in a questioning way.

"There is nothing to say," I assured her. "I am relieved."

She raised her eyebrows and her eyes retained their bitter look. "You left this morning without telling me anything? I thought something happened to you."

"It took longer than I expected. There were last-minute negotiations." I stopped myself from saying anything more.

"What is it?" she said. "What is wrong?"

What good would it do to tell her, I thought. And yet I did tell her then, because silence was no longer an answer.

"Dufois is in New York. He will stand trial there for the allegations against Compagnie Financière."

"When did this happen?" she said, looking directly at me, and I saw fear mix with anger and resentment.

"I found out today. He consented to extradition and went to the United States voluntarily." I tried to reassure her. "I have finished with Compagnie Financière. I have no connection anymore to Dufois." Only the bitterness in her eyes belied everything that I said. Her expression had become the mirror of what I felt and could not show.

"Why would he consent to extradition?"

"I was not told. Obviously he felt it was to his advantage."

Her eyes widened, and I thought I knew the source of her anxiety. "Michael Chase is not involved," I said.

She was silent. She seemed to be thinking rather than waiting for me to say anything more. I did not believe it was necessary to tell her that I was blamed for what was happening to Dufois, or that it was perceived that I had made an arrangement with Michael Chase.

"Will you sit outside with me?" I said.

She merely nodded her head.

It was pitch dark as I lit the thick candle in the center of the table, watching the small flame, blue at first, before turning yellow and rising in a burst of light. Three gray moths chased one another to the flame. She came out a few minutes later with a small carafe of mint tea and two glasses. I felt a faint touch on my shoulder as she rested her hand there. A burst of flame illuminated her face before swallowing it in shadow. I ran my finger along her cheek and drew her closer, feeling lost, with only the trembling glow of the candle to reassure me as I placed a kiss on the top of her brow just below the hairline and saw her eyes floating beneath me.

I loosened my tie and slipped it off. She reached out and took it from me, folding the blue silk around her hand and placing it on the table beside her. Her eye went to the lighter on the table.

"Are you smoking again?" she asked.

"Today," I shrugged.

I thought with irony of the comment Dugommier had made, "I see you have stopped smoking. You are becoming American." And not an Arab as you have become, I answered.

Black ants scurried across the table onto a wilting sprig that had fallen from the tree. She brushed them to the ground. Through the gleam of the candle a weary expression appeared in her resolute eyes.

"You worry too much," I said, trying to be gentle.

"I know what my role is. I am the one who will bear witness. I know I will see it through to the end. No, it is not for myself that I worry," she said with the calmness that comes with resignation.

I made an image of her in my mind at that moment, something that would stay with me, her belly swollen with pregnancy, her face full like a cherub, only her hands seemed unchanged, her long, graceful, white fingers. She might otherwise have been a stranger. I took her hand; it was cold, but her arm was warm. "You have to take care of yourself," I said with the tenderness that I might have used in addressing a child. She leaned closer to me and put her hand on my arm. The expression that appeared on her face was like a small stone thrown into the water, rippling briefly before the water covered over it.

"The things we are waiting for are not the same," she said.

I saw her studying my face, and yet I remained impassive.

"What will you do?" she asked. The vein in her neck had become more pronounced.

"I am not sure it is best for you to be in Rabat," I said.

"I thought after today your dealings were finished," she said with a hint of sarcasm mixed with accusation.

"For the future, yes. But that does not change the past," I answered.

"No, we cannot change the past," she said.

I heard the remorse in her voice. The first night we were in Rabat came back to me, but my heart was so heavy it aroused no feeling.

She lifted her eyes and let them meet mine directly without answering. Then after a moment, "I am tired, I am going to bed," she said.

I made no effort to follow her. I too was tired and we would talk again in the morning. I felt a shiver run through my body; the temperature had dropped. I smoked and listened to the night noises drown the silence left by her absence. I lost track of how long it was or how many cigarettes I smoked before I went upstairs to the bedroom.

She was sleeping silently on her side, her delicate features obscured by her heavy dark hair spread across the pillow. Only her arm, bare and rounded, had slipped free of the cover. Lying there, she seemed timid and vulnerable. I heard the relentless groan of the surf against the emptiness as I crossed the room to the window facing the sea. The moon had risen and a mist hovered over the water. The night was calm in contrast to the confused agitation I felt. I stepped back into the room. The bed seemed a refuge against the open space. I took off my shirt and sat at the foot of the bed. A moment later I felt her hand on my arm.

"I woke you, I am sorry," I said, covering her hand in mine without lifting my head.

"I wasn't really asleep. It's never a deep sleep anymore," she said quietly. We sat for a minute or more in a vigilance of silence.

"Something is going to happen," she said in a low voice.

I lifted my head without looking at her, but I could see her out of the corner of my eye. "Are you afraid?"

"Today, when you were gone and I didn't hear from you. Now that you are here, no," she said with gentle sincerity.

I put my arm around her shoulder. She seemed eager to take refuge in that false promise of security. "I thought I would know what to tell you, what you should do. I am uncertain of everything. What is right and what is wrong and most of all what is best."

"Right and wrong don't matter anymore. We can do nothing about it," she said. Her half-whispering voice was like the murmur of the water frapping against the shore. "Just tell me when the time comes you will accept the child. Tell me now, while nothing is certain."

"You said yourself, we can do nothing about it." But I could see this last remark hurt her, and I had no desire to hurt her. She pulled away from me. I thought she might cry, but silence had taken the place of tears. In a wave of tenderness, I took her hand and covered it in mine.

I dozed off, awakening abruptly a short while later. The night was lifting and soon the dawn light would filter through the windows. It was the time when Muslims say the *salat as-subh*, the first prayer of the day. I watched her as she slept, gently stroking her shoulder. Soon it would be light in the room. Then we would awaken from the sad dream. I got up and dressed.

325

She stayed in bed until almost noon. When she came downstairs I told her I was making arrangements to return to Paris.

"What if there is a warrant?"

"Someone from the consulate here has inquired of the embassy in Paris. There has been no request for extradition." I smiled in an effort to make light of her concerns. "We will not be inconvenienced at the airport when we arrive."

She looked at me with a grave expression. "The proceedings in New York could take a long time. Because there is no warrant today does not mean a month from now it won't change."

"If it does I will be in a better position in Paris than I was in Rome."

Again she seemed to hesitate. "You might not be able to buy your way out," she said. "If you believe Rabat is no longer safe, why return to Paris now? Why not somewhere else? No one needs to know where we go when we leave Morocco. You buy time that way."

Her eyes did not blink or shine as she looked at me. She looked at me without judging me, as if what she said the night before were true; all those eyes could do were bear witness.

"I have no delusions about the consequences of returning to Paris. Of course I am afraid; I no longer have the arrogance to pretend I can avoid the forces against me." My gaze fixed on hers, though my voice was gentle. "I want to be an honest man again."

She pressed her hand to her brow; her fingers seemed swollen. I wrapped my hand around her wrist.

"Our child will be born in France. Isn't that what you wanted? For me to accept the child."

"Yes, yes, but I want what is safe for you too. Why go back now when things are still uncertain? Why not wait?"

I smiled ironically, "Rabat, then Geneva. You said it yourself, for as long as I run, they will own me. I have decided this is best. Trust me, won't you?"

Her complexion had turned pale. I could see I had upset her, and yet I was certain that my decision was right.

"You don't look well," I said, taking her warm, damp hand in mine.

"I'm feeling a little nauseous, that's all. I have gone too long without eating."

I went to the kitchen and asked Fatima to bring toast with confiture and tea for Juliet.

We sat outside in the courtyard. I noticed that it was becoming difficult for her to walk. I helped her into the chair. The air was sweet and in the shade where the table was it was cool.

Fatima came out carrying a large tray. Along with toast, there was fresh orange juice and a bowl of figs from the fig tree.

The fig was so soft it broke open in my hand. " A fig tree is a giving tree. The more you take, the more fruit it gives, " I said. I handed a piece to Juliet. As she took it, she lifted her eyes to meet mine.

"You don't have to go back now and risk the whole thing starting all over again. I will return to Paris if that eases your mind, and you will be free to do what you need."

I smiled. "Do you think I could leave you alone now?"

A little yellow bird appeared and perched on the ledge of the fountain. "I will miss him," she said, throwing a few crumbs in his direction.

She let her gaze meet mine and rested her fingers against my cheek. I felt a shiver of hope like light as it traverses a wave. At last the past was finished.

I knew there was no point in arguing any further. His mind was made up. I felt a pang of pity that must have shown in my expression.

"That first morning after we arrived here, you promised we would return to Paris. Do you remember?"

A sad look passed over his eyes that I felt mirrored in my own.

There wasn't much to pack. We had never lived here; it was always temporary, like an indefinite stay in a hotel. I felt a lightheadedness that had as much to do with my condition as with our return to Paris.

The light filtered through the fabric where the tea-stained drapes had been worn by the sun. I went to bed earlier than usual. I was not feeling well. When I awakened a short while later, I felt a cold wet sensation across my legs. I reached for the light beside the bed. In the tinted glow of the lamplight I saw the stain of bright red blood spreading on the sheets. When I tried to move I felt a sharp pain. I called out for François, who was somewhere in the house.

"Are you all right?"

"Call the doctor," I said.

I heard him on the phone. After he hung up, he came over to me in bed.

"He will be here soon," he said to reassure me, and yet he seemed as anxious as I was.

"It was not supposed to happen for another month," I said. "It must be the heat."

"You are in pain," he said, pushing back the hair from my brow.

"It comes and goes."

He went out to look for the doctor's car, then he came back. With an impulsive gesture he kissed my hand, which was wrapped tight around his. "Stay with me," I said. I do not know how much time passed before we heard the sound of a car.

He went downstairs. I could hear voices. A minute later the doctor, who was French, came into the room. He had a Moroccan nurse with him. She was young with a long, oval face and dark eyes, made to seem larger still by the black foulard around her head.

"Why must she wear black? Tell her to take it off," I said. François remained standing in the doorway. His face had lost its color and he appeared reluctant to come into the room. I know what he will say, I thought. There are no omens. Only consequences.

"It would have been better to do this in hospital. It is too late to move you," the doctor said. He seemed annoyed rather than concerned. The nurse placed a mat under me and folded a sheet over it. I could hear the running faucet and the doctor washing his hands in the sink. The room smelled of alcohol. The doctor began giving orders to the nurse.

"Not much longer," he said.

From the bed, I turned my head to look for François. In spite of the shadow in which he was standing, I saw the strained expression of his face and eyes. With each pain I had the sensation of a hammer pounding a nail, a rhythm of agony then respite.

"Come close to me." I gestured to François.

I felt his hand around mine and I clutched his wrist, smooth and cool against my burning skin. As I gasped to keep from screaming, my fingers dug into his skin.

"Can't you give her something?" I heard his voice.

The doctor gave me a whiff of morphine.

"It's better if you go. I don't want you to see me this way." Then I shut my eyes. I could no longer keep the pain inside.

"It will be fine," I heard the doctor say. "She will push better if she feels the pain."

"*En plus*," the doctor said in French.

My hair was matted to my face and my back was wet with sweat. The nurse placed a cool cloth on my forehead.

"Push. Harder. Once more. I see the head. A few more and it will be over," the doctor said.

I shut my eyes.

"A son. A son is good. Call the father. Tell him he has a son."

"*Allahu Akbar*," God is great, the nurse said.

I heard the baby's cry, high pitched and breathless. The doctor held him up for me to see; his dark hair was wet and stuck to his head. His little face with tiny features appeared to smile.

"Your son," the doctor said, handing the infant to François.

The nurse asked for a mop to wash the blood from the floor.

"It's best to burn the sheets when there is so much blood," the doctor said.

François handed the baby back to the doctor and came to sit beside me on the bed. He took my hand to his lips and kissed it. I saw the scratches where my fingers had dug into the skin. Tears swelled in his eyes, which he hid by pulling away. I tried to smile but I was too exhausted. "You are a mother," he said. If I detected a note of bitterness, it was in my mind not his.

"You will see how I will love you." I whispered. With his other hand he stroked my cheek.

The nurse wrung the bloodied mop into a bucket and a thin red mixture of water, blood and vinegar overflowed down the sides of the bucket. I turned my face to the wall and slept. When I woke up the room was clean. The night was lifting, giving way to heat and light. Soon the call to prayer would rise like the sun. I felt weak and very thirsty. A carafe of water was left on the bedstand. François poured out a glass and handed it to me. I drank it at once. A few minutes later the baby let out a feeble cry. François went over to the cradle and took him in his arms. I watched as he placed a light kiss on the baby's head.

It became necessary for us to remain in Rabat a while longer. The baby was not strong enough to travel.

The doctor came each week. "You understand, he weighs barely three kilos and his lungs are not yet adequate to withstand travel by airplane."

I looked at the scrawny little red body lying naked on the white sheet. The doctor must have seen the concern on my face. "He will be fine. He needs time to grow," he said.

"There is nothing pressing us to leave now," François said reassuringly. "We are fine here. We have everything we need. You will rest too."

I did not turn my gaze from the infant at my breast to see what his eyes might not have been able to disguise as he stepped aside and allowed me my bliss. The truth is that I was relieved. I was not ready for what a return to Paris might mean.

"Yes, it will be good here," I said.

The long afternoons of heat and flies surrendered imperceptibly to night. The days changed, tomorrow into today into yesterday. If I was sad it was because I felt time slipping away from me; each moment with the new life in my arms was precious compared to the harsh indifference of time. A small sigh escaped from the baby's lips as he slept, lying on his back with his arms resting palms up alongside his head.

"It is a sign of health when a baby sleeps that way," the nurse said. Then she added as was the custom, "You have been given a gift of Allah."

Nearly a month passed before the doctor determined that he was strong enough to withstand the trip. It was midsummer and the fig tree had stopped giving fruit. As Fatima helped me with his morning bath, she asked me if it were true we were going back to Paris.

"Yes," I said. François had made arrangements for us to leave on the following Sunday.

She seemed hurt.

"We will pay you wages for the month," I said, and this seemed to reassure her.

"Ahmed has asked if he could work at the house for you when you are gone," she said.

"The house does not belong to us," I said.

The baby let out a loud cry as I poured water over the back of his head. His little body was beginning to look plump I thought with satisfaction.

From the window I could see the brazen sun reflected

against the water. The houseboy was walking along the beach in the direction of the harbor.

"Where is Ahmed going?" I asked Fatima.

"There is nothing for him to do, Madame, so he has gone for the day."

François had been in his study most of the afternoon. We did not have a chance to speak until dinner. Fatima had prepared a couscous of eggplant and chickpeas with fresh mint and yellow peppers from the garden behind the house. Afterwards we drank champagne. Throughout, we made small, pleasant conversation. He told me that he had made arrangements with the guardian for the apartment in Paris to be ready for our arrival. I tried to read his expression in the light given off by the candle, but his face was obscured by darkness. Wanting to reassure him, I reached out and clasped his hand.

"Something will be negotiated. There is a chance after all this time no one will care as much and it will all be over relatively quickly," I said.

Without answering me, he pressed my hand to his lips, a gesture that belonged to him. My fingers rested there, listlessly. We seemed lost in the same dream of the past, a dream broken again and again by the anguish of insomnia.

When I passed the kitchen I was surprised to see the houseboy had returned.

"Why is Ahmed here so late?" I asked Fatima who was putting the last few dishes away.

"He came back because he forgot something," she said.

He merely nodded without lifting his eyes.

"Now it is late and you will have to be careful going home."

I went back upstairs to the bedroom. The baby was sleeping restlessly. He would awaken soon for the next feeding. My eyes were drawn to the sea outside my window, so calm and serene. A white streak of moonlight stained the water like a tear. Soon we will be gone from here, I thought, feeling a rush of melancholy come over me.

I heard Juliet's footsteps, light and eager, going up the stairs after dinner. She seemed content. I headed back to the room I used as a study. I had spent the day writing the last of the letters to my former investors, thanking them for their continued support, expressing my regret at having let them down and offering the promise of making it up to them in the future. This was the letter that was expected of me. I thought about writing another letter, this one intended for Dugommier alone, putting down on paper the words I had carried in my head for so long... *I am aware of your view that the actions that have led me to this point were motivated by money. Regrettably, it is true that I allowed myself to be bought. The first time, while money changed hands, I assure you, it was hubris, and not the desire for wealth that caused me to act as I did. On the second occasion, since you delivered the terms, I trust you will agree that money did not enter into my decision. Nor was it hubris that time. Where I was there was no place for hubris, only nemesis...*

I reached for the pen when in the same instant I felt a jolt that stopped me from breathing and a sudden, deep thrust, followed in an instant by the raw sensation of pain. The blood gushed over my hands as I pressed them to my neck. I gasped for breath, opening my mouth as if I were drowning, struggling for air as I staggered uncontrollably toward the door. My eyes went black and my thoughts were empty.

I was lying on the floor and my chest felt wet as if I had been immersed in water. I heard screaming but it seemed far in the distance. My body felt light. I felt the cold on my face as I shivered. I knew I must get up, that lying there was hopeless. The darkness seemed to come and go and the light was thin, transparent, out of reach. I saw Juliet. My hand slowly reached for her cheek as her head bent over mine, her eyes were so close they blurred into the darkness that was growing around me, still I could not reach her, my hand moved so slowly. She seemed frightened. I called her name but I had no voice and the effort to breath was terrible. My eyes went black. I could feel Juliet's face against mine. I could feel her breath in my mouth. I heard her voice, tender and desperate sounding, "Please, God, no, no, not now . . ."

Now and at the hour of our death. She will know. There are things that are broken that can never be made whole again.

The funeral was to take place in Paris. François always intended to return to Paris. The arrangements had been made. The heart breaks first, later it cracks in all the places it had repaired itself.

The two suitcases I was taking with me were lined up next to the door. The rest of our belongings had been packed and would be shipped in a day or two. Fatima stood in the doorway. She had covered over the furniture with sheets to protect against the wear and tear of time. Why had she bothered? Doesn't she know? Death is the only protection against time.

I looked back at the white house with the painted blue parapets, this place that I would carry with me wherever I went for as long as I lived. It appeared run down and defenseless standing alone on the sand's edge beneath the cruel midday sun. The houseboy leaned against the side of the house, sobbing loudly. Fatima went over to him. I could not hear what he was saying, only the sound of his sobs between words.

Fatima came to me and said, "He is crying because he loved Monsieur very much."

"He hardly knew him. He has no reason to carry on that way."

Her face had no expression and I knew it was intentional. She bent her head and muttered something in Arabic that sounded almost like a prayer. Her eyelashes quivered over her half-closed eyes. "He wants you to know he is sorry. He thought they were only going to rob you so there was no harm in leaving the door open."

I was more tired than there are words. Weary and emptied of everything save grief.

"Tell him to stop crying," I said in a flat voice.

Fatima went back over to him. I watched as he wiped his tears with the back of his hand. He walked over to the suitcases in the doorway and carried them to the car as if nothing had happened.

There was the faint scent of jasmine mixed with the scent of eucalyptus and salt and heat, faint at first, but growing stronger in the breeze from the sea. We were headed back to France, yes, and further, as far away as memory would allow.

I remembered it was raining the day François left Rebibbia. He was waiting under the trees. His clothes were wet, but he did not seem to mind; he was smiling.

It had been a little more than two years since I last heard anything about her. It was the week after Thanksgiving, and the Christmas season in New York was in full gear. I had been with a client all morning, a real estate developer, and we had decided to go over to Bice for lunch. That was when I saw her. A small child was sleeping with his head against her shoulder. The simplicity of her appearance was striking. Her dark hair hung long and straight over a black sweater. Her face looked pale, yet rested and youthful, with hardly any make-up. She was wearing no jewelry other than a large stainless steel Cartier watch. There was an empty coffee cup and a half-eaten dessert across from her. Whoever it belonged to had gotten up from the table.

She looked up over the head of the sleeping child.

"I live here now."

She said it with the seriousness of a confession. Her voice lacked the familiar tone of intimacy mixed with irony. Then she lowered her gaze to the head of soft curls resting silently on her shoulder.

I had no idea that she had a child or that she was living in New York. Yet I tried not to show my surprise.

I rested my hand along the back of the empty chair. "I am sorry about François."

She let her eyes meet mine through half-closed eyelids. I could not read their expression.

"You know I had nothing to do with the second case," I muttered.

"I know," she said.

She put her hand absently to her face as she looked away. The child woke up and lifted his head, his large blue eyes turning toward me as his chubby hand reached for his mother's cheek. He had a pretty face, like a doll. I glanced from the child to her. She kissed the child lightly on the top of his ear. I smiled back at the child who looked up at me for an instant before burying his head in her shoulder.

"New York is great this time of year," I offered after an awkward silence. Then I just stood there, feeling as if I had exhausted my repertoire of pleasantries for the occasion. I looked back toward the smoking section. My client was seated at his favorite table, and was dropping cigarette ashes on his tie while eating a roll. "My client is getting impatient," I said.

Something in her expression seemed to awaken, in her tilted face, in her eyes like two dark jewels. "It's good to see you," she said.